FREEDOM'S FIRE

WAR IN THE HEAVENS FOR FREEDOM ON EARTH

Book 1 in the Freedom's Fire Series

A novel by

Bobby Adair

Website: www.bobbyadair.com

Twitter: www.twitter.com/BobbyAdairBooks

Facebook: www.facebook.com/BobbyAdairAuthor

Mailing list for new book alerts:

www.bobbyadair.com/subscribe

Report typos:

www.bobbyadair.com/typos

COVER DESIGN

Alex Saskalidis, a.k.a. 187designz

COVER ILLUSTRATION

Illustration © Tom Edwards
TomEdwardsDesign.com

EDITING & BOOK FORMATTING

Kat Kramer Adair

SPECIAL THANKS

Mike & Re Kramer

Aaron Landau and the folks at
EVO3 Workspace in Frisco, Colorado

CHAPTER 1

It's up there right now, slowly killing my wife.

I hate it.

I mouth the words in silent syllables. I think them loud and feel them hard.

In my mind, I'm wrapping my hands around that thing's doll-sized ankles, swinging it like a bowling pin—bashing its head into the sidewalk, coconut skull cracking, splattering cerebral gel across the yard.

I savor the violence, like I'm doing it for real.

But I remain in my downstairs office, inert at my desk in the glow of a salvaged computer screen.

I want to stomp its spindly arms and grind them into the concrete. I imagine breaking its bones, though I know it has none to make the satisfying crack I yearn to hear. Its limbs are bendy-resilient like green twigs. They won't snap.

At least it bleeds sticky amber sap when its gray, dolphin skin splits.

There's that.

I hear a noise upstairs, small and shuffling.

I drive my criminal thoughts back to the dark place I keep in my soul, a hole so deep nothing can see inside. It's where I veil my secrets, hide what I am.

The mask the gray things see when their big black eyes scan across my face is servile. I look away. I fake a tremble. I gasp when I need to. And when they probe with their alien minds, they feel my weakness. They think my charade is as real as the power they lord over every hostage human on this earth.

They see a cog in their machine. A slave in all but name.

My disguise runs deep.

I look at the clock. Half past one.

It shouldn't be awake.

The things stay on a tight diurnal schedule set by the spin of the planet on which they evolved—three hours awake, three hours comatose. It's rare for one to deviate from its sleeping pattern, especially one so young. Ours is three-and-a-half, still eighteen months from maturity.

Light feet are coming across the loft outside the room where I used to lie in bed with my wife, feeling her skin sticky against mine, hearing her breath hush across my ear.

Some memories sweeten with time.

Wood creaks.

A foot on the first stair.

Leech.

Tick.

Parasite.

I have more thoughts yet to hide.

When they awarded us the *privilege* of rearing one of their hatchlings, Claire was just as normal as the next wife down the block, but prettier—always catching the ire of those kinds of girls who like to envy. A wide smile and teeth so perfect you just knew they were fake. Corn silk hair flowed over her shoulders. A seductive curve traced from her waist down to her hip.

The way her breath would catch in her throat when I unbuttoned her jeans.

Memories I shouldn't be indulging.

Instead, I recall her eyes—plastic ice, blue and false—showing me for a time that she and I were the same, two imposters, each behind a façade, each with an aspiration buried too deep to see.

The wood of another stair bends.

I cock my head.

Is it that thing?

Full-grown they only weigh about forty pounds. Ours is maybe twenty-five. It likes to creep through the house on fairy feet that grow more silent every day, trying to catch me unawares, suspecting my truth and wanting to get close enough to feel my deception.

I kill the contraband video I'm watching, eject the fingernail-sized memory card, and slip it beneath my keyboard. I alt-tab to a mindless game, focusing on colors of red and black while filling my head with hearts, diamonds, spades, and clubs.

More squeaks on the steps.

Its pace quickens, caution gone.

I don't look through the wide doorway between the first-floor office and the living room where the staircase stands in the night shadows. I don't want it to know I'm aware. I know it thinks I'm a dexterous monkey with rudimentary mental capacities and a dependence on sound for communication—no better than an ant secreting hormones into the air for all to sniff—incapable of hiding my plots.

The most believable lies are the ones we tell ourselves.

Still, it sneaks.

"You still up?"

Startled, I look, and instead of that thing, I see Claire, standing on the landing halfway up the stairs, her wrinkled skin drooping off sinewy arms, crackly gray hair, and eyelids hanging tiredly away, exposing pink flesh beneath. Surrounded by whites veined in red, her irises have turned to haze.

As I imagine cold air drying out those eyes and making them sting, I sympathetically blink.

She doesn't.

It's like she's unaware, protected from the world's rough touch by an opioid addiction that casts every day in a numb blur.

Naked and Holocaust-thin.

I'm thirty-three. Claire and I were born at the same hospital just a few months apart. Now, only the rows of faultless teeth assure me she's the young woman I married just ten years ago, and I know there can't be eighteen months of life left in her.

Worms of guilt burrow deep into my soul, biting and pissing, affirming the cost of my mistakes.

We all have sins to pay for.

"He's asleep." The girlish lilt of her voice has long since gone. Now it sounds like tearing paper modulated into words.

I look into the darkness above her, toward the bedroom. "You're not supposed to be away from it while it's asleep."

"I need you."

I hide my cringe. The thing upstairs has aged fifty extra years out of her.

She caresses one of her sagging breasts and licks her lips. She shows me those glistening teeth as she stretches a smile. "Don't you think I'm still beautiful?"

I hide the *NO* in the dark part of my mind with the rest of my secrets. I can't let her see my truth because if she comes to know my feelings, then that thing will know, too.

I stand and wheel my chair away from the desk as I reach up to loose the buttons on my shirt. "Come."

She slinks down the remaining stairs and crosses the floor, closing on me in a sultry rush of grinding knees and wheezing breath. Her fingers find my skin, and I smell the odor of the thing upstairs seeped into her wrinkles, a urine-soaked diaper left to ferment for an August week in the back of a car.

She fumbles to get my pants down and pushes me onto the couch. She climbs on top of me, her body desperate for pleasure.

I don't resist.

I participate—enough.

She puts my hands where she wants them.

She tells me to squeeze, to caress, to kiss. She always liked to be in control.

We wrestle rhythmically.

Thankfully, not for long.

She gets where she's going and howls loud enough to wake the neighbors. Then stops, gasping.

I pretend to get there, too, get caught in the lie, tell her I'm tired.

Too much pressure at work.

Afraid for friends who've gone off to the war.

Last week's shrinking rations.

Too many problems. Not enough room for all of them in my head.

She doesn't care. She only wants a fiction she can pour into the void that grows inside her as her body wastes away.

Leaving me on the couch, she crosses the shadowy room, mounts the creaking stairs, and balances herself with the railing all the way up. She crosses the loft and goes back into the room we used to share, gently closing the door behind.

More soft steps.

The bedsprings meekly groan as they take her weight.

She's under the covers, cuddling that thing warm again, content to let it leach the last of her life away.

I exhale my guilt into the cold house and peel myself off the couch, leaving my clothes on the floor. I cross to the kitchen, and open the fridge. I find a beer way in the back. I pop the cap and gulp it to wash the taste of her out of my mouth.

It's all I can do.

I'd like to shower and soap the smell away, but I can't. She'll hear the water running, and the insecurity she fosters will make her ask why I had to clean myself so quickly after we'd made love. I'll have no answer, and she'll suspect the truth of me not wanting to feel her touch. That will lead to a more painful truth I have difficulty admitting. Disgust. And then she'll churn the truth out of that feeling and she'll see my hate.

I can't afford hate—not from her and not from that gray thing upstairs.

I won't waste my years of deception when finally I've reached the eve of the beginning.

Elfin monsters like the one wrapped in my wife's arms don't belong in my house, not in my town, in my country, or on my planet.

Before the sun sets tomorrow, I'll cease being a disgruntled servant accepting those twiggy things as my overlords. I'll stop researching, and learning, and practicing, and wishing. I'll stop recruiting and scheming. My cocoon of lies will split open and I'll emerge a man who'll never have to face his masters again without a weapon in his hands and murder in his eyes.

I'll live for the dream of freedom and I'll fight for a single cause.

Revolution!

Chapter 2

The cold morning air bites my skin as I look up at the sky.

Fitting. It's gray.

I check my bike's tires for air. They're worn smooth. Replacements are almost impossible to find. In the three decades of the Grays' dominion over the earth, they've allowed very few resources and little manufacturing time to be set aside for products that only serve to make humans happy. Every item available on the black market is either salvaged from things built before the Grays arrived or is creatively surplused out of their supply chain.

With the new war in our solar system in its second year, those surpluses have dried up, and most of the salvagers have been drafted into the Solar Defense Force. The rest snuck away into the mountains with their families, hiding from a world that changed too fast, hoping to ride out the hostilities in safety.

Good thing the bike only needs to make one more trip.

I pull the garage door shut on a car built before I was born. It runs well for its age. I'll leave it for Sydney, Claire's sister, who lives in our basement. She won't be able to barter for much gas, but I've left seventy gallons in cans lined along the back wall. My job at the grav factory affords me a fuel ration for my commute, but not much more. In the spring and summer, when there wasn't snow piled on the roads, I biked to work and saved my ration. Some of that is in the cans. Some of it, I used to drive down to the illegal market on the south side of Denver and trade for things I wanted.

Back when everything was good with Claire, I'd occasionally burn some of my saved gasoline to cruise up one of the old mountain roads. She and I would find a place with nobody around for miles. We'd shuck off our clothes, lie in the grass, and revel in the pleasures of being young and wrapped in each other's arms. Afterward, with the breeze blowing cool across our skin, we'd look out over the trees and watch the clouds float above peaks stretched to the horizon.

We didn't care then that the earth was ruled by little gray creatures from a faraway star.

We were living what seemed like a romance story from the pre-siege videos.

We were in love.

At least, I thought so at the time.

Throwing a leg over the bike, I shrug my backpack into a comfortable position, slip my gloves on, and zip my jacket all the way up. Rotating my neck for a good fit, I can't help but look at the gray ribbons tied into bows on the limbs of the fir tree in our front yard. Some of them are crisp and shiny. Most are dull and frayed, there since the day Claire brought the hatchling into our home.

The ribbons piss me off.

They're pointless offerings of respect and solidarity. Tokens from neighbors to honor Claire's sacrifice for the good of us all.

Residual sighs of relief—*better your wife than mine!*

The ribbons are wasted resources when everything is in short supply.

A reminder I'm the bastard to blame for her choice, although adopting the baby Gray was solely *her* decision.

"To hell with you people." Nobody's outside to hear me mutter.

I stand on the bike's pedals and roll down the hill.

I ignore the guilt, and the wind numbs my face as I pick up speed.

The hill curves with the shape of the mountain. Tall pines line the road and fill the gaps between old ski condos. I make my way to the south end of town before turning north for a last trip past the nineteenth-century buildings on Main Street. Breckenridge is dead so early in the morning.

On the flat, empty boulevard, I pedal hard to get my blood flowing, and trace the center stripe on the road with my tires.

I'll warm up soon.

The old-timers still talk of what a bustling town Breckenridge used to be back when it was a ski destination. Before the Grays.

I realize then, too many of my thoughts carry that before-after qualifier.

Before the Grays. After the Grays.

Before the siege. After.

Human history ended an era and spawned a new one three decades ago when those rubbery imps arrived to claim us as their property.

Before, tourists flew in on commercial jets from all over the country. Three hundred people at a time, coddled on cushioned comfort in aluminum tubes that guzzled jet fuel by the ton, burning more gas in a minute than I'm rationed for a month, just to tear across the high atmosphere and vacation far from home. I've never even seen an old gasoline-powered airplane fly, let alone one big enough to carry three hundred people across the continent.

It strains the imagination—so much wasted back then when we have so little now. If only we'd not lavished ourselves in frivolities but spent our efforts preparing for the inevitable.

And contact was inevitable.

Too many stars in the boundless void for it not to be.

The only thing in the sky these days are the gravity lifts hauling shipping container loads into orbit, and an occasional battle cruiser rising out of the shipyards down in Arizona for her maiden voyage around the moon.

Or rushing to the war.

The war is everything.

It's bleeding our planet of people and resources. Hell, they're even pulling up the rails the trains used to run on. One hundred and fifty thousand miles of tracks, sixteen million tons of steel, just lying on the ground. We don't use the railroads anymore, but the fact we've become desperate enough to dismantle them frightens me.

A day will come when there's nothing left.

A worse day will arrive when these new invaders set their Neanderthal feet on earth's sacred soil and massacre us all.

It's because of the Grays.

They're the true bastards in every tragedy, intimate or grand, on this weary planet. They're the ones my neighbors should point their accusing fingers at. But the ribbon-hanging bumpkins on my block, like most people I know, are too brainwashed by the Grays' lies to see the truth.

Maybe they're too lazy to look for it.

Maybe they're just afraid.

I'm out of the city as I lose feeling in my ears. Downtown Breckenridge is only eight blocks long from end to end, and it's colder this morning than it seemed when I got on the bike.

The road down the valley to Frisco won't be busy. Still, I jump a crumbling curb and bounce down an embankment to access the old bike path close to the edge of the river. There's no ice in the water this time of year, yet the peaks on both sides of the valley are tipped in snow left over from last year, and this season's blanket is already starting to build.

Water gurgles over the rocks as I fly past. I feel like I'm racing it down to the reservoir, but mostly I'm listening. It's my solace, and has been for all the years I've sweated through twelve-hour shifts in the grav factory.

Near the marshes at the shallow end of the lake, the bike path curves around the old high school. I reflexively gag. The whole building was converted into a hatchery for the Grays back when I was a kid, and stinks up this end of the valley. Like the grav factory, the hatchery runs twenty-four hours a day, six days a week.

Everybody is allowed one day off.

It's an alien labor management protocol. As little as the Grays value humans, they don't work us to death. They want us energetic enough in our free time to produce more little versions of ourselves that'll grow up to serve their insignificant empire.

Insignificant?

Do I dare call it that?

Yes.

That's been the rumor this past year with the war going so badly. The Grays are an insignificant life form in our end of the galaxy.

And whatever crumbs of pride we humans fostered in our hearts after the siege and before the new war started have now turned to self-loathing, because thirty years ago, the insignificant Grays conquered us.

Once past the hatchery, the bike path runs up a hill through the pines on the west side of the lake. Along the crest, a condo complex had been under construction back when the Grays laid their siege. It was never completed. Now it's a maze of culverts, concrete walls, rusting rebar, and thin, white-trunked aspens covered in quaking golden leaves, ready to drop.

Between the trees, I see the little town of Frisco a few miles ahead, also on the west bank. Tiny Dillon is on the east. Silverthorne, not much bigger, spreads into the valley below the aging dam. Heading north, the spaceport's warehouses, barracks, admin buildings, and launch pads fill every flat space between the mountains as far as I can see.

Grav lifts are setting down in the spaceport, loading and launching back into the air in quick turnarounds. Many more than usual. They climb in the shade between the summits. Through the low-hanging clouds they drag trails of mist, catching the sun shining over the peaks as they ascend. For a few moments, they glow like escaping stars. They accelerate at altitude and the sonic booms echo down as they blast past the speed of sound.

The Grays are moving two SDF divisions into space today, including the one I've been attached to.

I'm anxious to be fitted into an actual battle suit for the first time and to step onto a grav lift bound for the endless void.

Well, just the solar system, really.

It'll be the beginning.

A war. A revolution.

And maybe my death added to a billion others. At least I'll die a free man.

After a life of servitude, what price wouldn't I pay for just one breath of freedom?

The bike is coasting.

I check my watch. I need to ride a little faster.

The Grays are not lenient masters. They don't understand tardiness, which seems odd for a species that had no concept of measured time before they arrived on our planet.

They're a telepathic race, always in communication with one another, living in the now, recalling their history from details parsed among them. When they're ready to do something, they act by consensus, though there is a flexible hierarchy of dominance between them no human understands.

Their telepathy is the reason I hide my thoughts. The gel in their skulls—the goo which passes for a brain—functions so differently than our mass of neurons that making a telepathic link from one of them to one of us is laborious. The microelectrical activity their minds sense in our heads is mostly incomprehensible.

However, some of them learn, and some of them grow adept at reading humans.

Those are the dangerous ones.

Especially for people like me.

Chapter 3

Chafing inside my containment suit, I smell my sweat. Worse than usual. I drank too many beers in the wee hours and they're now seeping through my pores.

For closure? For celebration? Regret?

There's no answer to the *why*.

There's only the future.

I've chosen my path. I harbor no uncertainty about where I'm going.

Unfortunately, at the moment, my headache is growing so intense it's hard to focus. And at the gravity factory, focus is everything.

I'm nearly four hours into my shift, my final. A partial day.

From the speakers mounted on the ceiling, the shrill voice of a Korean woman bleats monotonic, rhythmic sounds into the sweltering air. The first break of the day is coming. She tells us to pull strong for a few more minutes. For the war effort. For the fate of our eternal brotherhood with the Grays.

Everything depends on the grav plates we produce.

Quality.

Quantity.

We have to do our share.

Every shift she goes on like that. The words stay mostly the same, yet they roll off her tongue a little differently each day. I can't shut her up, and I can't tune her out. Most of my adult life I've worked in the factory. I've had plenty of time to fantasize unusual and intricate pain for the woman behind that voice. At the moment, I only hope she hates the monotony of her job as much as I do in the swampy air on the production floor.

It's fitting.

But distracting.

I'm counting the last minutes of my factory life, feeling them drip by while I'm surrounded by scores of people in bio-containment suits.

We're all draped in drab blue, shapeless, with a filter apparatus over every face, clear goggles protecting every pair of eyes. We're social animals who spend eighty-two sterile hours a week with only a single dimension through which to distinguish one another, to communicate, to form the intimate bonds every human needs.

Besides our eyes, we're all the same, except for Phil.

I look down the line to see him, my estranged brother-in-law. With the extra weight he carries around his gut, he makes his bio-containment suit look overfilled. Everyone on our line is habitually checking on Phil. We can't have his suit catching on something and tearing. That would shut down the line and maybe the whole factory. We don't wear the suits for our safety—no, they protect the microbes we inlay on the plates.

At the moment, Phil is etching the last of the paper-thin, ceramic composite plates I'll ever have to work.

After him, cleaners flow chemicals and distilled water over the rotating discs before warm, filtered air dries them. They ensure that no micro-particle remains on the surface, organic or otherwise. Inspectors follow, looking for flaws in the etch, for resilient contaminants.

Humans, trying to be perfect.

Our line crew rotates among the stations at every break, every shift. It helps keep us fresh. It reduces mistakes.

Right now, it's my turn on the most challenging step in the process, the secret sauce that makes this alien tech the kind of invention we humans couldn't possibly have stumbled across on our own.

And I realize immediately how wrong I am.

We humans have a long history of serendipitous breakthroughs. One of those breakthroughs is proving itself out in the factory right now.

The war is going so badly that the Grays have finally rescinded a cardinal rule and allowed their mechanically clever monkeys—us—to merge our computer tech with one of their most treasured technologies, gravity manipulation.

Using computers, two lines in the factory have been converted from manual processes to automated ones. Now, each of those lines produces more by itself than the whole factory did prior to the upgrade.

Nevertheless, I'm required to finish my shift.

I place a dinner plate-sized disc in the bottom of an open-ended leaden cylinder large enough to store a few basketballs within. I lean the faceplate of my suit onto the top of the tube, sealing it closed with a rubber ring around my visor. I tune out the noise and ignore the acrid fumes that find their way through my protective layers of Tyvec.

Sweat beads tickle my skin as they run down inside the suit.

Concentrate.

I open and then close each of three gas valves to send small clouds of minuscule organisms into the leaden cylinder. The microbes in the vapor are each married in symbiotic pairs. All of the Grays' advancements over humans depend on biological technology, most of which utilizes organisms inextricably bound to others.

Even me.

As the newborn son of a woman working in the molybdenum mine a half hour west of Breck, my mother made the bold choice to give her son the only advantage she saw in a world run by Grays.

A choice she hoped would lead to a life of privilege, it carried an unquantifiable risk she was only able to ignore because she was making the decision in the shadow of my father's death.

My mother didn't want a laborer's short life for me. In those days, there were only two ways out of hard labor in the service of the Grays. One of those was to be born a North Korean. They'd made their deal with the Grays and earned their special place while the rest of the world was foolishly trying to stand united against the alien invader during the siege. Since neither of my parents was Korean, that left my mother a single choice, to allow the Grays to implant a symbiont in my head. So few humans were chosen for the privilege, it must have felt like a lottery win to my mother.

Now I'm a member of the first generation of humans to have an alien bug implanted at birth. An avocado seed of a thing with a thousand hair-thin follicles rooted into my cortex.

And the privilege came.

I have an enviable house, a car, gasoline to run it, food at every meal, plenty to sate my hunger—mostly—and even meat on occasion.

However, I'm the Grays' tool, bound to them by the bug.

They see the thoughts in my head—they *believe* they see them all.

The bug has rudimentary telepathic abilities, so by using it, I have the capacity to control the biological switches in the Grays' machinery. That makes me useful in a Gray world.

The bug is able to see gravity, so in my mind I see it, too, a 3D picture of the world augmented in colors and intensities normal humans can't perceive.

The alien symbiont made me into a lesser version of the Grays, more capable than normal humans, and more valuable. So it almost goes without saying every unenhanced person I've ever met resents me.

Especially the North Koreans.

In the grav factory with my face against the tube and my eyes closed, I use my bug—not even thinking of it as anything other than a natural part of me—to precipitate millions of symbiont pairs out of the gas, coaxing them to settle onto the etched disc in just the right orientation, in the perfect spots, touching one another just so.

An intricate lattice of life.

To lay all those microbes on a grav plate in the few minutes it takes requires all the attention I can bring to bear. Doing it as quickly and flawlessly as I do makes me the rarest of people. Even among those with bugs in their heads, I'm recognized as a talent, ripe for reward.

With the war having burned through a whole generation of North Koreans who'd been implanted with bugs and sent into space to navigate the Grays' ships and aim their railguns, the Grays decided it was time to give their loyal servants from other countries a chance to sacrifice their lives for the cause. They allowed the lines in the grav plate factories to be automated so people like me could be spared to fly into space with the last of earth's defenders.

Like most masters, the Grays have a peculiar sense of reward.

The thing they didn't understand, though, was my officer's commission and my attachment to an SDF division was exactly what I'd wanted from the day the war with the Trogs began, when I learned the Grays were putting weapons in the hands of humans.

A weapon in the hands of a man who grates at the manacles of his servitude is a dangerous thing.

Breathing slowly to take my mind off my plans and refocus on my job, I lay the last of the microbes in their nirvana spots. I remove the disk from the leaden cylinder and carefully pass it on to the next step in the process. Before any of the unsuspecting little creatures has an inkling of what's coming, a blast of UV light kills them all.

The carcasses are then dehydrated where they lay. A protective film is spread over the cemetery disc to hold the special arrangement of their mineral remains in place.

The finished discs are stacked, all oriented in an exact direction, the edges lined up to form a solid contact for DC to flow in one of two directions. The whole pile is snugged into a titanium housing, and the grav plate is finished. Run a current through one way, and you get gravity. Reverse the current, and you have anti-gravity.

Combined with the Grays' fusion reactor technology, it's the power to travel the stars and to conquer backward apes like us.

That power, too, will soon be in my hands.

Chapter 4

I wear my stale odor like I wear the smudges on my knees, evidence of a life fading into the past.

Before being granted permission to leave, I had to kneel at the tiny feet of the factory's six Gray overseers.

Please, foul little creatures, grant me permission to stand tall like a man.

It was foolish to think that heretical thought so strong, chomping at my reins, prematurely feeling my freedom.

Two of the factory's Korean toughs looked on, or that's to say, looked down on me as I bowed. Dead, coal eyes. Jet-black hair. They're all fuckers.

To them, I'm subhuman.

And then my Gray masters dismissed me so I could bike the last few miles from Frisco down to the spaceport.

Each bug-headed line worker in the factory bowed the same as me, one at a time, asking permission to go and serve the next overlord in line. In doing so, the Grays, blinded by their pride, willfully sent a host of scheming insurgents into the midst of their last great effort to save themselves from the creatures invading the solar system.

Back in the moment, I breathe my last peace along the bike path, feeling the crisp, late-morning air. Around me, tall mountains are broken by jutting rocks, blanketed by the carcasses of long-dead evergreens, splashed yellow with autumn aspens.

I'll never bow again.

Never again.

It's as much a promise as a prayer.

I pedal past the reservoir, over the dam, and then back along the burbling river until I roll beneath the interstate highway. It's clogged both east and west with buses and semis bringing in two SDF heavy assault divisions, their equipment, and support personnel. All virgins to war. It'll take the rest of the day to have so many soldiers fitted into suits, ferried into space, and loaded onto the newly designed assault ships, the mysterious wonder-weapon that's supposed to turn the tide of the war.

Not likely.

I come to a stop. The bicycle path is blocked by a fence. Like everything else on the north end of the valley, the recreational path has been subsumed by the spaceport. I hop off my bike and lay it in the grass by the river. No lock. No need. I open my bag and find a pen and notepad. I write out a message and tuck it into a gap in the headlamp bracket.

TAKE THE BIKE IF YOU WANT.
I DON'T NEED IT ANYMORE.

Then I wait. I'm supposed to meet Vishnu, my contact with the Free Army, for any last-minute instructions he might have for me before I lead my ring of traitors into orbit.

Enough time passes to make me uncomfortable, and I decide there must be nothing new. Everything is going as planned.

I climb a steep bank to get up to road level.

Chaos.

Soldiers in uniform unload from their transports and try to figure out where to go. Boys just starting to shave. Middle-aged men with gray-flecked hair. Girls, not old enough for legal sex. And mothers wearing the scars of war's intimate touch, wrinkles eroded deep by worry, loss in their eyes. Third and fourth choice demographics for the draft. Maybe fifth. Sixth, even. All the strong, the young, the fast, are in suits up there among the asteroids, already fighting, or drifting lifeless in the void as the moisture from their cells leaches into the vacuum.

Our history could be written in the tales of our armies, their glory and their victories, all forged in the fire of discipline, tradition, sacrifice, and maybe a thousand trivial rules and rituals that don't make any damn sense to a civilian looking in from the outside. Those ingredients, when drilled into a recruit in the right proportions and reinforced through the camaraderie of soldiers who believe in a cause and know victory is their destiny, turn a regular person into a soldier.

Sadly, all of those ingredients were left out of this batch.

We're soldiers in little more than name. We're familiar with the words we're supposed to have memorized and we've all passed our multiple-choice tests, yet we know nothing about marching, taking orders, sacrificing for our brothers and sisters, or any of the steps in-between.

We're sandbags being thrown into the breach in the dike.

Most of us will wash away.

Others will sink under the weight of the dead, piling on top.

No, not soldiers, not us. We're draftees sprinkled with a few volunteers.

At thirty, still young and strong, I am an oddity among these dregs.

As sure as I know I'll never kiss my shriveling wife again, the Grays will bleed our planet to a husk. They tell us it's the survival of our species we fight for, but I darkly suspect it's only their pride we defend.

MSS men—Ministry of State Security—are in their gaudy uniforms everywhere. They're all North Koreans, of course. It occurs to me that I refer to the Koreans the same way the old men in Breck do, as type 'North.' The NORTH is a moot distinction. Soon after Pyongyang made its traitorous deal back in the days of the siege, the Grays thanked them for their fidelity by obliterating South Korea. China also paid a price for having nudged too hard, too often, to keep their nasty little subdivided neighbor in line with global norms.

Now there's only Korea, bordered on the south by a wasteland peninsula and a desert of destruction on the north.

I stand on a curb and look around to get my bearings.

The MSS autocrats are stopping every man and woman, affirming their authority by leaning in close to faces, yelling instructions, pointing, and keying in arm tattoos.

"You!"

"You!"

I realize one of the MSS men is pointing at me, mouth loud and arrogant. A lieutenant.

"Here!" He gestures at the fragmented asphalt where he expects me to come and plant my feet.

Normally, I'd hurry to act when ordered by an MSS man. Not today. I don't feel the fetters of their authority so tight. In the midst of twenty thousand SDF wannabe killers, I don't even fear the randomness of MSS violence.

I saunter toward him.

His face turns redder with each casual step I take. His accented words become harder to understand. He has one hand waving his data pad and one on the butt of his pistol.

I jog the last lazy steps.

"I could shoot you for delaying! Are you coward?" His accent gets stronger with emotion. "You deserter?"

"Clearly." My tone sparkles with sarcasm. The idea of liberty has made me brave and a little foolish. A lifetime of pent-up scorn is trying to burst out. Still, I'm hours away from having a weapon in my hand.

Just that much longer.

Forcing myself to look at my feet instead of into the lieutenant's eye, I wrap my next words in humility. It's a trap I'm laying. "Clearly, I'm not a deserter, sir. I rode my bike down the path, sir. I just came up from the river, sir." Holding out my forearm for him to see, I say, "I need my assignment, sir."

My arm, from the crook of my elbow to my wrist, is tattooed with an alphanumeric code written in Korean letters two inches tall.

He reads.

He keys it into his data pad.

And then he freezes.

I look up at him. The trap has snapped.

He knows.

I try not to smile.

His world just took a turn into the surreal, and he's confused, afraid. A Caucasian commissar outranking an MSS lieutenant, the Korean nightmare coming true.

Much more gently than the first time he did so, he takes my wrists.

Still, he doesn't believe. I can see it in his body language.

His voice is syrup and sugar now. "May I read you again?"

I nod so he knows he's not worth the effort it takes me to release a word into the air.

He looks at my tattooed skin. Carefully, he keys one symbol at a time into his device.

No mistake.

His face is animated with the thoughts running through his head. Meekly, he says, "Major Commissar Kane?"

Satisfaction.

Oh, glorious satisfaction.

For years, I worked hard to be the most productive bug-headed drone in the grav factory, and every time the Grays invasively probed my thoughts, I showed them the enthusiastic servility they hoped to see. I convinced them past any wisp of doubt I was just brimming with that one human characteristic they value above all others—loyalty.

So much loyalty, in fact, they believed I would be an efficient proxy for squeezing it out of other humans.

So, without one shred of military experience, they commissioned me *Major Commissar Kane*, an unflinching enforcer of the Grays' will in their flawed military.

Now I'll be expected to raise my weapon and gun down human cowards and mutineers.

Only I won't need to.

As the highest-ranking officer on an assault ship, only the Korean captain and communications officers will be outside my direct authority, though not necessarily above it. Mortified with the way the war is going, the Grays, instead of blaming themselves for their feckless strategy and ruinous weapons prohibitions, put the fault for the mess on their Korean lapdogs. The shift in power away from the Koreans is their punishment.

As for the two American members of the bridge crew and every SDF soldier we'll be hauling into battle, they'll all have to answer to the officer above them in their chain of command. They will also have to answer to me. To make sure that authority is real, every battle suit worn by every one of them will be coded to special gravity switches embedded in my helmet. I'll be able to magnetically freeze the metallic parts in their suits at will, rendering them immobile, and also be able to turn off the life support—in the worst cases, instantly kill any one of them or all of them with a high-voltage jolt from the micro-fusion reactor that drives their suits.

I'll be the most powerful man on the ship.

Feared.

Hated behind my back.

Plotted against.

The system is designed for that eventuality as well. I can opt to link my gravity switches to a biosensor in my suit. If I stop breathing, they all do, too.

They can't murder me.

When we go into battle, they'll do everything they can to protect me even though I'm not expected to fight.

Regardless, I'm ready for war.

What no Gray is aware of, what none of the MSS men realize, what not one of the twenty thousand combat troops flowing into the spaceport knows, is that I've run through every simulator on every weapon. I learned about the tactical roles of each man in a squad and platoon in every situation the simulators had to offer. I've familiarized myself with every job of a naval ship's small human crew. I think I understand space warfare in three dimensions with variable gravity.

Hopefully not false hopes from book-learnin' bullshit.

The only thing I've actually done with my own real, live body in three dimensions was that I spent hundreds of hours in a zero-g training room put together by me and my grav factory coconspirators with reject plates in an unused theater. A friend let me onto the rifle range at the spaceport from time to time.

I'm a pretty good shot with a railgun.

My biggest concern? I've analyzed the rumors trickling back to earth so I can understand why—if the whispers are true—we've lost every major battle in this conflict so far.

Besides a fair number of the sergeants, men promoted from those few lucky enough to have survived a battle or two, I might be the most combat-ready soldier in the spaceport.

"Major Kane, sir." The MSS lieutenant is pointing over the throng moving through the gates. He wants me away from him before I decide to do something about the disrespectful tone he took when he first addressed me. "Staging J-33. The hangar with the curved, red roof."

I look at the vast rows of warehouses and buildings, spotting J-33 painted in tall letters on a wall a half-mile ahead. "I pick up my gear there?"

"Yes, sir. They'll have your lift assignment, crew and platoon rosters, and assault ship designation." He taps his data pad with a finger. "I have you checked in." He cordially waves me to start moving. "This way, please."

I nod. No more words for him.

It's petty revenge.

Like every other human on the planet, I despise the Koreans, not only for the betrayal, not only for the collaboration, but for the way they relish the brutality they dole out to the rest of us.

Like the Grays, soon the Koreans will exist no more in earth's solar system.

One more item of my list of gruesome to-dos.

Chapter 5

It's been hours.

I worked through the crush of bodies moving toward their assigned armory buildings. At the door of Hangar J-33, I was scanned again and told to wait in one of eighteen lines.

Now, the toes of my shoes are touching a yellow stripe across the floor I'm not supposed to cross until I'm called.

Next in the queue to receive my equipment.

I'm hot, and I'm bored.

In the lines around me, I've spotted several of my coconspirators. Some are already through and on their way to their muster stations. Others, like me, are still waiting. We'll all be commissars. J-33 is the commissar equipment building.

Vishnu's promises, so far, have been kept.

Past a female commissar finishing up at the station with the techs just in front of me, past a staging area where workers in coveralls scurry, busy at tasks moving pieces of equipment needing to go here or there in a hurry, I see into the bowels of the warehouse.

Racks stand in rows forty feet tall. Technicians push ladders on wheels up and down the aisles. Near the front, they're moving coffin-size lockers on and off the shelves. Each of the coffins is open on one side, and contains a full commissar kit—weapon, ammo, undergarments, and battle suit. A modified construction suit, really. Each is sized—height, weight, arm and leg length—for the soldier intended to wear it.

Further into the warehouse, people are working at putting the kits together from racks that contain the individual pieces.

Past them, rows and rows of technicians toil at stations, repairing damaged suits and testing the systems contained in the integrated backpacks.

At the far end of the warehouse, through the open doors, out in the sun, laborers are unloading dumpster-size containers. Scarred, limp battle suits tumble out onto expansive metal grates above drain culverts.

No bodies inside, just the suits.

Also guns, empty magazines, boots, and helmets.

People in coveralls rubberized up to the chest use pressure washers to clean the salvaged suits, inside and out. Water sprays in white and foamy, and drains down reddish-brown.

A tech stomps a lump to push it through the grate. It looks like the flesh of an animal killed on the road. Then it's gone, washed away with swirling water.

I come to realize none of the equipment is new. The Grays don't waste anything—anything except people.

"Step up, dumbass! How many times I gotta ask?"

The commissar who was being equipped ahead of me is gone. Moved out through a side door. In her place, one of the coffin-sized lockers is standing, full of my equipment.

"Waste of my time." It's the sergeant in charge of distributing my new equipment. His patience seems to have been used up years ago. "I'll be fitting this suit on someone else tomorrow." He goes on to mutter, "Might as well go up naked and save me the goddamn trouble."

I step across the line and hold out my forearm for him to read as I take my place in the designated spot.

The guy glances at the tattoo and enters my info into his data pad. Without looking up, he says, "You saw what everybody else did, strip." Again he rhetorically mutters. "Why do I gotta ask?"

I drop my bag, untie my shoes, and peel off my clothes.

"Jesus, you got a Gray stink on you."

I ignore him.

He starts his interrogation.

"Any injuries?"

"No."

"Open wounds?"

"No."

An assistant bags my belongings and writes my name and ID on the plastic.

"Bad teeth?"

"No."

"Venereal diseases?"

"No."

The list of questions goes on. I drone the same answer over and over. I figure my responses are irrelevant. I'm a hot carcass on the cutting line. The war needs bodies to bleed. I can do plenty.

It's not a hard quality to measure. Five quarts of corpuscles? I've got that.

Another tech comes up and fetches an apparatus of tubes and connectors from my kit box. I know what's coming. I cringe.

The sergeant sees my reaction and glances at the tubes. He laughs.

"Ever had a catheter?" the second tech asks.

I shake my head, wishing he were female. Somehow, that seems like a better way to go. "Is that recycled too?"

"Waste no pennies, want no pennies?" The tech says it like it's a question as he looks at the sergeant for confirmation. "How's that phrase go?" His hand is already on my penis like it's a piece of meat on a backyard grill. Nothing special. Not sexual. Not repulsive. Just plumbing.

Everybody gets used to their job, I guess.

"The suit is a self-contained life support system," he tells me as he works. "You'll be like a frog in your own personal terrarium."

The catheter slides in. I tense, but it's not as bad as I thought it was going to be.

He says, "It'll give you all the air, warmth, and water, you need for three months or three years without cracking open, as long as you change the calorie packs and hydrogen cells. Occasionally, the recycler unit in the backpack will eject a solid waste pellet. A little flat disk about an inch across. Don't be alarmed when you see it."

"How often?" I ask.

"Depends on the person. Your metabolism. Your activity. What residual solids are in your system when you start."

I continue to wait for an answer.

He makes a guess. "Once a week? Once a month? It varies."

"Three days out of a cal pack," the sergeant tells me. "Your suit comes with one in the mount." He points at my shoddily-repaired orange gear hanging in the coffin. A dented thermos—the calorie pack—is attached to the backpack integrated with the suit. It looks to hold a little more than a liter.

"Turn around," the catheter tech tells me. "Gotta catch the outflow. All of it."

I turn.

He roughly goes to work prepping me for the second tube. "The suit recycles just about everything. Hell, if you keep the hydrogen cell swapped, you could spend the rest of your life in this thing."

The sergeant laughs and looks at me, taunting me with his aversion. "Don't worry about how long the cal pack lasts, you won't make it to your first change."

I ignore him.

"You been on a liquid diet?" asks the guy handling my plumbing.

"Yes."

"How many days?"

"Three."

"Did you drink your prep kit liquids?"

"I did."

"What did your last bowel movement look like?"

"Rocky Mountain spring water."

"Hope you enjoyed the one before it. It's the last real shit you're gonna take until this suit comes off."

The second catheter goes in.

Chapter 6

His work done, the catheter tech leaves.

Another technician arrives, a woman. She helps me into my suit's undergarment, a skintight layer, thicker than a t-shirt, thinner than flannel. It's translucent green and webbed with coppery filaments that'll regulate my temperature, cold or hot, and wick away perspiration to the suit's moisture recycler. It'll self-seal over smaller wounds, retaining blood inside my veins to keep me in the fight a little bit longer. It even has a bio lab on a chip installed in a small module pressed against one of my thighs. The device can sample my blood and diagnose a range of conditions as well as administer coagulants, morphine, and the one everyone seems anxious to try—Suit Juice—an amphetamine cocktail created to keep a sleepy soldier's eyes open and pump him or her full of confidence.

The micro-fusion reactor in the integrated backpack will power my new veneer. Once I'm encased in the ragged orange relic, the undergarment will keep my temperature in a normal range at any place I'm likely to end up in the solar system.

Of course, the sun's corona is on the list of notable exceptions.

Time for the outer layer, a repurposed and reassigned space construction suit.

Through three decades of occupation, earthbound factories have produced these suits in the hundreds of millions to support the Grays' ambitious lunar and orbital building projects. Like all of the suits, mine is orange, formerly bright, now dirty and scuffed. My name, rank, and an alphanumeric code in Korean are stenciled on the chest.

The remnants of a previous owner's letters have left a ghostly haze.

The gruff sergeant hauls the suit out of the coffin on its hanger. He hefts it on his fingers as he shrugs. He wants me to know how light it is. Coin-sized patches mar the surface in seven or eight places, but the sergeant runs his fingers over a large repaired tear across the torso. It's clear the suit was nearly ripped in half. "Wonder how that happened?" he muses.

"Don't be an asshole," the female tech tells him.

The sergeant's disdain for me is starting to grate on my tired nerves. "Has the repair been tested?" I ask. "Will the suit function?"

The sergeant points vaguely toward the men and women working at the repair benches down at the far end of the hangar. "Those people slave around the clock for you spaghetti-heads, and that's how you show your appreciation? Slagging the quality of—"

"Sarge," says the female tech, getting his attention, "you're talking too much." She looks up at me and winks. "The major could slap an insubordination charge on you and hand you to one of the MSS dinks outside. It's been a long day for all of us. Be smart. Clamp it."

The sergeant huffs, thinks about things for a moment, then leans in close to my face. "Jokin'. Stress and all, you know, with the Trogs conquering the solar system and coming to cannibalize my kids for dinner. You understand."

He sees only dead ice in my eyes. I know, because his expression changes. His breathing quickens. His posture droops, just a hair.

I don't know if I'm as dangerous as I'm pretending to be at the moment. He knows I'm willing to find out.

And that's enough.

"Cannibalize isn't the right word." The female tech smiles like she's trying to hold in a laugh. "We'd have to be the same species as the Trogs for it to be cannibalization."

"The suit's been tested," says the sergeant sheepishly, as he moves to help the female tech stuff me inside.

The explanations come now without any editorial inflection.

The suit will protect me from the vacuum of space and high pressure up to thirty-eight atmospheres. It was designed to shield the wearer from cosmic radiation, micrometeors, and other bits of high-velocity space trash, though the repaired holes attest to its limitations in that regard.

It's a marriage of the Grays' alien tech and human ingenuity. Far from a magical weapon of war, it'll help keep me alive in an environment that would snuff me in seconds given half a chance. And with the suit's tiny, built-in gravity plates, it might even sway the odds a bit in my favor.

It feels a little bulky now that it's on, although not much more so than wearing a few layers of sweats. It's completely flexible but can go rigid in small areas or wholly. It shouldn't impair my movement once I'm used to wearing it.

"It's getting warm in here," I tell my dressers.

"Don't worry." The woman moves around behind me and seats the hydrogen cartridge into the backpack.

I feel a mild vibration.

"The micro-fusion reactor kicks on automatically as soon as you plug in the hydrogen fuel cartridge." She picks up a second hydro cartridge and straps it into a place made for it on my thigh.

My skin starts to cool. "Feels fine," I tell her, nodding. "Thanks."

"If you're out in the vacuum, I wouldn't go more than five or ten minutes without a hydro pack. You'll have time to swap it when this one runs out, but don't lollygag." She smiles again.

I like her. Working with her is how things should be.

Sarge stays quiet as he fetches my boots.

Together they help me push my feet in, and then they seal them to my suit. The gloves follow a similar procedure. Finally, the helmet engulfs my skull with the smart-glass out of its seal and slid up over the top.

The whole integrated ecosystem doesn't weigh thirty pounds.

We run through a series of tests to make sure each subsystem works.

It feels rushed, like we're bumping up against a time constraint nobody acknowledges.

I'm shown how to switch the calorie cartridge. It works just like the hydrogen cell. Calories on the left, hydro on the right. I try each once, burning the exercise into my memory as I go. My life depends on getting it right when the time comes to do it myself.

The woman mentions the suit's gravity controls but figures since I've worked in the grav factory, I'm likely to know way more about it than she ever will.

They give me a pistol-shaped weapon. Being a commissar, I'm not assigned a rifle.

The female tech, not chiding, tells me I'm lucky to get the pistol. Shortages and all.

The pistol is a mini gravity-drive railgun. It runs on the exact technology behind all of the Grays' and Trogs' kinetic weapons.

My gun shoots tiny projectiles that look like short, headless nails. Each weighs a bit more than a gram, but at the velocities they travel, they'll punch with the momentum of a .45 slug. My magazine holds nearly three hundred, alternating between titanium-tipped armor-piercing rounds and those of a softer lead alloy designed to flower out on impact and shred soft flesh.

Unlike the rounds for the rifles that had been the mainstay of terrestrial militaries for centuries, my projectiles aren't powered by a chemical reaction. So I don't need the extra weight and bulk of powder and brass in the magazine. I carry just the slugs.

The woman says, "You're lucky, both divisions going up today will be carrying the new guns. Everything before was single-shot. These will go full-auto."

"Gray rules," grouses the sergeant. "They tie our hands. If they'd let us build the kind of weapons we used to make when I was a kid, this war would be going differently, I'll tell you that."

And that's the thing about Grays, they're a status quo, no-imagination bunch. They have scads of mandates designed to keep humans from creating new things and combining our technologies with theirs, especially when it comes to weapons and gravity tech. It's only the war we're losing that's altered the policies.

Ignoring the sergeant, the woman says, "Your gun runs off the energy from the micro-fusion power plant in your suit. All the power you'll ever need. But if you go full-auto, which you shouldn't with your pistol because you won't be able to control it, you'll burn through hydrogen like nobody's business. The three days you're supposed to get out of a cartridge happens only if you're doing a lot of nothing, like watching TV. If you're using lots of grav and shooting, you might get three hours." She slaps the spare hydro cartridge on my thigh. "Don't lose track of how much H you've got. It's your life."

Nodding, and pointing to the empty magnetic mounts around my waist, on my thighs, and up my chest, I ask, "What about extra magazines?"

"Grab what you need off the dead troops," Sarge tells me. He's happy to say it, not because the other soldiers will be dead, but because it means I'll soon be dead, too.

The female tech nods to confirm. She's sad and serious. "We can't build this stuff fast enough."

Thinking of my long hours in the grav factory, forging and inlaying plate after endless plate, one of hundreds, maybe thousands of such factories across the globe, I can't help but think other war industries must be producing just like we were. "How is that kind of shortage possible?"

"The Ticks don't understand mass production," says the woman, slipping into the derogatory slang for Grays. She probably didn't even realize she'd done it. "They can't manage a supply chain to save their life. And their concept of math…" she shakes her head and waves at the air.

"Fuckin' Grays," adds Sarge.

It surprises me, but it turns out he and I at least have something in common.

CHAPTER 7

An American woman in a Korean uniform with large gold and red epaulets walks up. She's a colonel, and she's stiffer than the starch in her clothes.

Sarge salutes her and sulks back a few steps, his posturing ended.

"Is he ready?" asks the colonel.

"Yes, ma'am." Sarge hurries away with the female tech in tow.

The colonel lifts her data pad but focuses on me. "I'm Colonel Blair. Have you completed your online training?"

I nod.

"'Yes, ma'am' is the proper response."

"Yes, ma'am." The reasons are different, but I decide I don't like this woman any more than I liked the sergeant.

"This is your first day, but next time you come into the presence of an officer, salute."

"Yes, ma'am."

"You are Major Commissar Dylan Kane, Solar Defense Force Heavy Assault Division 743." She looks down at her data pad, "3rd battalion, 6,736th Regiment, Charlie Company."

Heavy Assault Division sounds badass to me. I like it. "Yes, ma'am."

"You know what everybody calls the Heavy Assault Divisions?"

"Yes, ma'am. Grunts."

"You know that's not a sanctioned SDF term, correct?"

"Yes, ma'am."

"Do you know why they call themselves Grunts?"

"Are we making conversation?" I ask, "Or are you testing me?"

She doesn't answer my question, but instead looks at her data pad. "You're married?"

"Yes, ma'am."

"And your wife is rearing a Gray hatchling?"

"Yes, ma'am."

"You know that exempts you from the draft, don't you?"

"I volunteered."

"Volunteered?"

In a tone with a deniable level of sarcasm, I say, "Service to our brotherhood with the Grays is a human's highest calling."

"You believe that?"

I look down at the shitty orange spacesuit I'm wearing as if that's a sufficient answer.

"Caring for the Gray hatchling should be your most important concern," she tells me. "You know that?"

"My wife's sister lives in our house and will care for my wife and the hatchling in my absence."

A long pause follows while the colonel scrutinizes me. Finally, she says, "Show me your d-pad screen. Does it work?"

I lift my arm and turn my palm up, showing Blair the screen built onto the inner forearm of my suit. The LED panel flashes to life. It's designed to activate whenever it's in my line of sight.

"Half the damned things break on the first deployment." She steps back and looks my suit up and down. "A wonder this thing still holds air."

Nothing but sunshine here.

She nods at the d-pad on my arm. "Call up your ship assignment under the Priority Orders tab."

I look at the screen. The software is not the version I trained with in the simulator.

"Flashing red," she tells me as she reaches over and points. "That one."

I tap it.

"Your ship assignment, Assault Ship Alpha Delta Kilo Seven Eight Nine Tango Three. You'll go out with First Platoon. The company's commander is a Captain Milliken. You'll be on the same ship as him. The ship designations for the other three platoons are here. One platoon per ship." She points again.

"Got it."

Her finger hovers over another part of the screen. "For the company roster and ship's officers, there. Muster station, here."

I nod and then remember to add, "Yes, ma'am."

"After we finish here, you'll follow the map on your d-pad to your muster station where you'll be loaded onto a transport and taken to an earth-side staging area. From there, you'll board your ship. With any luck, in a couple of hours, we'll be in space."

"Earth-side, ma'am? We?" Two questions that are competing for answers.

"I'm your CO. I'm going up with division command." She points at my d-pad again. "You'll see me in the Chain of Command tab."

I activate the touch screen and look. She reports directly to Lieutenant General Lee, I assume Korean. Seems like half the MSS are named Lee. I click on Lee and see that he is indeed MSS. MSS has control over every SDF unit through a political command structure that parallels the SDF chain of command. As a commissar, I'm part of the MSS hierarchy. So, in the eyes of the men and women in the platoons I'm responsible for, that'll make me MSS, too.

Getting past that is going to be hard. The company's trust will come at a steep price.

"Arizona is where we're headed," Blair tells me. "The yard there has built out eleven hundred of the new design assault ships. We'll be taking almost half of them up."

Security around the design has been unusually tight, and nothing I'd heard through the online rumor factories was verifiable. I'm curious. "Anything I need to know about these ships?"

"New ships," she tells me, "new tactics." Then, in a surprise I didn't expect, her voice turns to a whisper just loud enough for me to hear. "'Bout damn time, too. The Troglodytes have been handing us our asses in this war since day one."

The official word on the ground has always been that we're winning. Only the loyalists and people who like to keep their heads in their asses believe that, though.

Colonel Blair steps back and examines my face like she's searching for something false concealed under my skin.

The things I'm hiding are buried too deep for her to even guess at.

She points to a side exit. "Walk with me."

My suspicions tingle.

No officer came to escort the commissar who'd kitted up just ahead of me.

Blair turns to go, and I follow.

What choice do I have?

CHAPTER 8

Blair says nothing else. She just walks.

She leads me away from J-33 and down an old road turned to dirt that runs behind the warehouses. The path will take us to the muster stations near the lift pads a mile or so further on in the valley.

Around us, men and women in spacesuits are shuffling in the same direction. What passed for exuberant patriotism among many of them when they were coming in through the front gate earlier in the day is mostly gone. Now we all have plastic tubes stuck in places we once thought private, and we're geared in battle suits still damp from the steam that cleaned out the remnants of the previous owners.

Feet autopilot their way forward.

Soldiers' eyes search the snowy peaks above, looking for inspiration or God or who-knows-what to fortify their shivering souls.

Fingers tap frustration into d-pads, as men and women who scammed their way through their military courses try to figure out the software that runs their suits, maintains communication, and keeps them alive. Too many of them never expected to need their training. They never thought they'd wear the orange, let alone queue up in front of a grav lift designed to haul cargo into orbit.

Despite our new weapons, many of us will die soon, not just because we're overmatched and outnumbered, but for those most rudimentary of reasons historians like to say should have been obvious at the time.

Number one on that list will be the Grays' conceited disinterest toward their chattel—us. The telepathic little monsters can't get past the human necessity to spend undue time learning. Grays easily share with one another what they need to know and believe we should do the same with our rudimentary substitutes for telepathy—the internet, telephones, and TV.

And fucking books, I guess.

To them, sending a productive worker away from a job for ten or twenty weeks to learn about weapons, tactics, and war is a colossal waste of time. It was only the reviled Koreans' incessant arguments for training camps in the fashion of those utilized by earth's pre-Gray militaries that we have anything at all.

The compromise the Grays allowed was better than nothing, but not by much.

Every able-bodied person sixteen and up is required to demonstrate proficiency on a battery of military simulators, some with goals as simple as learning military hierarchy so would-be soldiers will know who their boss is. Other sims teach about d-pads, weaponry, and zero-g maneuvering.

The simulator program is supplemented with privatized hands-on certification courses anybody can arrange to take in their time off from work. Few take advantage of these courses, because people just can't resist the temptation to take the shortcut.

So comes the second guilty reason behind the coming slaughter.

Anybody with a measure of motivation to shirk the responsibility of military training can find a way out. Cheats for all of the sims are available in any black market for the price of a meal. Most of the private certification enterprises are rubber-stamp operations, designed to herd students through as fast as possible with no regard for the value of the outcome. They operate according to their incentives. Owners get sweatless work and full bellies. Students meet their training obligations with little effort.

Hence us, the planet's home-schooled army.

The leftovers.

Gristle for the grinder.

I find sudden certainty in the thought that a battle-hardened Trog is going to shoot me, or hack me, or break my bones so violently their jagged shards will tear through my secondhand suit. My blood will boil into the vacuum as I try to bite back mouthfuls of air escaping my lungs, my breath abandoning me when I need it most, the last oxygen I'll ever taste.

Some time later, my suit will be fished out of the void and recycled back to earth. After the remains of my body are washed out, it'll be patched again, half-ass tested, and wrapped around the shivering body of another unprepared recruit.

Fly.

Die.

Repeat.

Until there aren't any humans left on our pale blue planet to massacre in the heavens.

Revolution will be a moot idea, a wispy dream in the senile minds of those too old to raise a weapon.

The Trogs will come to harvest the Grays, rooting them out of their cold warrens on the moon. They'll invade mother earth and find every wrinkled hag hiding a hatchling in a stinking bedroom, and then our parasitic overlords will meet their gruesome end.

Karma.

At least there's that.

The colonel, unaware of the dark future my thoughts are wandering through, says, "You can gravity compensate by ten or twenty percent, so it'll be easier for you to make the walk."

"No thank you, ma'am," I tell her. "This will be the last natural g I'm likely to feel for a while." Maybe forever. "I'll carry the load."

"Drop the ma'am for now. That's for when we're in front of the non-coms and grunts."

We're not exactly in private, but I say, "Okay."

Without any hint of what's coming, she says, "Your contact was compromised."

The phrase, sudden and shocking, means only one thing to me. I feel like ten pounds of ice just dropped into my stomach. She's talking about Vishnu, my contact with the Free Army. I stumble.

Blair reaches out to steady me. "You all right?"

I smile my lie. "I should have g compensated." I add the twenty percent and pretend to concentrate on my balance as I concoct an escape plan. I have a pistol. I could put a dozen rounds in Blair's chest and hope she doesn't have a kill switch linked to a biosensor under her uniform. Then I could max grav my ass the hell away from here.

The orange battle suits are built to handle enormous construction loads, but I've heard a brave—crazy—person could use the embedded gravity plates to accelerate the thing to Mach 1 in atmospheric flight. Of course, the suit, not being aerodynamic by any measure, would likely kill me at that speed.

Blair stops walking. "Go ahead, get yourself right."

"I already have." I prepare to yank my pistol off its magnetic mount.

"Now stop being coy, and let's talk."

"About?" I ask, not ready to give up on coy. I tell myself she can't know everything about my contact or I'd already be in cuffs.

"The MSS picked up Vishnuvardhen this morning."

They have his full name, but I don't respond, deciding instead to let her keep fishing. I might learn enough to keep myself alive until I can warn the insurgents—my friends—I've recruited over the past several years.

"I know what you're thinking. We don't have time for it." She lets that hang in the air, but if she truly had any idea what I was thinking she'd be running in the other direction.

"I don't know what you're talking about." The cliché is the best I can come up with at the moment. I need to calm myself. I need to think clearly.

Blair huffs, grabs me by the arm, and leads me away from the other soldiers on their long walks toward the lift pads. We crunch our way through brown grass between two hangars. No one else is between the buildings.

We're as alone as we can be in the midst of two SDF divisions being processed through a spaceport.

I'm thinking it'll be a good place to shred her with a burst of high-velocity metal.

Few eyes to see.

Better chance to get away.

Chapter 9

"Penny Reed and Phil Barber." She looks at me to see if I recognize the names.

Of course I know the names. Phil's my best friend, my brother-in-law. He works at the grav factory, as does Penny.

I show Blair nothing.

She proceeds down her list, naming a dozen more of my coconspirators from the factory. "Do you want me to go through all of it?"

Sure, if it'll buy me time to make the necessary choice.

If I kill her, I give up on all I've worked for. My revolution ends here. Shortly after they catch me, my life will end in an MSS interrogation chamber with most of my favorite pieces missing.

I don't think there's another way.

I glance right and left and casually move my hand over my pistol grip.

"Listen to what I'm telling you, Kane. I know you're suspicious. You should be. But if I already know everyone in your network, why wouldn't they be under arrest already?"

"How do I know they're not?"

"You'll see Penny and Phil when you board your ship. You three are assigned together. That's what you requested, right? And that SDF sergeant and the captain Vishnu asked for, I don't see how you could have pulled them into your network, but they're on your ship, too."

I don't know what sergeant and captain she's talking about. I don't have any contacts in the military, and everything about the Free Army is supposed to be compartmentalized for security reasons. There's got to be a mountain of important things I don't know. In fact, I'm counting on it. The revolution can't be just Vishnu, me, and my friends.

Which, of course, means Vishnu had to have his contacts up the chain.

"Listen to what I'm telling you, Kane. Who do you think made the assignments you asked for? These are military ranks and positions on ships of war. Vishnu is a black-market salvager. He doesn't have that kind of authority."

By guessing my thoughts, she has me. I'm still having trouble with the fact she's an MSS colonel.

Then again, *I* am an MSS major, and I'm a rebel.

"You made the assignments," I conclude, glancing around for uniformed MSS goons, thinking they'll be cockroaching out of their crevices to arrest me now that I'm incriminating myself.

"We don't have time for your games, so I'll just tell you what you need to hear. Vishnu was captured alive." Blair's disappointment looks real. It runs deep. "They'll torture him. He'll talk. Nobody holds out for long. You and I both better hope we're off-planet by the time that happens."

If Blair *is* telling the truth, then my friend is suffering, and soon he'll be dead. I grimace. Too much is changing, and it's changing faster than I'd like.

She goes on to say, "There's a coded message on your pilot's d-pad. There's an encryption key on yours. Drop them both into the same folder. Among other things, they'll give you a location for a rendezvous. We don't know when each ship will be able to sneak away, probably in the chaos of the battle once we get up there."

"This is really happening, then?" It's a childish question, an incriminating question, a hopeful question. I've put years into this dream. I don't want it to fail. I want to believe Blair.

"Yes," she tells me, with a look in her eyes that tries to erase my doubts. "Get your ship to the…" she pauses and looks left and right, "to the Free Army's base. However you need to do it. You understand?"

I nod. Mutiny is easy in the abstract, but by the end of the day, I'll need to test my mettle and actually kill a North Korean officer.

"Once we have our forces at our bases, we can start running this war the way it needs to run. We can win it. And then we can win the revolution."

I ask, "Where is the rendezvous?"

"Asteroid belt. A mining colony where the people are sympathetic to our cause."

It sounds like a base to me. Good. There is more to this rebellion than my do-nothing conspiracy and a dodgy MSS colonel. I figure I'll press her for information I know is secret, test her. "I've heard a lot of conflicting rumors about these assault ships we're supposed to be taking up. I've heard they're not built for deep space." Meaning we won't make it to the asteroid belt. "Do they have the power to make light speed?"

"1.2." Blair shrugs. "On average. Some barely make it over the hump. Some'll do 1.5."

A range for the top speed? Not something specific? That worries me. And even worse, 1.5 is nothing close to the hyper-light velocities the big Trog cruisers do. They'll blaze across the universe eight times faster than a photon in vacuum. "Are these assault ships another shitty Gray design?"

"I don't think the Ticks are capable of creating anything new." Blair looks around, worried. She's just uttered a heresy, an illegality. Everybody on earth is habituated to take that cautionary glance when they voice the unspeakable. "I think everything the Grays make us build for them is based on designs they stole from wherever they came from. You've probably heard the Trogs use pretty much the same tech we—" Blair thinks for a moment. "Their cruisers are exactly like ours."

"Exactly?"

"Exactly."

I shake my head. I'd long ago stopped believing the news feeds, instead, trusting my instincts to ferret through old histories and current rumors to find my truth. The stories of Trog cruisers being exactly like ours, that one seemed beyond belief.

"These assault ships are all us, but with all the damned Gray laws about what we can and can't do, humans don't have enough people with the right kind of expertise anymore. Things aren't like they were before the siege." Blair sighs. "These ships were fast-tracked through design and rushed into production. You'll see what I mean when you lay eyes on one. They look like something you'd find in a junkyard."

"Great." Full dose of sarcasm on that one.

"They will fly. They'll do what they're designed to do. But light speed..." Blair sighs again.

"What does that sigh mean?"

"You can ride a brick into space if you attach a few grav plates and a power source. No big deal. But generating a grav bubble robust enough to warp space into a localized wave you can surf past the speed of light..." Blair pauses and switches to a different subject. "You know how the Grays are, they don't name their ships, their space stations, not even each other. So there wasn't a name for this assault ship design. Once the engineers understood what they were creating and how it would be used, they started joking around about what to call it."

I understand where she's going, so I ask, "Which was?"

"Kamikaze."

"Great." It's a good day for sarcasm.

Blair says, "The name stuck during testing when nearly one in twenty came apart trying to make it to light speed. The more you fly 'em, the worse your odds. That's why the SDF decided on an official designation for the type—Spitfire. They figured a name like kamikaze would be bad for morale."

Skipping the sarcasm for a moment, I start running numbers in my head to calculate how many of my friends these ships will kill by day's end. The result of my calculation is, surprisingly, more sarcasm. "These ships sound wonderful."

"They've got their flaws, but they'll do what they were built for. Human ingenuity." Blair nods proudly.

Nobody says that kind of crap anymore. I wonder if it's real or part of her act. "So what does an assault ship do, besides assault?" I'm thinking D-Day landing craft and high casualty rates.

"At sub-light speeds they'll pull twelve g's all day long."

"All day?" I laugh a bit too derisively. I don't need to do much math in my head to know it won't take long at twelve g's to start bumping up against light speed, and then infinities in the equations start making everything impossible.

"That's not what I meant," says Blair, "They'll do twelve g's when you need it. And they're maneuverable because they're small. Those big Trog cruisers max at four g's."

"So we can dodge their railgun fire and win with numbers?" I ask. I'm trying to guess the tactics and wondering why ships with such small crews have such a large contingent of grunts onboard. "What are the armaments?"

"None."

Sometimes, even sarcasm isn't enough. "Because?"

"Weight."

"Please tell me you're getting to the good part."

She nods. "Our physicists have engineered a gravity lens."

"What the hell is that?"

CHAPTER 10

"This is our best-kept secret," says Blair. "A decisive weapon. Invented by humans, manufactured by humans."

"With permission from the Grays," I add, "because we're losing the war so badly?"

"Exactly," answers Blair. "If we were winning with their weapons, they wouldn't give us permission to do any of this stuff. You'd still have a single-shot pistol, and you'd die trying to reload it while a thousand Trogs swarmed over you."

Yeah, well, she's mostly right there, but training draftees with the damned weapons would go a long way toward making them more than squishy speed bumps for the invading hordes. "What's this gravity lens?"

"It's built from specially shaped and configured grav plates controlled by computer."

"Computers and grav tech?" I ask, shocked, but completely out of habit. Mixing the two technologies used to be a death penalty offense.

"The assault ships were built with special permission," Blair tells me and then taps the underside of her left forearm. "Just like the computer enhancements to your suit."

The computer-controlled features of the suits have been in existence so long they've become mundane. Proof that if the Grays would get out of the way, we could do so much more. "Tell me about this gravity lens."

"It focuses an ultra-intense gravity field down to a narrow point."

I'm thinking of a magnifying glass and cooking ants on the sidewalk with the sun's rays.

"The lens forms a conical anti-grav field that narrows on a 3D parabolic arc toward the tip. It pushes matter away from it."

I'm trying to imagine how such a thing could be used as a weapon.

"Think of it as a lance, like knights used to joust with in the Middle Ages. The lens is the handle, the anti-grav cone is the long pointy part."

I'm stuck on the jousting image and can't get past it. "What do we do with that?"

"These assault ships are built like battering rams," she answers. "All steel, fusion reactors, and grav plates, with just enough room inside for a platoon of SDF troops."

I get the picture, and I really don't like it. "We're going to ram Trog cruisers in space?" I'm recalculating the number of my friends I think will soon die, and the mortality rate is soaring. It's odd how quickly math converts to sarcasm. "Why do they call them kamikazes?"

Blair contains her exasperation over my thinly veiled disdain, and says, "You'll have some time at your muster station to gain an understanding of the technology and the tactics. The information is on your d-pad. Yes, these assault ships were built to ram Trog cruisers."

I'd have preferred not to have that confirmed.

"It sounds bad," admits Blair, reading the look on my face, "but if all goes well, your ship's hull will never actually collide with the cruiser's hull. The focused gravity cone is so intense that with the momentum of an assault ship, no material we know of can hold together against it. The gravity cone will pierce the target cruiser's defensive fields and impale the hull, creating a hole large enough for the assault ship to slip right in. Of course, the whole process is extremely violent on the cruiser's side of things."

"And on the assault ship?" I ask. "Aren't we going to be inside?"

"Like I said," she answers, "the assault ship is made of steel, reactors, and grav plates. No comforts. They're built for this, and this only. They have enough plates and they can generate enough reactor power to create an inertial bubble around the crew compartment. You won't even feel the impact. The trick is coming in fast enough to punch through the defensive grav fields and the hull, but not so fast that you obliterate both ships in the collision."

"In ships where one in twenty falls apart when you step on the gas?" I make it sound like a question, yet I'm just making a point. "So far, this revolution isn't sounding anything like the one I envisioned."

"We have to win this war," says Blair, "or at least drive the Trogs out of our system. Without an end to hostilities, revolution is pointless. First one, then the other."

I don't need that point clarified for me. I understood it from the day the Trogs first set foot on the moon, blowing everything to hell and trying to kill everybody up there.

"If things go well after you ram the Trog cruiser, you capture it," says Blair. "That's the idea."

"The hope," I translate, for both our sakes.

Ignoring my comment, Blair says, "With these assault ships and our new tactics, we'll destroy enough enemy cruisers and the Trogs will go back to where they came from. If we capture enough ships, we'll make the Free Army the preeminent power in the solar system, and then we can rid ourselves of those little Gray miscreants and their Korean lapdogs."

"All with a gravity lens." I want to believe it, I really do.

"The Grays conquered us on the back of two technological advantages," argues Blair, "fusion power and gravity manipulation. That's all they had over us, and it was enough."

I nod. I know that's true, though the MSS propaganda machine would have us believe the Grays are our benevolent big brothers in the universe, and that our acceptance of their rule over us was voluntary because we sought a path to physical and spiritual transcendence through their guidance.

Total shit.

Chapter 11

Blair leaves me and heads back up the road to fetch another commissar like me in need of final instructions.

I walk on toward my muster station, thoughts swirling with what-ifs and feelings that don't want to be ignored. Vishnu is as good as dead. I can't indulge any emotions over it.

Around me, soldiers are stopping and looking at the sky.

At first, it's just one or two, and I ignore them. I've got no time to stare at a cloud that looks like a bunny or a horse on a pogo stick. I'm thinking about the tactics of ramming another ship in space and how difficult it's going to be to keep the assault ship moving in that window of relative velocities that'll produce a successful attack and not kill us all.

The thought bothering me the most is that our commanders might not care much about our success in that regard. If one assault ship and its platoon are obliterated while taking a Trog cruiser out of action, it would be an easy trade to justify—forty or fifty soldiers for thousands of Trogs and a capital ship. Any admiral would make that choice.

I can't help but consider the possibility that perhaps these assault ships aren't meant to survive at all. Maybe the platoon rides along as a way to spoof the pilot into thinking he has a chance to survive the collision. And that's how the SDF convinces the pilots to do it.

Suicide zealots are hard to come by.

I don't want to believe I'm kamikaze bait, but it would account for the apparent quality of the troops the SDF is sending up today.

I bump into a man who's stopped but barely takes notice when I excuse myself. It's then I see *everyone* has stopped, not just some of them. They're all looking at the sky.

I stop walking and look up, too.

Way above the clouds, a misshapen blob glows white like the daytime moon, but about half as big. It's moving across the sky fast enough to make a full orbit in ninety minutes. Lights sparkle and flash around it. Sprays of fireworks' explosions streak through the atmosphere, far away and silent.

Only they aren't fireworks.

The blob is one of the twenty-six asteroids towed in from the belt over the years and placed in orbit around the earth two hundred miles up. Each is roughly a mile across. They've all been drilled, cut with tunnels, and honeycombed with dormitories, armories, cafeterias, and storerooms, everything an orbital fortress would need to survive a battle or a drawn-out siege.

I've watched enough vids on the Internet to know it's an attack I'm seeing. The Trog cruisers are up there pounding the fortress with railgun fire, trying to destroy the defending guns buried inside. Hunks of stone are being blasted off the surface. Some of the rock is hitting the atmosphere as meteorites and burning up. Some of it, maybe lots, will impact the ground below.

"Is that where we're going?" asks the corporal I'd bumped into moments before.

"I don't know." I hope it's not. I pray command wouldn't send us off the ground and straight into a firefight. No general could be that stupid—that wasteful—with the lives of the men and women in his command.

Unless we are just kamikazes.

The lights of the battle cross out of sight behind the mountains, and people scan the sky looking for more. Another asteroid comes into view, glowing white as it catches the sun high above. It's on a different orbit, moving southwest, away from the battle that went east, maybe to swing around the backside of the planet and fire on the Trogs from a direction they aren't expecting.

That's the genius behind the orbital arrangement of the asteroids. None share an orbital plane. None share an orbital radius or an orbital period. They're all around, two hundred miles up, crisscrossing the sky in no apparent pattern. When any of the asteroids are attacked, they receive defensive help from others that happen to be close. Attackers need to defend themselves from all sides, so they can never fully focus on the particular asteroid fortress they're trying to destroy.

But the genius part of our orbital defense is also the most boring part. It's all mathematics and orbital mechanics, and nobody likes to think about that. The flashes of light are gone. People start to walk again.

Most continue to glance at the sky, whether looking for more flashes or worrying about the same things as me, I can't tell.

Chapter 12

No tarmac seals the ground, and no lights stand on poles along the perimeter. The spaceport's landing pads are just squares and rectangles, hundreds of them, marked by pale-colored rocks in a pasture of beat-down grass, a new set of Nazca lines some far future generation might speculate about if the Trogs win this war and choose to annihilate mankind.

As I follow the directions on my d-pad, I walk past platoons scattered in many of the squares. Some are loading into grav lifts. Others are sitting, talking to pass the time, or staring at the sky, waiting for the next hint of war to slip by in an orbit way overhead.

I know I'm getting close when I start to see friends of mine from the grav factory, my insurgent recruits, standing in twos and threes among soldiers waiting to go up.

Apparently, none have been arrested by the MSS. One bucket of worries empties down the drain. That means Blair must have been telling me the truth about being my new contact with the Free Army.

I hope.

Yeah, I'm that much of an optimist.

A new worry bucket starts to fill with the possibility she could be playing a deeper game than I've guessed. That's a symptom of growing up under the boot of an oppressive regime, never believing you're winning, just knowing you're too stupid to figure out how you're losing.

Despite that, I move forward.

Freedom calls.

Station 13C suddenly presents itself in front of me.

Penny, my pilot, is standing by herself, looking away from me, down the valley. I don't need to see her face or read the name stenciled across her chest to know it's her. She has a shape to her, large-breasted, wide hips—voluptuous they might have called it in another time. She spends her free time in the gym, so she has an athletic build. In fact, she's more muscular than most of the men I know.

She bleaches her hair and wears it short and spiked. We've even flirted over the years when one or both of us were going through a rough patch in our relationships at home. The timing never worked out, and our friendship remained flirtatious and frustrated.

Penny turns and spots me. She waves.

I cross the stone boundary to officially enter my muster station as I spot Phil talking to a sergeant.

It looks like the entire platoon has arrived ahead of me. The troopers are lined up sitting on the ground in squads. The sergeants are on their feet, walking among them and answering questions. A short distance away from the rows stand two officers, the platoon's lieutenant and the company's captain, talking with another two men I know immediately are Koreans. They've got Asian features and unblemished, crisp suits. The assault ship's first officer and captain.

"Glad you made it," says Penny, as I walk up.

"Been here long?" I ask.

"Half-hour." She nods toward Phil. "Adverb got here first, a little bit before me." 'Adverb' is her nickname for Phil because he never *just does* anything. When he walks, he does it *tiredly*, or *slowly*. When he worries, he does it *loudly*, pulling any passerby into his anxiety. When he sighs, it drips with boredom. He talks *quickly*, and *sadly*, and *excitedly*, always glazing his words in the emotion at the forefront of his troubles. When he despises the nickname Adverb, he despises it intensely. Lucky for him, everybody at the grav fab tired of the nickname years ago. Penny, though, finds her fun in his discomfort. Something inside her smiles whenever she prods his sensitivities and he reacts with a whine.

I notice neither Penny nor Phil is armed. The Koreans, the only other two who'll be on the ship's bridge, are. All the soldiers have rifle-sized railguns, and three pairs of them share the load of larger railguns, each with a mount. Those are the platoon's only heavy weapons. I turn my d-pad up so I can see it, and I start tapping. "Do you know anything about these assault ships we'll be flying?"

Penny purses her lips, and her eyebrows draw close to one another. She knows. "Got my briefing while they were suiting me up." Penny puts her hands on her hips and snorts. "I thought all that simulator training about high-speed docking maneuvers didn't make any sense when I was going through it. Now it does."

I grimace. "What do you think? Can it be done?"

"Damn gravity lens better work, is all I can say."

"Can you fly the ship?"

"If it works like the simulator." Penny shrugs.

Of all the pilots-in-training in the web of my conspiracy, Penny did a little better than average in the flight simulators. I know she's a quick learner and she's fearless. At least she pretends to be.

"Did you hear anything about the light-speed capabilities on these ships?" I ask.

She doesn't answer, but looks at me instead, scanning my face, looking for something. "You're asking questions because you're nervous."

I shrug. I don't feel nervous, not really. A lot is running through my mind. Troubles are piling up.

"We'll make it up there, and we'll be prepared or we won't," she says. "We'll do what we need to do, or we won't. Time for what-ifs is long gone."

"I can always count on you for a dose of sunshine."

"You can."

"What about your…" Penny looks around, checking to make sure no one is close enough to overhear, "friend. What's the word?"

She's asking about Vishnu. I can't tell her the news. Not right now.

"What's wrong?" she asks.

"Some hiccups. That's all. We're good to go." It's my turn to look around suspiciously. "We've each got half an encrypted file on our d-pads. We can merge them to find the coordinates for a secret Free Army base out in the asteroid belt. Our orders are to get the ship out there."

Penny glances over at the officers. "What about them?"

It's a question that's always gone unanswered. Mutiny was easy when we were planning and plotting. "We do what we need to do."

And just like that, I've failed to answer it again. I wonder whether I'll have the balls to do what needs doing when the time comes.

"So this is for real?" asks Penny.

"We're all here," I answer, as I scan across the field, seeing more of my coconspirators from the grav factory, mixed with their SDF units. We're all ready to turn on our masters and join the Free Army. How many of these soldiers will raise their weapons to kill us once they realize some of us are traitors?

Chapter 13

I don't have much time to study the assault ship's tactics. There isn't much I need to know. Penny's the pilot. She understands the ship's flight capabilities. That much, if not the details about ramming other ships, was included in her simulator.

More technical aspects, such as grav controls, navigation, and ship fusion reactor systems, were included in Phil's simulator courses. The only new parts for him are those covering the grav lens. It's unfamiliar to all of us, but only Phil needs to have an intimate understanding, since he'll be in charge of that part of our ship.

Assault ship tactics aren't hard. It's all guesswork. Nobody on earth has engaged in this kind of warfare since ancient times when Rome and Carthage sent their navies out to ram and board enemy ships. Effective modes of attack may exist, but we'll have to learn those by trial and error once we're in outer space fighting the Trogs.

A flock of grav lifts descends on the regiment's muster stations.

Watching them come down, I realize I'm out of time for prep. I'm as ready as I'll ever be.

The platoon's senior sergeant—a lean, intimidating man named Brice—orders everyone to their feet.

Butterflies fill my gut as our assigned lift silently settles onto the short grass in front of us. Like all the other lifts, it looks better from a distance. Up close, I see it's a forty-foot shipping container, older than any of us, rusted by age and pitted by countless trips through the atmosphere. Attached to the container is the actual lift, little more than a rigid frame for holding the container in place, embedded grav plates, and a small fusion reactor. The pilot sits in a half-bubble cockpit on one end.

Soldiers close their faceplates.

I take my last breath of earth air and do the same.

Penny nudges me and smiles. She's more than ready, she's anxious.

I wonder if her confidence is as fake as mine.

I'm listening in on the platoon comm. Brice's orders are curt and clear. He's a guy who's used to having soldiers do what he says, like he's used to being right.

Then again, maybe that's me projecting hope.

The doors on the grav lift's container swing open.

"Hazardous Mangos!" Brice's strong voice addresses the troops in their brightly colored suits. "Move your feet and stay in line. Pretend you're real soldiers, or first graders. You pick. Move!"

Men and women are on their feet, jogging toward the vessel.

Moments later, I'm inside with all the others. There's nowhere to sit—the container is just an empty metal box built to haul twenty-ton loads of equipment, workers, and raw materials into orbit. It was never meant to make anyone comfortable.

I look around for Phil. He's near the door, one of the last to step inside. Through his glass faceplate, I see anxiety on his face, not unusual for Phil. I hope he's ready for what's coming.

Penny nudges me again, advertising her excitement. "It's really happening!"

Is it the revolution or the flying she's talking about?

"Grab a handhold on the wall," the sergeant tells us from where he stands in the center of the container. He reaches up and clutches one of several thick wires strung across the box just overhead. "Or a cable."

I grab a handhold that was welded to the wall so recently the raw metal hasn't had time yet to rust.

The grav lift's captain powers his plates, and the vessel starts to rise.

I feel the downward pull of the earth as we accelerate away with wide-open doors.

Plenty of troopers have something to say about that, mostly versions of 'Holy shit!'

We're a few hundred feet in the air already and starting to veer when the ship's single crewman swings the doors shut, leaving us in darkness.

My eyes adjust.

Spears of light shine in through gaps around the door and holes in the walls where the metal has corroded through.

A soldier falls to the floor and knocks another over.

"Grav compensate!" barks Sergeant Brice. "Or hold on."

Suit lights mounted on helmets and left shoulders come on, casting beams at odd angles all through the crate.

Wind starts to howl through the gaps as the lift picks up speed.

The g's start to weigh on me, and I feel like I'm being stepped on by a giant. My back strains and my knees hurt. My readout tells me we're pulling two g's.

Soldiers lean on one another. Good thing we're packed in pretty snug.

A woman's knees buckle.

Another trooper goes down.

"Auto-goddamn-compensate!" shouts Brice. "It's the slider on the left end of your d-pad. Use your favorite nostril finger and move it up and down. Remember your training, people!"

The metal wall I'm standing next to starts to flex, buffeted by the wind outside.

The wind's howl turns to a screaming whistle.

The container shudders like it's going to fall apart.

I glance at Penny, letting the concern on my face ask my question.

"This is normal," she tells me. She used to date a grav lift pilot who'd take her on occasional joyrides. "Only the old ones fall apart."

I glance around at the oxidizing walls and look back at Penny.

She's grinning, and I'm wondering which part of what she said was the joke.

The shaking grows worse.

People start talking, letting fright run away with their words.

A grav lift ride was never in any of the simulators. None of us but Penny knew what to expect.

I decide it's time to stop with pointless machismo and set my suit to ninety percent auto-compensate for the extra g's. My bones thank me by only hurting a little bit less.

Penny is looking at her d-pad, unconcerned about the grav lift. "The trip goes faster than you think."

The whistle changes.

The ship's shudder dissipates.

The push of the ships acceleration lessens.

I feel the lift lean.

The pilot is letting off.

Sound dies away. A moment later, all sense of weight disappears.

"We're at the edge of space," Penny tells me.

The troops around me notice, too. One of them whoops, and a few more copy. For most of them, this is the first time they've felt actual zero-g.

Feet come off the floor.

Hands grip everywhere.

A few steps in front of me, a man's visor screen splatters yellow from the inside.

I'm thankful the smell of his vomitus is contained in his suit. Lucky for him we're touching down in Arizona before boarding our ship. He'll have a few minutes to open his faceplate and clean the mess out. Unfortunately, taking off his helmet or suit aren't options, so whatever drips down inside, he'll have to live with for days or weeks, maybe more.

He starts to complain loudly over the platoon channel.

"Suck it up," Brice tells the whiner. "Maybe put that waggly tongue to work and lean forward and lick it off your glass. It all goes back inside anyway. Might as well get used to it."

"He's no Marine," jabs a woman, like any of us have earned the right to label ourselves.

"None of us are," says another, and more of them laugh.

That's the joke, really. We're part of a Heavy Assault Division, yet all of us know—whatever a Marine was fifty years ago—it's not us.

"Kill some Trogs," says Sergeant Brice. "Live to tell about it, and I'll call you whatever you want."

That gets some nods from the platoon.

The lift executes a spin maneuver that throws everyone off-balance.

"At the top of a parabolic path," Penny tells me. "Like a ballistic missile."

"Are you trying to make me feel worse?" I ask.

Penny grins.

I guess that's my answer.

"The pilot needed to reorient the ship for deceleration." She reads the time off her d-pad. "We'll be there in seven or eight minutes."

The floor starts pushing up on us as we decelerate at the same rate we ascended.

We're back in the atmosphere again, and the wind whistle starts. The container shudders.

The platoon settles down as we continue our descent. The soldiers know we're coming to the end of this leg. Like me, they feel they've been through the worst of it. From here on out, we know what to expect.

Something buffets the lift, and a rumble rattles my teeth.

"What the hell was that?" I ask. A gust of wind? Thunder?

Everyone is alert.

Looking at silent Penny, I ask again, "What was—"

The lift bounces left on turbulence, and the unmistakable roar of an explosion stuns us.

Shit!

I think we're crashing, but realize immediately I'm wrong. We're still decelerating, not falling. Something's not right.

"What do you think?" Penny asks over the comm.

"I was hoping you had the answer."

A guy starts hollering panicked gibberish and falls to the floor. The first of us to crack and we haven't even seen a Trog yet.

He crawls toward the doors we entered through, pushing and elbowing past boots and knees.

Brice orders him to stop.

Another explosion bounces the ship, yet we still descend.

The company captain squawks some noise, and the lieutenant immediately parrots it.

I glance at Penny, and I can tell she's concluded the same thing as me. If the panic spreads, we're all screwed.

Sergeant Brice is moving toward the crawling man, and not getting there fast enough.

I identify the man by the gravity signature emitted by his suit. They're all unique, and thanks to the spaghetti bug in my head, I can read it. I kill his outgoing comm link and reluctantly issue the command to paralyze his suit.

He freezes stiff.

The platoon channel goes silent as they all realize what just happened. Some of them look at me, relieved. Other eyes accuse.

The lieutenant shouts something pointless that sounds like a question.

Nobody pays attention.

"We'll be down, soon," booms Sergeant Brice's voice. "Disembark like soldiers, and scurry your dainty butts to the assault ship. No time to sightsee once your feet are on the ground. No time for longing looks at the lovely sky. No time for goodbye kisses and happy wishes. It seems some Trogs are in the neighborhood and they want to kill you. Don't make it easy."

Another explosion rocks us.

The press of deceleration disappears, and the ship starts to maneuver in fast jukes.

We're all getting bounced around inside.

"A couple hundred feet up," Penny tells me.

Another explosion rattles the shipping container—not close, but distinct—and if any in the platoon had any doubts, they've disappeared. We're coming down in the midst of a battle.

CHAPTER 14

The shuttle pulls hard around a tight turn, grav plates stressing under the load. Thanks to the bug in my head, I see the grav fields glow brilliant blue. The cargo doors swing free and squeal on their hinges.

Hundreds of assault ships—maybe thousands—are lined in rows on the desert floor, all the way from the sprawling shipyard factories in the south to the foot of the mountains in the north.

Rusty and coarse. Brutal and hard.

Iron berserkers.

Enders of life.

They're shaped like the Apollo rockets of the last century, only in the crudest way. Those ships were flimsy and clean, perfect and smooth, painted white and packed with the most ingenious devices of their day for keeping men alive on the first trip to a world beyond our own. Those ships were built for explorers.

These in the desert are machines of war.

We'll ride the corroded brutes into the void to harpoon star-faring dreadnoughts a kilometer long. If the technology supposed to keep the vessels in one piece works, if the enemy ships don't disintegrate, if we live through the collisions, we'll pour out with weapons blazing.

Maybe we'll capture our prey. Maybe, we'll die.

Ifs and maybes.

Desperation and possibility.

I'm hoping again the mundane new wonder-weapon lives up to expectations and does what our generals tell us it will do, praying my life isn't part of a ploy to trick the pilot into a suicide run. We're losing this war so badly. I don't put anything past the North Korean epaulette-trolls in their buried bunkers planning our fate.

An explosion startles me and the shuttle lurches to the left.

I grip a handhold to keep my balance, as a thought about the randomness of death in war reminds me of how little control I have over my fate.

In the distance, a lance of perfectly straight lightning pierces the sky and pricks an assault ship. The vessel shatters in an eruption of smoke and fire.

A pressure wave dominoes down the line from the blast, blowing dust off each ship as it passes. The wave punches me, not hard enough to hurt, still intense enough to make it real. The sound rumbles through my helmet.

Our shuttle touches down, nobody jumps out. The platoon is paralyzed. None of us expected to descend into a bombardment. None of us was ready for the carnage to come so soon.

"Move it, move it, move it!" yells Brice. He's the only sergeant in the platoon who's seen war with his own eyes, fired his weapon at the enemy, and watched his friends die.

The rest of us are virgin shock troops, a new kind of soldier with new equipment and new tactics, tasked to storm the heavens and turn the tide of the war.

But we're soft.

Another explosion rocks our shuttle, closer than the last, though out of sight behind us.

Wannabe killers are falling out the door, hitting the desert dirt and scrambling to the assault ship.

Brice is yelling. "I've never seen a bunch of fruit-flavored fuck-nut nitwits as disappointing as you! Don't you know to hurry when a bunch of idiotic cavemen are shooting at you from space?"

Orange-clad soldiers are shaking off their paralysis and trudging toward the doors with the weight of death riding on their shoulders. White-helmeted heads sway, awkward and tentative. None of us is yet used to the suits we first donned just two hours ago.

I see panic in the eyes behind smart-glass faceplates. I hear rapid breathing over the platoon comm.

Sergeant Brice is at the door of the shuttle, pointing while waving the rest of them out. "That ship, right there. My God, it's the closest one. It's the easiest guess."

I'm starting to think it won't matter whether our assault ship was designed to be an elaborately disguised kamikaze or not. I'm a sim-trained novice in the company of amateurs already reeling from war's brutality and we're still only spectators.

We'll all be dead five minutes after we face our first Trog horde.

A useless thought.

All I can do is move forward and try to survive.

I jump out of the battered metal freight box that brought our platoon to Arizona, and my boots hit the sun-bleached dirt.

Plumes of smoke rise in every direction. Dust wafts between the ships.

Bits of gravel rain around us.

Another hypersonic bolt lances down from above and hits the ground.

I feel it.

I hear it.

Instinctually, I avert my eyes to protect them.

I look back up to see where the bolt came from and I spot three slivers of frosted glass glued to the sky. They're Trog battle cruisers, above the atmosphere, sun rays blazing against their hulls, so goddamn proud and invincible they can peg themselves to a geosynchronous spot right above Arizona and fire their railguns down like there's not a goddamned thing we can do about it but look and see and piss ourselves.

I guess leaving more than a thousand secret weapons standing in the desert is no way to keep them hidden.

It's like the bunker troll generals want us to die.

No wonder we're losing this war.

Frantic, the platoon's lieutenant—Holt—is shouting, trying to follow Brice's example and be a leader, only he's failing. He's unraveling already frayed nerves and confusing the platoon.

Milliken, the company captain, was yappy enough when we were at our muster station in Colorado, now I don't hear him on the comm and he's disappeared from sight—I can't imagine where he's gone. His four platoons are on the verge of disintegrating under enemy fire as they disembark from their shuttles and scramble to their assault ships. I find myself hoping a lucky slug from one of the enemy's railguns has vaporized him already.

Penny stumbles out of the shuttle.

Instinctively, I reach to grab her arm, asking, "You okay?"

Her feet somehow find their way beneath her, and she straightens up tall as if she meant to come out the way she did. "Fine."

A soldier jumps to the ground beside us, glances at us standing there like we're insane, and sprints for the assault ship.

"Go!" Lieutenant Holt shouts. "Go, go!" He's out among them, and he's not even pointing at the right ship.

"Somebody's gonna frag him," Penny tells me over a private comm connection like we're talking about the length of the grass in his lawn.

I nod like I know, although I don't. I've only heard what I've heard. Demoralized troops tired of watching each other die to support a strategy they don't understand find it easy to blame their officers and rough out their justice with a grenade or hypervelocity slug. The practice has turned into an epidemic in the SDF, and it's the reason my job exists.

Something flashes above us.

An explosion knocks most of the troops off their feet.

The pressure wave pushes me into Penny, who seems unaffected.

Looking up, I see a shuttle has been hit. It's broken into pieces and its grav plates are driving the parts in cockeyed directions as soldiers in orange suits tumble out.

A thick dust cloud blows over us, obscuring everything more than a stone's throw away.

"This whole thing's a damn mess," says Penny, before pointing at the sky. "At least the Trogs won't be able to see us with all the dirt they're kicking up. They'll be shooting randomly now."

I figure they already are. The Trogs don't have the kind of accuracy to hit one of these ships from space with anything but luck. Nevertheless, they're doing a pretty good job with that. "We need to fix this mess right now if any of us are going to make it off the surface."

Penny looks at me. She knows what I'm saying, and she knows the risk of pushing my authority so soon.

Unfortunately, I don't see a better way. "You find Phil and make sure he gets to the bridge. I'll load the platoon onboard."

Penny is already moving as she tells me, "Yes, sir."

It's weird, hearing her say it. Until we were officially inducted a few hours ago, we were equals, two worker bees doing the same job on the same production line. Now she's a lieutenant. I'm a major.

I activate the grav plates built into my suit, and they push against earth's gravity field, sending me sailing over the heads of the soldiers in my platoon. I aim for one of our assault ship's open side doors.

A third of the length of the ship, maybe sixty feet off the ground, I grab onto an exterior beam and plant my feet on a steel shelf covered in new, orange rust. I don't think once about the poor aerodynamics of our medieval battering ram of a ship. Once out of the atmosphere, it'll spend its existence in space. There's no friction out there between the planets. This machine doesn't need to be sleek. It only needs to be sturdy and fast.

A woman is at the top of the ladder below me, just entering the door. "Hurry," I tell her. And then over the platoon comm, I cast my first official order as I point at the other open doors on this side of the ship. "Don't run, use your grav. Get in here."

Sergeant Brice immediately shoots off the ground and perches himself outside a door twenty feet above me. "Do it, now!" he reiterates. I'm both pleased and apprehensive. I need Brice to follow my orders without question, however, if his fealty to the SDF is unbending, it'll be a problem.

Lieutenant Holt isn't as experienced as Brice, and Holt starts to squawk at me over the platoon comm about chain of command. I cut him off before he has a full sentence out. I'm not going to let him get my company killed.

My company?

Not yet—I'm going to make it so.

Soldiers start to float. Several soar smoothly toward the open doors.

One activates his suit's gravity drive and shoots off the ground at rocket speed.

Before I can do anything to stop him, the streaking soldier slams headfirst into the top edge of the doorframe Brice is perched beside. I hear the crunch of bone over the comm as his helmet splits. Blood and gore rain down in bits as his suit's gravity drive continues to push, jerking his body in spasms and mashing his head into the steel.

A few screams echo over the platoon comm.

Over the noisy channel, Brice announces, "That's what a dumbass who scammed his way through his sims looks like."

I realize the suit's grav controls were damaged in the collision.

One of the younger soldiers starts to sob. I identify him and kill his comm.

Thinking quickly, Brice reaches around to the dead soldier's integrated backpack and deftly removes the hydrogen pack that powers the suit's micro-fusion reactor. That cuts the suit's power, and the body falls to the ground as his comrades dodge out of the way.

"Careful," Brice tells them all. "If you can't fly the suit, climb one of the ladders."

Novices and amateurs.

Every gap in training is going to be deadly.

The three other platoons in our company are disembarking from their shuttles and loading into nearby ships. I comm connect to the lieutenants of those platoons and loop in the absent company captain. "We don't have time here. Tell the ones who can use their grav to fly to the upper doors. Put the rest on the ladders through the doors near the ground. Do it!" I don't wait for a reply.

I switch my comm to link the small bridge crews of the four ships. I leave out the ships' captains and first officers, the North Koreans. "Everybody answers to Penny," I tell them. I don't need to be overly formal with this group. Like Penny, they all worked with me at the grav factory. We know each other well. I tell her, "Get those reactors powered up. If the ships' captains gives you any crap, loop me in."

We can fly the ships without them—the North Koreans, that is. They're here for political reasons only. Still, overriding their authority will put me in a world of shit if the plan doesn't work out. "Leave laggards on the ground. Launch at your discretion, but the longer we stay here, the more likely we'll be hit. Penny, let me know as soon as our ship is ready."

Looking down, I see her and Phil moving through the thick door just above the reactors and the aft drive array. They'll be on the bridge in the pressurized portion of the ship in thirty seconds.

Our platoon's lieutenant is in a tizzy. He's gesturing, yelling silently inside his helmet, and pushing his way up the ladder to get near me.

I don't have time to finesse my way through his offended feelings. I decide to take a step I'd hoped to avoid altogether. I override his suit's control system and lock it, freezing him in his pose.

Looking down the length of the ladder, I see his face go red as he understands what I've just done.

I laugh a little because I know he's going to hate the next part even more. I take control of his gravity functions and I remote-fly him off the ladder and through the open door beside me. I deposit his stiff body against the back wall of the platoon compartment. I leave his comm cut. I'll deal with him later.

Penny comms me in. "I'm in the pilot seat. The captain is shouting crazy Korean jabber at me, however, he's got the reactor already purring. I'm goosing the hydrogen flow so we'll be at max output before you can piss off another officer."

"Let me know if the captain becomes a problem. Give me a grav bubble in the forward compartment as soon as you have the power."

"And just so you know," Penny adds, "The company's captain, Milliken, is strapped into a jump seat on the bridge, staring at the wall."

Another problem to deal with later. At least he's staying quiet.

Lights come on inside the platoon compartment. The doors we're not using on the other side of the ship grind closed. I feel momentarily disoriented as Phil activates the gravity field inside, canceling out the earth's pull and making the interior a weightless environment.

I comm the platoon and tell them to expect zero-g.

A narrow flame cuts the air nearby as a sonic boom pounds my ears.

The flash blinds me for an instant as a nearby ship explodes. Fire and huge shreds of iron soar into the air. The blast throws me against the hull.

Most of the soldiers still outside are knocked down.

Our ship leans and I fear it might fall. Penny is already compensating.

"I got it! I got it!" She yells.

Everyone is hollering on the platoon channel. Some are hurt. Others are panicking.

Brice is trying to help them refocus.

The troopers already inside are drifting in the weightlessness, holding on, or strapping themselves into seats. One of them pops open his faceplate and pukes. It floats there, an amorphous blob, as I wonder why the anti-nausea drug laced into the suit's water supply isn't working.

Another explosion's shockwave ripples over us.

It's time for desperate measures.

I freeze the suits of everyone in the platoon except for the bridge crew.

Brice curses and I realize I should have left him active and autonomous. He's the only reason the platoon didn't fall to pieces the moment the shuttle sat down.

I unlock his suit while I shut down the platoon comm so only he and I will be heard. I quickly apologize to Brice, and say, "They're coming your way."

"No sweat," he answers. "None of you new officers learns shit from those computer games, but you'll pick it up." He laughs. "Who the hell am I kidding? You know the attrition rate for officers?"

Brice doesn't bother to tell me any number, so I figure the question was rhetorical, and that's worrisome.

My experience in the factory makes the next part easy. I take grav control of a corporal's suit and fly her up to Brice's door at a speed that would frighten anyone. "Dunk her."

Brice pushes the frozen woman into the zero-g compartment behind him just as another stiff-suited soldier arrives.

"You ignorant, mutinous pig!" It's the ship's captain over the bridge comm. He's talking to me, of course. "My ship. My command. When I report the—"

I shut down his comm and freeze his suit. I tell Penny, "If that first officer starts in, let me know and I'll lock him out, too."

Everyone on board is going to hate me, still, at least they'll be alive.

More fire lances down from the sky.

"We gotta go," Penny tells me. "The reactor is at full power."

"Thirty seconds," I respond. "How are the other three ships doing?"

She gives me a quick report as I move soldiers.

One more to go.

I send him up.

Brice pushes him through the door into a 3D jigsaw puzzle of floating soldiers.

I scan the area around the ship as I realize I don't have time to search for anyone who might be missing.

"Get inside, Brice." I look up to see him jump in. On the bridge comm, I tell Phil, "Close the doors, and give me radial grav at point-two-g inside the bubble."

I unfreeze the platoon's suits.

The last open doors start to grind on sturdy gears. The radial grav nudges the drifting soldiers toward the walls where they start to strap into empty seats.

"Done," Phil tells me.

"Go, go, go!" I shout, "Penny, get us off the ground!"

Chapter 15

The ship shudders and the steel walls glow blue with bands of energy that resemble propane flames dancing over the rust. The glow is a visible artifact of imperfections in the grav field surging off the plates under a heavy load.

Welded joints groan and metal flexes. It doesn't seem possible so much steel wrapped around the long tube carrying the platoon can bend.

But it *is* bending!

And shrieking.

Soldiers are busy trying to strap themselves into the rows of seats lined along the walls of the tube. That's really all it is —a metal tube, formerly a tanker car, part of a train that hauled oil across the country, repurposed surplus from an obsolete industrial age, like the ransacked steel tracks bent in a crisscross pattern, embedded with grav plates, and welded five deep around the tank.

Steel, thirty inches thick, squealing as it's pushed between the power coming out of the drive array behind us through the back half of the ship, and the weight of the gravity lens up front—a conical hunk of solid steel, titanium, and specialized grav plates, the mojo in our wonder-weapon that's supposed to make this whole quixotic dream real.

God help us, we're flying into space, encased in junkyard surplus to ram starships with an invention never tested in battle.

More in the platoon are panicking as the contagious thought of the ship coming apart spreads.

"Sergeant Brice," I order, "get the stragglers in their seats and under control."

"Yes, sir." He firmly starts in on the soldiers, many of whom are having trouble with the radial gravity because it's not consistent. The field is flexing with the ship and pulsing with the electrical current flowing from the reactor.

I link a private comm to Lieutenant Holt. "I need you to help Sergeant Brice situate the troops. Provide me a status report on the platoon—how many can fight, and a no-bullshit assessment of what they can do. I'm guessing we'll see action before we're ready for it."

Completely ignoring my request, the lieutenant starts in on me about how I'm overstepping my authority.

"Dammit!" I yell at him. "Do your job now, and bitch later. We don't have time for this shit." Some people only respond to the harshest of words. "I'm opening your comm to the platoon. Grow the hell up and get me that status report."

It works.

The lieutenant busies himself, following my orders.

I'm a little bit surprised.

I don't know that I'm a natural leader, but I believe in my cause with all my heart, and I hate watching knuckleheads sit on their thumbs while complaining about sore asses. Maybe the mix of those two is enough.

I aim myself down the center of the tube where the radial g in the platoon compartment cancels to zero. I push off.

Another soldier opens his faceplate and wretches into the air outside his suit. I point at the troop as I drift by and call Brice's attention. "This compartment isn't pressurized. In three more minutes, that'll be suicide."

"Yes, sir." To the platoon, he orders, "Lock visors closed." He proceeds to remind them of what they should have learned from their simulators about the effects of a vacuum on a human body.

Brice is still scolding the troops when I tune out of the platoon comm channel.

Wind is whistling through the gaps in the doors along the sides of the tube, and I still see daylight leaking in around the edges. The doors weren't built to hold in atmosphere. They were built to bear a structural load and to not jam shut. Considering what the ship is designed to do, the not-jamming part is important.

I reach the airlock door separating the platoon compartment from the aft half of the ship where we have a rudimentary sickbay, supply rooms, and the bridge.

A sonic boom rattles the ship as we blast past the speed of sound.

My God, this thing can push the g's.

I'm glad to have the inertial bubble protecting me.

I push the palm-sized button to cycle the airlock.

Nothing happens.

The blue glow in the grav field intensifies around the ship's structure.

I link into the bridge comm. "Phil, the airlock won't open."

"Give me a minute," he answers.

"I'll take it," says Penny.

"No," I tell her. "You've got to fly this thing." Taking up Phil's slack is a habit from our grav factory days I need to break her of. "Phil, tell the first officer to get busy on the comm panel and find our rally point. My guess is we'll be attacking those Trog cruisers as soon as we're up there. I need those details and the status of the rest of the company."

"I just remembered," says Phil, "the airlock won't cycle because we're still in atmosphere. It locks. It's a bug. That's one we know about. How many bugs do you think this rusty piece of shit has that we don't—"

"Adverb!" Penny's had her fill of Phil.

"Got it." I turn my back to the bulkhead and grab the handles on the wall—handles are everywhere inside the tube. Other than the two rows of facing seats, and the thick supports running through at regular intervals, the handles are the only interior feature. They'll come in handy when we're in zero-g.

With nothing to do for a second, I take a deep breath to clear my head. I can't let my nerves frazzle with everything moving so fast. Besides Brice, it's looking like there isn't a decent officer or non-comm on the ship. I hope the other three platoons are better off than we are.

As my gaze drifts over the compartment, I notice most of the troops are locked into their seats. Many of them are looking down the length of the tube, staring at me. Glaring is more accurate. I froze their suits and for a few minutes, they were powerless dolls. I can see some of them won't forgive me for doing that. Humans don't like losing control.

Don't they understand they've spent their whole existence with no say in their lives? Half of us were born slaves to a race of big-headed alien twig-runts who conquered our planet in the briefest of wars some thirty years ago. The other half suffered the more difficult pain of living life with no master and then having their freedom taken away.

I want to shout—*what's a few more minutes of no control?*

I don't.

There's something more important they need to know.

I open the platoon comm and mute all of them. "For any of you who didn't take the time at the muster station to view the company's command structure on your d-pads, I'm Major Commissar Dylan Kane." I hold up my arm and tap the d-pad. "You know why I'm here, so I'll be frank. Nobody gets fragged in this company, officer or otherwise. And just to keep you honest, I've initiated the kill switch, so behave, kids."

I cut the comm and hit the airlock button again.

The Solar Defense Force is serious about curbing the practice of troops killing their officers.

Now, the platoon knows I'm serious, too.

Chapter 16

The airlock's outer door seals shut with me inside.

I wonder for a moment who I am.

This morning, I was working a half-shift at the grav factory, and now I've just stared down thirty armed heavy assault soldiers—or however many are left after that fiasco at the shipyard—and told them if they didn't behave I'd kill every one of them.

Has my rank made me stupidly brave? Has it turned me so quickly into a tyrant?

I tell myself it's neither. I'm only working through unforeseen minutiae in a plan that's been growing in my head since I was still figuring out no Easter Bunny was ever going to leave colored eggs in the spring snow and no Santa Claus would be bringing good-behavior bribes down our chimney at Christmas.

I wonder sometimes if my childhood had been different, would I have grown up wanting to change the world so badly?

My father was a hoist operator who suffocated under a cave-in at the molybdenum mine two weeks before I was born.

My mother worked twelve-hour night shifts in the molly mine over by Leadville, hauling ore over the same ground where my father died with eighty-two others. She came home each morning, dirty and tired, and made me breakfast with what little food we had in the house. While I ate, she read me stories from our history—human history—and I learned about a time from before the siege, back when humans arrogantly thought we were the only thinking beings in the whole endless universe.

What a painful punchline that joke turned out to have.

Before I learned to read for myself, I was familiar with stories about presidents, generals, dictators, and kings. She and I talked about the choices those men made and the consequences of their actions, and she asked me questions that forced me to think. They were all simple stories and basic questions at first—they became more complex as I grew older.

Together, she and I learned about the different ways political power shapes the world and the lives of the people in it.

She wanted me to know what military might could do in the hands of geniuses, fools, and mediocre officers trying to keep their soldiers alive, or in the hands of men willing to trade those lives for glory.

She didn't talk much about the leaders who embarrassed our species when the Grays arrived in our solar system just before I was born.

In fact, for an event so momentous in the evolution of a species, for a war so pivotal in the history of humanity, there isn't much to tell. The contact and the subsequent war were devastating, decisive, and anticlimactic all at the same time.

We weren't a spacefaring species then, not in any real sense. We'd landed some men on the moon, left people in earth's orbit for long periods of time, and shot fragile little probes into the solar system to gather bits of data about the infinite black void and its hunks of orbiting rock. We had tens of thousands of ballistic missiles we could pop into low-earth orbit in the blink of an eye so we could obliterate each other on some future day when that perfect mix of nationalism, enmity, and stupidity convinced our kleptocrats that a dead planet was preferable to living under the yoke of some other culture's facade of good governance.

And that's one of the defining aspects of human DNA. Something unique in our double-helix of proteins makes abhorrent the idea of kneeling to someone who doesn't look like us, sound like us, or hate like us.

Maybe for that reason, the war with the Grays eventually turned me into what I became.

The siege started a year or two before I was born, when the Grays' single kilometer-long ship blipped out of hyper-light travel one day and floated into an orbit some twenty thousand miles above the earth's surface.

Of course, it was a surprise, and based on the videos I've seen from that time, hope and fear were palpable in the air. Everyone had a theory about the contents of the craft—if anything—and what it had come to our solar system to do.

Every attempt was made to communicate with the ship's occupants, but as far as anyone could tell, the ship held no living creatures. It responded to nothing.

After a few weeks of earthly governments making their plans on how to send a vessel out to the interstellar cruiser, it suddenly zipped off to land on the bright side of the moon, right where any knucklehead with a telescope could see it.

Still, the ship did not respond to any messages from earth, no matter what medium was contrived to send them.

Eventually, the ship's occupants started building subterranean structures of all different sizes with strange little holes on top. That's to say, it was deduced the aliens were building the structures, as no one on earth ever got a glimpse of one of them outside the ship.

A cottage industry grew up fanning the speculation of why the aliens had come and what they were up to with all their activity on the moon.

Nothing more of consequence happened.

The aliens' odd little farm continued to grow.

Time passed.

Most of the people on earth eventually grew bored with guessing about a construction project two-hundred thousand miles away that didn't have any impact on whether they could pay the rent, buy a shinier car, or get laid on the weekend. Our governments didn't lose interest, though.

Earth's technologically advanced countries chose to collaborate on the design of a rocket to ferry a pilot, copilot, a few military men, and a half-dozen scientists to the moon.

We needed to find out what was up there.

An astronaut selection process turned into an international drama, re-captivating the world's entertainment-hungry masses. Construction began on a ship that would take the crew to the moon, not an easy feat in those days since no country on earth had landed a manned mission on the moon in half a century.

Eventually, they finished building the ship, and they scheduled a launch.

Chapter 17

Not since the days of the Apollo missions had so many people been glued to a television to watch a rocket ascend into the heavens.

The cameras were all turned on.

The signal was broadcast across the globe.

The countdown ran its course.

As expected, the engines roared and mountains of clouds flooded over the launch facility.

Up the rocket went.

Three days passed while nearly everyone on earth sat riveted to a television screen or computer monitor watching what might as well have been ten people on an RV trip from New York to Los Angeles, all taking turns peeking through a few tiny windows without ever stopping to go outside for a walk.

At the end of it, the ship went into orbit around the moon and made five or six circuits before the final decision came to land. People cheered. There was a certain giddiness to it. Earth's cultures had finally come together around a common goal.

By itself, that would have been a significant step forward.

Without incident, the ship touched down on the moon within a quarter mile of the alien vessel.

The engines cooled. The crew prepared themselves to exit the lander. And then, without warning, a small projectile fired from the alien ship. It blasted right through the lander's engines, disabling, but not destroying them.

The world erupted in crazy talk and unhinged behavior.

Some thought we'd offended the aliens.

Others believed our ship had tripped an automated self-defense system set up to protect the empty vessel.

Still more accurately guessed the earth had just witnessed the first shot in an interstellar war.

Amidst the furor, nobody seemed to notice that no attack followed. However, a door opened on the side of the trespassing ship.

An invitation?

More speculation.

The astronauts lingered in their lander for two weeks, confirming and reconfirming they had no way to repair their ship and return from the moon. The mission wasn't designed to last more than three weeks, and the astronauts ran low on food, water, and oxygen.

Finally, accepting they were in a position where there was no other choice, they all left the ship together, crossed the moon's barren surface, and disappeared through the alien craft's open door. The door closed behind the astronauts and then not much happened on the moon for about a year, except the subterranean construction continued, and the aliens put the astronauts to work slowly disassembling their spacecraft and hauling pieces inside the vessel.

On earth, the public went back to theorizing and making bad choices.

During this time, it was leaked that most of the governments on earth had agreed the planet was under attack and they were actively working together on a countermeasure. The hush-hush version had the governments of earth building fleets of ships and training soldiers to fly to the moon for an assault.

Something else odd happened while the world was in limbo about our new neighbors on the moon. Ever the international pariah, the North Koreans launched a rocket that appeared to be a copy of the one the rest of the world cooperated to build. It also orbited the moon a handful of times and landed near the spot where the other ship had sat down. Only instead of lingering inside, three astronauts immediately exited the vehicle and walked right up to the alien vessel.

To everyone's surprise, the aliens let them in.

That didn't sit well with the rest of the nations on earth. North Korea was pressured for information. Sanctions were stiffened. War was threatened.

Before that situation got out of hand, the calendar flipped to the anniversary of the first lander's arrival on the moon and a video signal was broadcast from the alien vessel using the lander's equipment. It showed one of the world's chosen scientists standing alone in front of eighteen little Gray aliens arrayed in a semi-circle behind him.

The short version of what he told the world was that the Grays were a telepathic species with a history stretching back a million years. They were learned and wise, and they had declared themselves humanity's guardians. In that role, they would shepherd our species through the next ten or twenty thousand years of evolution and help us ascend to our full potential. The small price they required for this benevolent tutelage was our complete obedience. In fact, by their plan, we'd be little more than a slave species.

Earth's choice in the matter was to accept their authority without reservation or to submit to them by right of conquest.

Just to make the whole thing a little bit more like a bad joke, they told us there were just eighteen of them. On their ship, they'd brought with them a few thousand members of another lesser species—slaves. During a question and answer session, the scientist ventured a guess that the Grays' humanoid slaves were descendants of Neanderthals taken from earth sometime in the distant past.

And yes, he told the world at least a dozen times, it truly was just eighteen Grays.

As anyone who knows anything about human behavior might guess, there was no submission. The aliens were told how quickly they could go to hell, and were given the ultimatum to return our astronauts and to get off our fucking moon or suffer the kind of full-scale, pain-soaked annihilation humans had been dishing out since we first fell from the tree branches a few million years ago and started beating each other to death with rocks and brittle bones.

That's when the war started in earnest.

Earth launched its quaint fleet of chemical rockets stuffed with as many spacesuit-clad soldiers as could be crammed inside.

Like nearly every case in human history, when a technologically backward army attacked an advanced one, slaughter ensued. Not one of the hastily constructed spacefaring warships came close to landing on the moon. The alien vessel's railguns shredded them en route.

Thus began the final phase of the war.

Humiliation turned to devastation.

The alien ship lifted off the moon and spent two days destroying every human-made satellite in earth or lunar orbit. It then went back to its previous resting place. To earth's chagrin, nothing could be done to stop them.

The Grays decided it was time to show earth what they'd been constructing on the moon the whole time—huge railguns, driven by gravity, powered by fusion reactors. Those two technologies turned out to be a decisive combination.

While the Grays had the slaves building their battery of weapons, they'd also had them smelting the moon's ore into metal casings around slugs made of solid moon rock. The slugs weighed anywhere from a few hundred pounds to a few hundred tons. Fired by those railguns, the projectiles hurtled toward earth at speeds as high as sixty thousand miles an hour.

When the kinetic energy of the heavier projectiles converted to heat on impact, they produced blasts on par with small nuclear devices. No fissile material and no chemical reaction required, just simple physics producing the kind of violence that's been shaping the universe for fourteen billion years.

On the first day of the bombardment, a dozen small towns sprinkled across the globe were obliterated.

Earth's leaders made speeches about putting on a brave face and preparing for an invasion. They told the people humanity would never submit to a gaggle of effete gray monkeys no matter what technological advantages they possessed.

As was the usual case in matters of war, defiance was paid for with the blood of people not involved in making the decision.

The Grays set about raining their meteoric projectiles down on military installations and nuclear missile sites the world over. In the process, they worked their way through a list of the earth's largest non-capital cities. Shanghai, Karachi, São Paulo were destroyed. St. Petersburg, Munich, Los Angeles and a dozen others went the next day.

After working through a list of cities, the aliens contacted earth again, only this time it was one of the North Koreans speaking. He told us the Grays didn't mind destroying all of earth's population centers except those within the borders of North Korea, home of their newly converted acolytes on earth.

He said the Grays were gods who lived lives spanning thousands of years and they were a patient species. They didn't mind devastating the planet and then waiting while their North Korean friends repopulated and redeveloped it to their liking.

Earth's revised set of choices—let seven billion people die, or accept the absolute authority of the Grays over every living thing on earth to be administered humanely by the North Koreans.

That's the day the world's leaders set my fate. I was born a slave.

CHAPTER 18

We've reached the edge of space and the platoon compartment has emptied of air.

Sensing the external vacuum, the airlock door opens.

I slip into the airlock and turn away from the door's small window as I seal it closed. I don't need to see those soldiers' eyes drilling me with contempt.

Air hisses to fill a space large enough to hold a handful of soldiers in full gear.

I wait.

A tremor runs through the steel beneath my feet, and I hear the sound of a hammer striking an anvil.

More gravity stress on the hull?

The ship shudders as three more hammers pound in rapid succession.

I open a comm link to the bridge just as a hole punches through the hull in front of me. A sizzling beam of plasma cuts a diagonal line through the airlock, blasting another hole near my foot. The air flashes to fire, completely engulfing me, instantly dissipating as it howls into space.

Before I know I've been knocked down, I find myself on my ass, pushed against the door.

Even as I'm trying to figure out if I can breathe, if my bones are broken, if my suit is punctured, I think of the ship, and I understand what's going on. A railgun slug punched a hole through the airlock and burned the atmosphere as it tore straight through the ship.

The sarcastic genius that lives in my head tells me we're under attack.

I shout into the command comm. "Defensive grav!"

Another round hits the hull as Phil says something I don't understand.

The ship's interior grav bubble flexes, and disappears without warning as I'm smashed flat against a side wall under five or six g's.

The ship maneuvers and I'm thrown against the airlock door and the g's push so hard my vision tunnels down to a small pool of light in the center of engulfing black.

I realize I need to grav compensate with my suit just as my vision turns swimmy and reality skews off-kilter.

I'm not unconscious, though I'm not right. In truth, I'm not sure what I am. I'm on a sidewalk of dreams with memories parading past.

We met at a required-attendance social function, Claire and me. It was one of those monthly MSS things for all the singles in Summit County. Every locality has them. The Grays want fertile humans to pair up, spawn, and to push offspring into the pipeline that feeds the labor pool.

Under the Grays' management of earth, humans are little better than off-brand ketchup packets, out of which every drop of utility must be squeezed.

Phil was with me that night, as usual. We were making our perfunctory appearance—sign in at the desk inside the front door, stay past the first name check, get a free plate of actual barbecued beef, duck out the back. That was our play. Summit County in those days wasn't heavily populated with the unattached, and most of us singles knew each other already. Any sparks that were going to fly had already flown. Any carnal play that was going to lead to love, already had.

Twenty minutes into the event, as our stomachs were starting to grumble, Phil and I were near a window and bitching about the new North Korean overseer at the grav plant. That's when Phil spotted two girls signing in at the front door, Claire and her twin sister, Sydney. We'd never seen them before.

I've never been comfortable meeting new people, so Phil took the lead. He wasn't much to look at, but that never detoured him from giving a girl a go. Phil had an edge. He could do so much more with that bug in his head than the rest of us who'd been implanted at birth.

After introducing us, Phil bet the girls he could guess their names.

Everybody takes that bet. Why not? It's nearly impossible to lose.

They did lose, however, and that obligated them to be our dates for the evening.

It turned out Claire and Sydney were both born in Breckenridge and lived there until they were in grade school. As the Grays slowly appropriated the whole valley for their growing spaceport, supporting facilities, and factories, the girls' family relocated to Denver. That's where Claire worked in a sweatshop assembling wire harnesses for grav lift control panels, among other things. Sydney wasn't MSS but she worked for them as an auditor, employed by the Front Range Farm Bureau. Her job was to catch farmers cheating on their production quotas by skimming extra food for the black markets.

Both girls had come up to Summit County because—like Phil and me—they were bored with the prospects at their local social function.

What followed was an evening of laughs, dances, bellies full of food, and inhibitions dulled by beer.

By night's end, the pairing-off worked by some social magic I had no hope of understanding. I was in bed with Claire, naked, ready to unleash months of pent-up sexual frustration and she was greedy to accept it.

We were breaking the law.

That's not to say any rules existed against intercourse. The Grays, through their MSS mouthpieces, encouraged women to get on their backs and invite men in—to hell with human moralizing over which pairs of people could and couldn't procreate. Rituals be damned, they just wanted more human babies.

It wasn't the fornication that was illegal—it was, and still is, the contraceptives.

I explained to her that I had no condom. Prices on them had been going up at the black market down in Denver. Most times, you couldn't even find one for purchase. And packaging? Forget it. If you wanted one in a little foil pack printed with a brand name in full, shiny color, a well-preserved, sanitary relic from thirty years ago, those were pricier than a five-gallon can of gasoline.

Most guys settled for loose condoms sold out of a plastic bag slipped surreptitiously from another guy's pocket. Probably used before and rinsed clean-ish. It was often the best available.

Though I always aspired to own two condoms, one primary, and one backup, frequency of opportunity never proved out the necessity. Worse yet, in a desperate moment on a recent trip to the black market, I traded my condom for a computer network card after mine crapped out.

So, I would have happily been the lawbreaker, if I'd had the means to do so.

Claire told me not to worry. She was on the pill, making *her* the criminal.

I was mortified.

An odd emotion to have with an erection raging between my legs.

At the time, I still believed some of the MSS propaganda. I didn't realize until later that it was one-hundred-percent shit. I was under the impression that contraceptive pills slowly ate away a woman's uterus, and eventually filled the empty space with pus-dripping tumors that became infected and killed her. In fact, I believed that line of shit so deeply, I was afraid to enter Claire for fear that I might contract a contagious penis tumor that would eventually kill me off through pus leakage.

The MSS are a bunch of violent cretins, but their propaganda wing can spin some compelling shit.

As it turned out, Claire found a way to persuade me to ignore what I'd been told about the pill. She'd been on it for years, she claimed, without the slightest negative effect. She was healthy and raring to go.

In some ways, that was the beginning of my intellectual rebirth. I'd grown up a doubter and a rebel at heart, but society grinds that out of a boy with an endless, slow flood of peer pressure and propaganda. Claire's healthy, enthusiastic genitalia served as a glaring contradiction that exposed a huge MSS lie. It sparked my quest to see through the rest of their deceptions.

Just one more boy suffering a vagina-centric epiphany. A born-again minion for the golden beaver of truth.

A month after our first night together, Claire and I were married.

Three weeks later, Sydney and Phil tied the knot.

For a long time, a few years maybe, I thought I was in love. No, I knew it. I just didn't understand what my relationship was.

I'd seen love stories and romantic comedies in the pre-siege vids. I'd watched other people meet, mate, marry, move-in, and manufacture babies. Lots of them seemed happy, or at least comfortable with each other. I felt like I knew how love and marriage added up to something they were convinced was special.

I wanted that, too, probably because I believed it was the only way a twelve-hour-a-day drudge slave could find happiness in a Gray-ruled world.

What I never comprehended at the time, maybe the kind of thing no slave understands when he's in the sort of position I was, is that to most people I was affluent, or at least I was what passed for rich among the lowly hierarchies stacked beneath the MSS boot. I had a bug in my head, a big house, and more food than most. I was privileged. More than that, being a human capable of carrying on a productive life with an alien implant symbiotically living in my brain, the Grays wanted me to procreate, and procreate a lot, to make more little humans whose bodies wouldn't reject the bug.

By their laws, any woman I married would no longer have to work. Her sole responsibility under the MSS was to reproduce.

Phil and I both thought we were marrying for love. Claire and her sister were simply earning food enough to keep away the hunger pangs, and shucking off the requirement to toil twelve-hour days for the Grays.

They made their trade.

Over the years, both grew bitter about the choice.

Sydney's dissatisfaction with her deal turned into sharp words and cruel insults that she'd heap on Phil in front of anyone unlucky enough to hear. Toward me, Sydney was always sweet and flirtatious. More punishment for Phil.

Claire just turned cold.

And colder.

Any effort she put into acting the part of loving wife was transparently false by the time we'd been together two years. By five, it was absent. We became two mute automatons, sharing a house, and a bed, a place where we serviced the only apparent need Claire had, her still healthy and active genitalia, protected from pregnancy by her continued use of contraband pills.

We talked and touched enough to negotiate the coupling. She mounted me like I was a mechanical device and rode until she was satisfied. After she was done, at least she was considerate enough to let me fondle and pump until I reached my biological endpoint as well. No intimacy existed in the act, neither before, nor after.

Chapter 19

"Kane! Dylan Kane!"

"Kane!"

My eyes pop open.

My thoughts are treading through mushy neurons.

I'm piecing together I'm awake. "Penny?"

"Kane," she asks, "are you okay? Were you hit?"

I'm breathing. That's ultimately important. My arms and legs are still attached. No breach of my suit.

"Kane," Penny asks again, "are you okay?"

"I'm good." Though I'm not entirely sure. I glance at the two holes in the airlock. I see a spot of blackness through the one above, and I see vibrant blue ocean down below. Far below. We're still in space. "Status?"

"I hit full accel," Penny tells me, kind of apologetic, but not really, "at the same time Phil maxed the grav field on the hull plates to deflect incoming fire. You guys probably felt it inside."

No kidding.

"I spun the ship," she adds, "so the grav lens is facing the Trog cruiser firing on us."

"Great move." It's an offensive weapon, yet there's no reason it shouldn't deflect incoming fire, it just didn't occur to me to use it that way. Good thing it occurred to Penny. She was a good choice for pilot. "Are we clear now?"

"No," answers Phil, jumping on the line. At least I *think* he says that. The North Korean first officer is prattling through his bad accent and muddling the comm. Easy enough to fix. I drop him from the command link I share with Phil and Penny.

"There's a squadron of Trog ships attacking one of the orbital battle stations," says Phil, his voice barely containing his anxiety. "One of them is redirecting fire at us now. The shots that already hit us came from one of the three ships bombing the shipyard. We'll be getting it from two sides."

The grav lens won't be able to keep us safe, I deduce.

Penny calmly adds, "We'll be around the curve of the earth in about ten seconds. Safe from enemy fire."

"Unless there are more Trog ships waiting for us over there," says Phil. "Or they slow down the speed of their railgun rounds, so they'll follow our orbit."

"Kill the drama, Adverb!" Penny scolds, to end Phil's negative speculation.

"Can't we grow up?" mutters Phil. He really does hate it when Penny calls him Adverb.

Unfortunately, Phil's right. Mostly. We don't know how many Trog ships are attacking which stations around the earth. But the idea of one of them hitting us with a lucky shot around an orbital curve when they can't see us—not likely. They'd need a badass targeting computer to instantly work out the orbital mechanics and relative ship velocities for that kind of shot, and if the rumors are true, Trogs don't have computer technology of any kind. "Phil, how bad is the ship damaged?"

"Cosmetic," he tells me. "We got raked pretty good, but all the systems seem to be working. We've lost pressurization in the crew compartments. One of the hydrogen tanks is venting, and so are two of the water reservoirs." Phil pauses.

I think something ominous is coming next.

Penny finishes out the status report. "Captain took one through the chest just below the neck."

"Ship's captain or platoon captain?" I ask.

"Ship," answers Penny. "Most of him is still inside the suit. If it weren't for the first officer still being alive, you'd be in charge."

Command of the ship is a necessity for the plan. Ships are weapons and weapons turn subversive dreams into revolutionary reality. The captain being hit was unfortunate for him but a piece of luck for me. The first officer is a problem with no good solution. I need to deal with him, except I'm not looking forward to what I'll have to do. I shift gears. "Any word on the fleet?"

"It's chaos out there," Phil answers. "The first officer is talking on the ship-to-ship comm and switching from Korean to English and back again. He's freaking out. I can't say how many ships were too damaged to make it off the ground at the shipyard—most of them, maybe. With the Trogs targeting the airborne ones just as they leave the atmosphere…" Phil has a hard time saying the next part. "It looks like they're destroying most of them."

Is it bad luck that our new ships were slated to launch on a day when a Trog fleet happened to be in low-earth orbit attacking the space stations? Or is this another betrayal by those damned North Koreans?

"Phil," I say, "I need a bead on the nearest enemy vessel—velocity, flight path, profile of their defensive grav field. Penny needs an attack vector if we're going to be alive after we ram that damn thing. Too fast, too slow, neither works, get us those Goldilocks numbers."

"And the Free Army?" Penny asks. She knows our instructions are to go there with the company's four ships at the first opportunity. "No one will notice if we go now. The MSS will think we're dead with all the others."

But soldiers are dying, and Trogs are killing them.

As much as my humanity is going to be tested by the things I'll have to do to birth this revolution, I won't surrender it to what feels like cowardice. "We've stepped into a pile of dog shit up here. If something's not done about those three cruisers bombing the shipyard, there'll be nothing left of the two divisions." I pause as I start to rethink, yet I know it's the right thing to do. "We're attacking."

Chapter 20

Still stuck in the airlock, I'm hitting the door release so I can make it through to the ship's pressurized half. The door won't respond. "Phil, I'm stuck."

Phil comes on the line. "We've got some holes in this end of the ship. Now the airlock's sensors don't detect atmosphere inside but aren't smart enough to know the pressurized compartments in the rest of the ship are no longer airtight."

What were the designers of this ship thinking?

"Can you override?" I ask.

"On it," he tells me.

While I'm waiting, I connect with the company captain. "Milliken, any contact with the other three platoons?"

"Uhhh."

One syllable?

Are you kidding me?

"Milliken!" I shout. "Get on your tactical comm and locate those other platoons!" I'm hoping he'll be able to find some information the first officer isn't receiving or isn't sharing. "I need to know if they've made it up. I need to know what their operational status is."

He says, "I'm coming down there."

Christ! The guy is useless.

I switch to the platoon command channel—me, the three sergeants, and the lieutenant. "Lieutenant Holt, what's the situation? I need that status." I tap my d-pad, and it shows everyone in the platoon is still alive and uninjured. I know that's not true. I saw one of them die before liftoff and I know others are injured. I'm tempted to pound the d-pad with my fist, but I don't. I can't indulge the luxury of throwing a tantrum.

I hear a gurgling pant on the platoon command channel.

Brice comes on. "Sergeant Drake caught a piece of metal through the chest."

"Status doesn't show it," I say, regretting the pointless utterance even as the syllables form in my mouth.

The sergeant curses the d-pad.

I curse too. Most of our tech is nearly useless, worn out, damaged, and pieced together.

Brice says, "The corpsman put a patch on Drake's suit but he'll be dead before we can get him back to sickbay."

"Holt?" I call again, looking for him to say anything at this point.

"He's not responding," says Brice. "Is his comm disabled?"

Brice is asking if it was me who disabled the lieutenant's comm and left it that way. That would be an embarrassing screw-up that wouldn't help with my endeavor to gain the platoon's respect. I double check. According to my d-pad, Holt's comm should be working.

"No," I answer. "My d-pad shows his comm is active." It also displays a bar graph giving me an idea of how much time everyone in the platoon is spending on their comm links. The Lieutenant and Captain Milliken are chatting non-stop. Being the company commissar, assuming that feature of my d-pad isn't on the fritz, I can listen in or hear recordings of all the conversations they've had. They're supposed to be stored on my device, though none of them know it. *I hope.*

Nevertheless, I don't have time to listen. I assume they're bitching about me. That's expected, but they've got more important things to do. Me too. I tell Brice, "His comm must be malfunctioning. How many casualties?"

"One dead before we took off. Three more missing. Whether they didn't board, or were injured down on the surface, I don't know. Sergeant Drake was the only enlisted man in the platoon besides me with combat experience."

I gulp. That's going to hurt.

"A round came through one of the doors and ricocheted around inside the platoon compartment. Not counting Drake, four soldiers are dead, and two are injured. We have suit patches over the wounds, although we need to move them into the sickbay so the corpsman can peel off the suits and treat them."

Twenty-seven percent casualties and we haven't been on the ship ten minutes. I tell Brice, "We lost pressure in the back half of the ship when they hit us."

"When will we be able to re-pressurize?"

I look at the fist-sized holes above and below me in the airlock. I know there's at least one hole in the bridge, and I don't know where else. "Can't say. It doesn't look good. The airlock is damaged. Get your corpsman to haul the wounded into the infirmary. Maybe we can seal that room and pressurize it, however, they'll all be locked inside, with no way to move them out until we land or fix the holes in the hull."

"That takes our corpsman out of the fight." It's a crap choice, but Brice is decisive. "I say we do it. At least that way the wounded we have now will have a chance. The rest of us will just have to not get hurt."

"Agreed." Time for more drastic measures. "Sergeant, have one of your people recycle me a kit off one of the dead soldiers." Commissars like me are only armed with a pistol. Infantry have a pistol as well as a rifle-sized railgun, grenades, and ammunition for it all. "I'm coming with the platoon when we raid the Trog ship."

"Sir?" he asks. "You're not trained for—"

"Let's be honest," I tell him. "Except for you, none of us have seen anything but a simulator. I'm not sending the troops out short on noncoms with a lieutenant who won't communicate, and a company captain whose suit seems to have boarded without him in it. We go in together."

"Yes, sir," answers Brice.

I think I've scored some points with him. "Get my kit together. I need to move up to the bridge and resolve a situation. I'll be right back down. Make sure the platoon is ready to roll."

Chapter 21

Finally, I'm through the airlock's interior door and into the central hallway running down the axis of the ship. Phil has restored radial grav at point-two-g, so I close the door and shove off to float toward the bridge.

In here, where the ship was designed to hold air, the metal surfaces are painted, though the paint is already flaking, evidence of how hastily the vessel was thrown together. If the Trogs don't kill us, we'll be lucky to live through the day in our iron coffin.

The rear half of the ship is much wider than the front, so it has enough interior space on each side of the hall for the infirmary, a few storerooms, and the captain's quarters. The door at the far end of the corridor leads to the bridge. As I reach it, a Korean-accented voice blares over my comm. "Captain dead. I charge ship." It's the first officer. I've read his name off the crew roster, except I know I'll screw up the pronunciation, so I don't use it to address him. "We need to talk."

"You charge grunts," he tells me. "I charge ship. Go. Ready boots."

Boots?

I bite my lip to funnel my anger. It's insulting the first officer's English is so bad. It tells me exactly how little respect the North Koreans and their Gray masters have for the rest of us. That's nothing new. I try the handle on the bridge door. It doesn't budge. I try to unlock the mechanism through my link to the ship. Rejected. I don't bother to soften the edge on my annoyance when I say, "Unlock the door, lieutenant."

"You charge grunts," he shoots back.

"You get us in communication with our chain of command!" I yell in chopped, precise words. "That's your job. Do it now!"

"You charge grunts. Go."

Over the bridge comm, I say "Phil, unlock the bridge door." I don't want him to have to execute the first prosecutable act in our mutiny, but there's no choice.

The Korean officer hears my instructions to Phil and blows a tirade of half-intelligible orders over the command comm.

I try the handle on the bridge door again. It's free.

I slip through and lightly bounce up the six steps to reach the bridge floor level.

The Korean officer is yelling and facing Phil where he sits at a console for monitoring and controlling ship systems. He doesn't realize Phil has already done the thing he's trying to prevent. The officer doesn't know I'm on the bridge.

In the light-g, I shove off the floor to float toward them, pulling my pistol from its magnetic belt mount as I go.

If I can maneuver close enough and get the angle right, I can send a round through the circuitry embedded in a node on the backside of his helmet. It'll kill the helmet's communication systems, and consequently ruin the suit's life support system control computer. It won't be a death sentence. It'll just mean the first officer will need a replacement helmet off one of the dead soldiers. He'll have to suffer a few moments of vacuum while he makes the switch. Then again, the list of unpleasant inconveniences anyone will suffer to avoid dying is nearly endless.

Once the first officer is wearing a soldier's helmet encoded to my command authority under the company hierarchy, I'll have control over his suit and he'll be a manageable problem.

What I'll do with him then, I don't know—probably freeze his suit and store him in the captain's quarters until I come up with a permanent solution.

Unfortunately, the first officer senses something as I come within arm's reach.

He spins as fast as he can in light-g with only a grip on a wall handle.

His eyes narrow and he starts yelling at me, thinking he's putting me in my place, telling me what a stupid grunt I am. He's riled because I'm a political officer and my existence is an affront to the natural authority of Koreans over the lower forms of humanity, the rest of the humans on earth.

In truth, that's all in my head. It's what I imagine his rapid string of babble means, at least until I see in his eyes he understands I'm not here for a tongue-lashing. My pistol is in hand.

I reach out to throw an arm around his helmet so I can leverage him into place.

He's quick, and he manages to clasp both his small hands on my weapon, trying with all his effort to wrench it away, to point it at me.

It happens fast, two men grappling in light-g, with little leverage. I'm faster than him, not physically, but mentally. Or maybe I'm just better trained from all those hours in the simulator and zero-g room back on earth. I activate my suit's gravity and use my momentum to slam him into a bulkhead, thinking I'll knock the wind out of him and earn a few seconds to do what I need to do.

In the collision, my gun fires a burst of four shots.

The slugs rip into his chest and tear a path up his throat.

High-velocity metal bits ricochet inside his helmet and jerk it back and forth on his shoulders. Through his faceplate, I see his head disintegrate like a frog in a blender.

It's over as soon as it starts.

His grip loosens, and his body spasms.

Then he's still.

I let go of the corpse, and without taking my eyes off the unintended consequence of my mutinous act, I comm the remains of the bridge crew. "Penny, Phil, you good?"

"Yes," answers Penny, unfazed.

Phil's response is unintelligible.

"Revolution?" I ask, without looking at them, as I convince myself what I just did wasn't murder.

"Revolution," they each answer in varying degrees of enthusiasm.

It's the first time any of us have said the word louder than a whisper.

Oh, Christ!

I spin around, suddenly realizing I may have just made a fatal mistake.

The bridge isn't that large, and I'm confused.

I see the ship captain's body collaged in a mess of gore on one wall, held tenuously there by the micro-g. I don't see Captain Milliken. "Where is he?"

Guessing who I'm talking about, Phil asks, "You didn't see him? Milliken went forward before you came in."

I deduce the only possibility outside of Milliken being a magician able to materialize anywhere he likes, he must be in one of the rooms off the main corridor, having gone inside before I came out of the airlock at the other end of the hall.

Why would he be in there?

"How'd you know he didn't have a kill switch wired?" Penny asks me, motioning her head at the dead first officer.

I didn't. I guessed not. I hoped not. Being the company commissar, I was the only one onboard who was supposed to be able to set a kill switch. However, with the MSS so infiltrated into everything, such a duplicitous proxy of the Grays' authority over earth, anything is possible.

I decide to comfort my crew with something that sounds certain. "Nobody's life support turned off when the captain was hit." I let them finish the logical deduction that if the captain had no kill switch, then his lieutenant, of course, didn't either.

Pragmatic, Penny asks, "What next, Captain?"

"Like I said, we're attacking." I hand my pistol to Phil, and take the first officer's weapon off his belt and pass it to Penny. I like the idea we three rebels will have weapons, though for the moment, I have nothing.

Phil, looking emphatically at the dead first officer, says, "I can handle ship systems and gravity just fine. I can't do ship-to-ship comm, and my Korean is terrible."

That's one of the flaws in our plan. Everybody on earth who's not Korean hates them so much, few sully their tongues with the language. "I'll see if Brice has a Korean speaker he can send up to help."

"Is that wise?" Phil nods a few times at the dead first officer, evidence of the crime I just committed.

I shrug like it doesn't bother me. "The captain and first officer were killed when the railgun slugs hit the ship." It's the easiest lie to tell. "Just be careful what you say around the soldier until we know whether he's with us or not." I comm link to Sergeant Brice. "The first officer and captain are dead."

"Both the Koreans?" he asks, his voice ripe with hidden meaning. He suspects I fragged them. How could he not?

Or is it paranoia—or guilt—putting on a new mask?

"Do you have anyone who can work the comm panel who speaks Korean?" I ask.

"Give me ten seconds."

I click back to the bridge comm. "Penny, you have the ship. I need the soldiers to see me among them."

"You should stay on the bridge," Penny argues. "Captain the ship. That's what we planned."

"Milliken is an idiot," I tell her. "Lieutenant Holt isn't any better. I need to be with the troops when they go in." I hadn't expected anything to happen so fast, and not in this way. I'd figured I'd have a chance to bring the platoon, and then the company, to our side, maybe with a speech that ended in cheers. Silver-screen fantasies always look good when they roll through your imagination.

Now that I've seen the way the soldiers look at me, I know none of them like me, and many of them hate me. If I don't wade into the battle and shed blood with them, I won't gain their respect.

"Phil," I say, "Penny's in charge when I'm not on the bridge."

I see in his face he's not happy about it. He still nods.

Brice pings me. "I've found a competent Korean speaker. Almost no American accent."

"Send him to the bridge," I tell the sergeant. "I'll be forward momentarily. Is my kit ready?"

"Ready."

I cut back to the bridge comm. "Penny, we're going on the attack. I'd prefer not to go in alone. As soon as that soldier makes it up here, situate him with the ship's comm panel and tell him to find out if there's anyone out there who can attack with us."

With my business on the bridge done much more permanently than I'd planned, I head forward.

Chapter 22

A female soldier—a short woman with a serious face and kind eyes—is in the airlock when I step through the inner door. In her arms, she's holding an extra set of weapons. Another soldier, Jablonsky, shoves by me on his way to the bridge. He doesn't say, 'sir.' He doesn't apologize for bumping into me as he passes.

Jablonsky doesn't have the balls to say what's on his mind, but still wants me to notice his disrespect. He thinks I'm just a commissar, a stooge bureaucrat for the MSS, not a real grunt. It rubs me the wrong way because I know he's not a grunt either. He's not even competent with his equipment.

Back at the depot when we were trying to load into the ship, after he activated his suit's g, he was drifting in the air ten feet off the ground, struggling against the buffeting from the explosions when I remotely took control of his suit and moved him inside.

It's my bet Jablonsky's never spent any time in a zero-g room.

I stop.

I realize I'm indulging vindictive little emotions affordable to a line worker at the grav factory, but not to a major leading his troops into war. It's my job to win the men's respect, not simply to expect it. Getting used to my new job won't be as easy as it seemed back when I was sitting in dark rooms, plotting my treason.

"Sir, I'm Sergeant Lenox, sir." The soldier with my inherited kit is still in the airlock with me.

"Good to meet you, Lenox." I recall she was one of the first to board back at the shipyard. She was competent with her grav controls.

Lenox unloads the equipment by simply letting it go and allowing it to drift toward the walls.

Blood stains are on the gun, and I can't help but wonder if it's the blood of one of my soldiers or if the stains were left by a previous owner.

Lieutenant Holt opens the outer airlock door in front of me and steps inside.

The airlock isn't small, yet I'm not comfortable with the unexpected proximity. Over a private comm, I ask, "What do you need, Holt?"

On the platoon channel for all ears to hear, he says, "We need to talk."

"We can talk over the private channel." I say it in a scolding tone, though I silently admonish myself for doing so. I shouldn't disrespect my officers in front of their subordinates.

Damn, being the officer in charge is going to be harder than I thought.

Holt doesn't respond. He shuffles his feet and glances around. His mouth moves, so I see he's talking again—not to me.

Over the private comm, I try to get his attention. "Lieutenant?"

He ignores me.

He's going to be a problem. Yeah, I'm a deductive genius sometimes.

I tap my d-pad to see who he's conversing with. No surprise. It's Captain Useless.

Worrisome.

But enough of this. I break into the comm link to see what they're talking about and hear half a word before the line goes silent.

Holt looks up at me.

I start to tell him to get his shit together and act like an officer when something hard clinks against the top of my helmet. Instinctively, I jerk, and bump a body behind me. A localized gravity field centered on the crown of my head is suddenly pulling so hard it feels like my skin is going to peel off my face.

I try to shout at the pain but the g force notches up, overwhelming my resistance and slamming my head against the inside of my helmet.

I see stars.

More sensitive to gravity than me, my implant spasms, sending lightning bolts of pain through my skull.

Whoever is holding the small grav plate to the back of my helmet knows that. It's no secret what I am. My commissar status guarantees the truth of it.

My vision collapses to a dark tunnel.

I'm having trouble drawing breath and I realize my throat is being pressed closed by the g.

I try to squeeze out an order yet only garbled syllables choke through.

That's when it hits me what's happening. They're trying to kill me.

I trigger the freeze switches in everyone's suits.

Nothing happens.

Shit.

Lenox is raising her rifle and looking past me. "You'll get us all killed. What are you doing?"

"Stop," Lieutenant Holt tells her. "Everything's okay."

With her weapon halfway up, Lenox stops moving while still looking at the anonymous person behind me. "What did you do to the major? What is that?"

Holt says, "Lower your weapon, Sergeant Lenox. That's an order."

Lenox balks.

Soldiers start to crowd the door outside the airlock, trying to manage a peek inside.

Captain Milliken comes on the line. "It's a grav plate."

That's when I get it. That's who's behind me. Milliken must have been hiding in one of the side rooms, hoping to ambush me when I passed through the hall.

"It's pulling nine g's on the back of his helmet!" says Milliken. He shouts into the comm to make sure the whole platoon hears. "The remote control he has on all our suits, the kill switch he has on every one of us, it's a gravity switch mounted in this module on the back of his helmet. As long as this grav plate is here, he can't do anything to us."

Lenox glances between Holt and Milliken. "We're in the middle of a battle."

"He's a Trog spy," says Holt.

"What?" I manage to say through my constricting throat.

"Explain it," says Brice, suddenly squeezing past the soldiers and stepping into the airlock. He shoves Holt against a wall and holds him there with a hand pressed in the center of his chest. In his other hand, his rifle is raised and pointed at my face. He says, "Explain that, Lieutenant. Do it fast."

Shakily, Holt says, "I have a special comm signal tracer built into my suit."

I can see he's lying just by the look on his face.

God, I hope he's lying.

"And?" Brice asks.

"There's a reason we lose every battle with the Trogs," says Captain Milliken. "They have moles in our ranks who communicate our every move. That's why they're always ready for us. That's why we were just shot to shit."

"You're gonna say that to me?" Brice asks, glaring fiery eyes at Milliken. "You?"

"That business on Ceres?" Milliken asks as I feel him trying to get more of himself hidden behind me. "You're still carrying that cross? Put your weapon down, Sergeant!"

Genius deduction time: These two knew each other before our platoon mustered at the spaceport.

"Sergeant!" Holt reiterates. "Follow your orders."

I'm hoping Brice's rifle is pointed at Milliken, not me. From my perspective, all I see is the end of a railgun barrel that looks the size of a cannon.

Brice's brows grow heavy and his voice rasps like acid. "Captain Milliken, you're engaged in an illegal activity. Cut power to that grav plate. Step away from Major Kane."

Milliken huffs and says, "You'll do as you're—"

Brice pulls the trigger.

CHAPTER 23

I'm on the floor and looking up at red mist dissipating to nothingness. Small hunks of gray-red meat are drifting. Bits of shrapnel and glass are bouncing off metal walls.

Brice, Lenox, and Holt are looking down at me as I realize I'm not the one Brice shot.

Lenox leans down and disengages the grav plate stuck to my helmet.

Instantly, I can breathe. I can think. I can focus.

I hop to my feet, lose my balance, and have to catch myself with a hand against the wall as Lenox steadies me. I say, "I'm okay."

She doesn't let go.

I glance down to see Milliken's ruptured helmet, his head a mess, blood bubbling out of the gore and boiling into the vacuum. I turn back to Brice who still has Lieutenant Holt pinned to the wall.

Holt looks like he's peeing himself. Lucky for him, his catheter is recycling the urine into his suit's bio-support system.

Focusing on Brice with a humble expression on my face, I say, "Thanks."

"I didn't do it for you," he spits, and cocks his head toward the soldiers crowding the door. "Milliken gave me a legit reason, so I did it for them." He glances down at Milliken's corpse and then his hard eyes settle back on me. "Don't get them killed for nothing."

The message is clear. Brice won't mind fragging me if he feels it's deserved. All he'll need is half an excuse to legitimize it.

Humility time is over. I return Brice's stare. "I won't." I override Lieutenant Holt's suit and lock it. "You can let go of the lieutenant now. I've paralyzed his suit."

Brice glances at Holt like he wouldn't mind shooting him, too. "What do I do with the lieutenant?"

I answer, "We'll figure it out after the battle. Or maybe the Trogs will blow us out of the sky and we won't have to worry about it."

Brice laughs at that. Too many months spent in space fighting the Trogs have left him with a bleak sense of humor.

I laugh, too. Maybe I'm tweaked out on the giddy emotions of my brush with death. Maybe all this freedom has filled me with a heady rush. All I really know is I haven't seen a Trog with my own eyes, and this war business is already nastier than I'd have ever guessed.

Brice leaves Lieutenant Holt's stiff body against the wall in the airlock, gives me one final glance, and marches into the platoon compartment.

I think he and I have a bond now.

Phil opens the airlock's inner door and steps halfway in with his pistol unsteady in his hand. He spots Milliken on the floor and comms my private line. "I sensed a gravitation anomaly up here. Everything cool?"

"Is now," I tell him. "I'm thinking we should probably watch each other's backs until we figure out where the crew stands."

He nods. "I'll head back to the bridge."

"Will that communications guy work out?" I ask, referring to the rude soldier Brice sent back that way.

"I'm not sure yet. I think he'll do okay."

"Any word yet on other ships?" I ask.

"Other assault ships made it up, so it's not just us," answers Phil. "Some Korean colonel is making noise about leading a charge. Nothing clear yet."

Chapter 24

Tendrils of blue gravity ionization stream along the walls and the grav field inside the ship turns uneven.

Into the command comm, I ask, "What's happening?"

Phil is immediately on the line. "One of the cruisers attacking that battle station broke off and is firing at us long-range. I'm pulsing the defensive grav to deflect the rounds. We've got to get moving. We're not safe."

The ship accelerates, and both Lenox and I lean to compensate. Lieutenant Holt slowly slides down the wall. The inertial bubble isn't keeping up.

As if reading my mind, Phil comms in again, "I'm pulling power away from the interior grav bubble. You may feel some discomfort."

"Juji Station is coming up off our port side," says Penny. All of the battle stations are named after Korean mythological figures. "I'm going to fly beneath it. The grav lens deflects everything they shoot at us from the front, however, our flanks are vulnerable."

"Get us there," I confirm, as though she'd asked me for permission.

Seeing I'm busy, Lenox starts placing magazines on my belt magnets. "Two hundred and eighty rounds each," she says.

I nod as I keep tabs on the command comm.

She shoves the rifle into my hands. "You use one of these in the simulator?"

"Of course."

"You any good?"

"Expert Marksman," I answer with a grin, because it's ironic. "Like everybody else." It seems to me that much of the simulator training was geared to make us think we were much better than we were.

A confidence booster?

So we'll rush headlong into a fight with a false sense of competence?

I don't know if I'm that cynical, but then again, those fears disguised as questions did just cross my mind.

Gravity tugs to my left, and I shift my feet to maintain balance.

"Lots of debris out here," Penny tells me.

"I'm sensing two assault ships behind Juji Station," says Phil.

"What's the word from your comm boy?"

"Jablonsky?" asks Phil.

"If you say so."

"He speaks Korean just like one of them," Phil tells me in a rush.

"What's he saying?" I ask.

"Don't know."

"Well, find out," I tell him.

Lenox points to the rifle, "You shoot one for real?"

I nod. "I had access to the firing range down by the spaceport."

"You go a lot?" she asks.

I nod. "Expert Marksman rating with an *actual* gun."

"You know the rounds behave differently in atmosphere than in vacuum?"

"I do."

"This is the new model," she tells me. "You shoot one of these yet?"

Shaking my head, this time I tell her, "Only the old single-shot models."

She taps the electrodes on her palm. "Electricity from your suit's micro-reactor powers the gun through the leads in your palm, just like the single-shot models."

I look the gun over. Except for the magazine and an extra bulge at the rear of the barrel, it's pretty much the same as the old model.

"Just like the single-shot, this is a grav-drive gun," she tells me. "It'll send a slug downrange at near six k."

"Six thousand miles per hour," I confirm, "two thousand faster than the single-shot model."

"This one has a reverse-grav recoil compensator built in, so it won't kick the hell out of you every time you pull the trigger. Matter-of-fact, you'll barely feel it. The most important feature of this weapon and your pistol is they're both grav-integrated."

"They didn't mention that back on earth."

"Most people don't appreciate the significance of it." Lenox's serious eyes underscore the importance. "What that means is when your suit's defensive gravity field is turned on, it treats the weapon like a part of you. If it didn't, the field would be continually working to shove it away from your body, making it hard to aim."

"Good to know." That never crossed my mind.

"One other thing about defensive grav," Lenox's seriousness doesn't let up. "If you have it set too high, it will affect the slugs leaving the end of your barrel and ruin your aim."

"You know this stuff," I observe.

"Before they called my number, I was a certification proctor at the Omaha induction center for three years."

That piques my interest. "You know anybody else in the platoon?" It's a valid question. The way the draft works, inductees are pooled by an automated process not finalized until induction day—this morning for most of us. None of us met until we came together at the muster station.

"I talked to nearly everybody while we were waiting for our ride."

"Anybody else in the platoon any good?" I ask.

"Sergeant Brice is a pretty good shot," she smiles. The off-color humor is subtle and contagious. "Peters and Silva seem to know what they're talking about. No way to know until you see what they do with their equipment."

I nod knowingly as I realize at this point, all I'm getting from Lenox is talk. Maybe she knows her stuff academically, and that's the end of it. Nonetheless, she did handle her grav better than most back in the shipyard fiasco.

"Two things you should know," she says, patting the rifle in my hands, "because of that recoil compensator you'll suck down power twice as fast as with a single-shot model. You'll be more accurate, because it doesn't kick. If you go to full-auto mode, you'll burn through your suit's hydro cell pretty quick."

"How long if I'm firing auto?" I'm not happy with the info I was given back at the induction center, and I'm hoping for better news.

"In battle, using your suit grav to power around, shooting a lot, maybe three or four hours—then you better start looking for a new H pack to plug into your reactor. If you need to conserve power and you've still got Trogs to put out of their misery, you can switch off the recoil compensator." She shows me a small lever above the trigger guard. "You'll save half your energy on each shot."

"Gotcha."

The walls sizzle bright blue radiance. The grav bubble is straining. I brace myself. Holt, unable to do anything but be victimized by the tug of fluctuating gravity, flips to the other side of the airlock and slams against a bulkhead.

I don't say anything about it. I'm hoping he earned a few bruises.

Lenox apparently reads my thoughts through the look on my face, and in a low voice says, "He was a wormy prick, anyway."

"Sharp corner there," says Penny over the command comm. "We're coming in below Juji."

"Nobody can hit us here," Phil tells me.

Soldiers are coming into the airlock, hauling the wounded through.

"Anything else I need to know right now?" I ask.

"Final exam is coming up in a few minutes," Lenox smiles. "Let's hope you pass."

I force out a laugh, because it eases the tension kicking me in the gut, and it'll keep me from crapping a pharmaceutically-softened load into my suit's rectal catheter. And I laugh at that, too, because in this vacuum-packed, orange-suited army of sim-trained novices, anybody can get away with shitting their pants in the face of the enemy. What a brave bunch of heroes we are with the product of raving fear sucked away by our suits' recyclers so no one will ever see.

Chapter 25

Phil loops Jablonsky onto the comm line. "It'll be easier than me relaying," he says.

I don't want to talk to Jablonsky, but nobody ever said being an adult was easy. "Tell me what you know, Jablonsky."

"Juji and two other stations are dead."

Three of the twenty-six? Not good. "Where's the fleet?"

"They're gone."

"Where?" I ask. I need to know how far out they are, when they'll be arriving.

"Gone," reiterates Jablonsky. "Destroyed. Captured."

The command comm goes silent. Nothing but background static as me, Penny, and Phil try to fully grasp what that means for us. When the war started two years ago, our Gray masters commanded a fleet of sixty-two kilometer-long cruisers, all just like the one they used to conquer earth thirty years ago. Each one built by human hands. Each captained by a Gray and run by Gray and Korean officers, every single one with a human crew and SDF contingent totaling ten thousand, at least.

Penny breaks the silence first, "But the news—"

"Propaganda." Jablonsky doesn't leave any room for disagreement. "Lies. Everybody knows that."

Suddenly, I like Jablonsky a little more, though his assessment is wrong. Half the people I know back home gobble up every ladleful of lies the MSS defecates through their media outlets. Not only are we a race of conquered serfs, we crave self-deception because that wonderfully warped mirror helps us suffer the shame of our choice not to trudge the hard road to freedom.

And that's the thing that makes the road so steep—not the bullets in the air, not the blood-slick path, not even the bodies of our dead friends filling the ditches—it's those first ego-deflating strides into seeing the shiny, multicolor, self-confirming delusion for what it is, and understanding truth isn't what you believed.

"I heard from dependable sources," says Penny, defending herself, "not that MSS disinformation. We're still supposed to have seven ships."

"Can't say for sure," says Jablonsky. "Lots of chatter going on about another invasion attempt on the moon that started two days ago. The North Korean captains on the line are talking openly about things they shouldn't be, and I'm piecing it together, so I could be wrong. It seems the remains of the fleet were sent to the moon to repel the Trogs and the whole thing turned into a trap. All seven ships were destroyed with maybe twice that many Trog ships taken out."

"The lunar orbits are full of new wreckage," adds Phil, for confirmation.

"The Trogs can afford the loss," says Penny, zeroing in on the heart of the matter. "We can't."

"Two squadrons appeared out of nowhere to spring the trap," says Jablonsky. "Twenty-four brand new Trog cruisers straight from their home world. Nobody expected them to show up."

"So the only navy we have left are the assault ships on the ground at the Arizona shipyard." I say it because somebody needs to. "And they're getting shredded."

"It's a shit show up here," confirms Jablonsky. "Nobody's sure what things are like down there right now. All I can tell you for sure is casualties are… it's… a slaughter."

That silences the line again.

Phil's turn to break the hush with his despondence. "We've lost. The Grays should have surrendered to the Trogs a year ago."

"Adverb!" Penny uses the name the way a mother uses a child's name to let him know when he's stepping out of line.

Ignoring her, Phil's voice finds its familiar frantic edge. "I don't care who we lose to. One master is as good as the next. The goddamn Grays don't care if the war drags on to the last man, it's not Gray lives they're wasting, it's human lives."

True, mostly, but the Grays have been hatching little Graylettes by the tens of thousands on earth since they solidified their control of our planet. Plenty of them are being killed in this war, yet nothing like the hundreds of millions of humans who've been fed into the grinder.

"When things get bad enough," Phil continues, "All those Grays running this show from their cozy ship on the moon will bug out to some other unsuspecting planetary system on the other side of the galaxy with a technologically backward race of dumbasses just like us they can enslave." Phil deflates as he reaches his conclusion. "Then the Trogs will exterminate the rest of us and take our planet."

I don't know how much of that I agree with.

Something more important occurs to me, we're letting news of our defeat demoralize us into lethargy.

No, I'm in charge, *I'm* letting it demoralize us.

It's a sin strangers are paying for with their lives right now.

I have to get our ship into the war.

At the risk of hearing a number that'll worsen the mood, I ask, "Do we have a count of assault ships that made it up?"

Phil switches gears and offers his opinion. "There's so much debris from the space stations and so many wrecks, I can't tell." Like me, like Penny, Phil has an alien implant in his head. He's more sensitive to gravity than the rest of us—not as good as a Gray, but better than anyone from the grav factory. That's how he knows what's out there—everything with mass exerts a gravitational pull on everything else.

"I think forty or so are on the fleet channel," says Jablonsky. "The number keeps changing. Some take a hit and disappear. More hail the command frequency as they come up from the surface. I can't guess at the number of mayday calls."

"You said there was a North Korean officer making noise about being in command." I just know it's going to be that North Korean prick of an admiral in charge of the fleet. Trouble never seems to stick to guys like that.

"No flag officers are out here that I can tell," answers Jablonsky. "Mostly ships are asking who's in charge. I'm getting a periodic message from Pyongyang. It says the admiralty is ordering a withdrawal, telling all ships to take up positions around Imugi."

"I got a big Imugi in my ass." It's unusual for Phil to make a joke when he's stressed.

I don't tell him an Imugi is a big snake, that according to Korean mythology, might turn into a dragon one day. Instead I ask a question to confirm what I'm not sure of. "Is that the big battle station over North Korea?"

"It is," Penny tells me.

"Yeah," Phil confirms. "It's the only one in a geosynchronous orbit. Tells you something, doesn't it?"

Apparently, our great leaders on the Korean Peninsula went through their own analysis of the situation and decided earth needed to spend the rest of its military resources saving their asses, probably so they'd have time to cut a deal with the Trogs just like the one they made when the Grays came in and took control. "Fucking North Koreans."

Chapter 26

"You need to decide," Penny tells me. "Now that we know the situation, do we bubble jump the hell out of here, make our way to the asteroid belt like we're supposed to, or attack those cruisers on our own—"

"Suicide," mutters Phil, letting us know exactly what he thinks of the attack idea.

"—or follow orders and go to Imugi Station?"

"I hate the North Koreans as much as any of you," says Phil, talking in slow, wooden words, like he always does when he's starting a new argument. "We need to remember they managed to make a deal with the Grays when the rest of the world was being bombarded in the siege. This war with the Trogs is lost, just like our war with the Grays. Maybe the North Koreans are the bet."

"Phil," says Penny, "I like you, but sometimes your limp dick routine rubs me raw."

"Just because I use my brains," Phil shoots back in soft words, like he expects to be punched, "instead of hiking fourteeners every weekend looking for a mountain goat with an attractive sphincter?"

"We're not going to bicker," I tell them, dead serious. "There's a reason we're all up here. All of us chose this."

"Not me," says Jablonsky, still on the command comm.

Shit.

Penny said too much.

Now Jablonsky knows desertion is an option. And if he doesn't know it, he'll certainly guess when he's trying to figure out what Penny meant about bubble jumping to the asteroid belt. Once he discovers the truth, it'll only be a matter of time before the other soldiers know, too. Not that he's a snitch, that's just human nature at work.

Now what to do about Jablonsky.

Pending decisions are piling up—big ones—and I need to figure out pretty quickly if I've got the mettle to make them.

If not, I need to step out of the way and put someone else in charge.

I flex my fists around my railgun as I think.

I've never had a real weapon in my hands, especially not a military-grade tool designed and built for wholesale murder.

I'm in command of a platoon of inexperienced soldiers I think want to fight.

I've got a bullet-shaped ramrod of a ship slapped together from two helpings of desperation and a trainload of steel smelted so long ago human flight was only a dream in a few crazy men's heads. Still, the rusty thing is a powerful beast wrought for killing graceful, star-faring leviathans full of Neanderthal-looking wankers who want to make my people slaves.

I have more power than I've ever had, or ever will again.

I've sniveled and sucked up to my Gray masters and their North Korean lapdogs my entire life, pretending in every moment I was the most loyal, diligent cog in their war machine, building grav plates, sweating twelve-hour shifts, keeping my insurgent thoughts buried too deep for them to see.

I did it all on the chance that one day I'd have an opportunity just like the one I have right in this moment.

Do I have doubts?

Yes.

Am I afraid I'll get all of my friends killed?

You bet your fuzzy 'nads.

From the moment our ship lifted off from the Arizona desert I've been free, and only one question matters now that I've had that small taste on my tongue.

Really, just one question.

Will I ever be able to kneel again?

Hell, fucking no!

And that's my choice.

I'll die a fat old man, standing on a beach, with a beer in my hand and warm ocean washing over my feet, while three kinds of ass cancer eat away at my lymph nodes, but I'll be free, or I'll die fighting.

First order of business: Gamble.

Because my goal is bigger than just my pride.

I open a comm link to everyone on the ship. "Our North Korean slave masters are calling for a retreat. They want us to take up an orbit a thousand clicks over Pyongyang." I know we can't geosynchronously orbit at a thousand clicks, however, we can easily grav stabilize there just like Imugi station. "They think we've lost this war. And they might be right."

"What you saw in that Arizona shipyard when we were loading into this rusty beast, that's it. That's earth's navy as far as I can tell, and most of them have probably already been blasted into space junk. The last of our battle cruisers was destroyed or captured in a battle near the moon yesterday. Three of earth's battle stations are slag, and the Trogs are out there pounding a fourth. Maybe that's the worst of it, maybe the truth isn't that bad, but you know how our North Korean masters like to keep us in the dark."

A few of the soldiers gasp. *Masters* is a word that would land me in jail back on earth. Everybody knows what we are, yet we're not allowed to say.

I exit the airlock so I'm standing in the platoon compartment.

The soldiers strapped into their seats and the ones on their feet all look at me.

I let everything I've told them sink in for a moment.

I continue. "I'll tell you what I think. You all saw each other back at the muster station. You know what we are—pimply kids, fathers, mothers, and daughters. We're not the cream of the crop. You've seen the ship. It looks like a rusty piece of shit, some kind of kamikaze torpedo thing with an untested gravity lens welded on the front. The MSS news vids tell us the war is going well, they even imply we're winning. That's bullshit. Look around." I point at them. "We are not what winners in war look like." I wave a hand at the ship. "This isn't what a victor sends to mop up their beaten enemies.

"We're losing badly."

Mouths are agape. Eyes wide.

I'm spouting firing squad-worthy truths, the kind your drunk uncle babbles about when he's sprawled on the couch, half-delirious from alcohol poisoning and carb-loading after a Thanksgiving Day binge.

Before I reach full evangelist mode, I tone down to a rational level. "Captain Milliken is dead. All of you know that. Our Korean ship's captain and first officer are dead. It's just us on this ship—just us Americans. That's the situation. Now it's time for each of you to decide what you believe. And it's time to decide what you want to do about it. I'm disabling the automatic kill switch on your suits." Using my implant, I toggle the gravity switches. "I've been a slave all my life. I'll not be a new master's slave, and I won't kneel again for my old one. Right now, in this moment, for the first time in our lives, we're all free."

I pause again, hoping I won't have to jump back through the airlock door to avoid the hostile fire.

Nobody moves.

I think they're all in shock.

"We're floating just below Juji Station. It's been slagged, but I'm sure rescue parties will be up from the surface just as soon as the Trog ships bugger off to wherever in the solar system their supply base is. Anyone who wants off this ship can hop through a door and go. Use your suit's grav to fly down to the surface. You'll be able to find a way inside. There are plenty of extra holes now, thanks to the Trogs. Your suit's hydro pack and calorie pack will last three days. That's only three days of power and food. There'll be plenty of suits on the surface with corpses in them, and all the half-full power and calorie packs you need to last a lifetime if that's what you want."

"Or," I tell them, coming to my closing pitch, "you can stay on the ship and follow me. I'm a rebel major in the Free Army, and I'm taking this ship to one of our bases out in the asteroid belt." God, I hope that part is true. All I have are Vishnu's and Blair's credibility on that. "I'm not going to take up an orbital station over North-fucking-Korea, and I don't intend to follow another MSS order as long as I live. I will find a way to live through this war, do my part to win it, and then I'll kill every Gray bastard I can get in my sights, and murder every North Korean stooge who gets in the way."

The speech wasn't planned, however, when I imagined how it would look in all those years I fantasized about this moment, it looked a lot like a Roman victory parade.

All of the soldiers are silent. Not one is moving.

Not one of the bridge crew adds a word.

"Talk among yourselves," I tell them. "You still have a couple minutes. Maybe. Phil, open some of the assault doors so whoever wants to go can get out. On second thought, Penny, drop us down to the surface real quick. I've seen these knuckleheads try to use their suit's grav controls." I look back at the soldiers. "You can step out onto solid ground. No hard feelings. Just don't come with me unless you're ready for revolution and ready to die for it."

Over a private comm connection, Penny tells me, "Ignoring orders from the admiralty is one thing, but you shouldn't have told the platoon about the revolution. You're endangering us all."

On the open line, I say, "Get us down to the surface, Penny."

Several of the assault doors slide open, giving everyone in the platoon compartment a dizzying view of the earth and the orbiting wreckage of ships and busted battle stations. It looks like interstellar defeat.

We close in on Juji.

Through faceplates I see lips move. Men and women are talking to each other over private comm links.

God, I hope there's not an eloquent loyalist among them.

I watch, hoping no one raises a rifle.

The ship jolts as we hit Juji's surface.

"Now's the time," I tell them.

Down at the far end of the platoon compartment, Sergeant Brice pushes past a few soldiers and somehow, without a single word, commands everyone's attention. He drills me hard with those war-weary eyes of his. "I'm in."

Chapter 27

Penny tells me I've pushed too far, too fast.

Phil curses at me on a private comm link.

I ignore it. That's just Phil. He and I have a steamer trunk full of baggage in our relationship, and his whining is, at times, insufferable. Nonetheless, he's dependable and talented. And sometimes, he's right. Just not now.

Lenox privately connects with me. "I'll roll the dice with you, sir."

I thank her and step back into the airlock. It'll be easier for the draftees in the platoon compartment to make an honest choice if I'm not staring them down. On the bridge comm, I say, "If you're all staying, we need to get in the game."

"Of course, we're all staying," Penny tells me. "What about you, Jablow-me?"

"Name's Jablonsky, skank."

Penny shoots back, "You're name's what I say it is until I know whether you're staying to fight or getting off the ship with the other pussies."

"I've got nothing to lose back home," says Jablonsky. "I'll fight."

"Phil," I ask. "I need to hear you say it."

We've talked about this for years. Late-night bullshit between half-drunk friends is one thing. Making plans and asking for support from people who don't think they'll ever have to follow through is another sort of thing, and they both add up to squat.

We're at the moment where words are tested.

"Well?" I ask again.

Phil says, "If you get me killed—"

"Quit suckin' your momma's titty and grow up," Penny tells him. "We're probably all gonna get killed. Do your job or let Jablonsky do it."

Jablonsky can't do Phil's job. He doesn't have an alien bug in his head, so he can't see gravity fields.

Penny says, "Phil, quit playing for attention and answer."

"You know you can depend on me." It's perfunctory when it comes out of Phil's mouth. However, it's the final commitment.

Good.

Time to do something for real. "Jablonsky, broadcast on the ship-to-ship frequency that we're rallying at Juji Station. As soon as we have five more ships, we're leading a full-bore attack on the nearest Trog cruiser. Be clear about this next part, don't *ask* them, *tell* them. If no one answers the call, we're doing it alone. Shame them. Phil, calculate an attack vector for Penny on the nearest Trog cruiser bombing the Arizona shipyard. Do it now."

Acknowledgements.

Double good.

I flip to the platoon command comm, now just me, Brice, and Lenox. "What's the status of the platoon?"

Brice links to the whole ship. "Close the assault doors. Everyone's staying on board. Grunts were born to kill, not kneel." I know among the SDF troops, the label 'grunt' is an honorific between comrades. From Brice, it's a compliment.

I don't know if it's worth anything, but I tell the platoon how proud I am. I step back out of the airlock and look at my soldiers while I address them. "Sergeant, the three machine gun teams will stay on board. After we ram that Trog cruiser they'll defend the ship. Take the rest and balance them into two squads—one yours, one for Lenox." None of us have fought together. In fact, the grunts barely know each other. Shifting the squad lineup now won't have any harmful effects on combat effectiveness. God, I sound like a real officer, at least in my head.

"We should separate them by ability," says Brice. "Put those who can take advantage of the gravity mobility and fly in one squad, the rest in the other."

That makes perfect sense. At least we'll have one squad that's fully capable. "Good thinking," I tell him. "As soon as we ram that Trog ship I want each squad to egress through separate assault doors, killing every Trog bastard we can while they're still too stunned to know what happened. As soon as we find our bearings, we'll make our way to the bridge and take control of the ship."

All of the soldiers are tense now that we're talking about fighting actual Trogs and pulling triggers. "One more thing," I tell them, "There are two kinds of grunts." I pause for effect. "The kind who piss their suits before they go into battle and the kind who lie about it."

They laugh.

I laugh.

Hell, even Brice laughs like it's a real joke.

CHAPTER 28

I comm link to the bridge crew. "Status?"

"I've made contact with the third platoon's ship," answers Jablonsky.

"Jill Rafferty?" I ask, hopeful. She's one of my commissar subordinates, a lieutenant, a coworker from the grav factory, and a coconspirator in our plot to mutiny and defect with our ships to join the Free Army.

"Yes," answers Jablonsky. "Both Koreans onboard her ship are casualties. She's captain now."

Casualties? I know exactly what that means. Jill's a silver-haired, blue-eyed mother left childless by this war, and she's tougher than any of us bug-headed freaks who came out of that factory. She harbors no illusions about who is to blame for the death of her sons. If anything, those North Korean officers on her ship were casualties to her vengeance.

"Two assault ships with crews from our factory," says Penny, relieved, at least a little.

Nobody mentions we're still missing two of our company's ships and six more of our friends, yet we all know it. Extrapolating that casualty rate to the rest of the people I recruited from the grav factory, half of my friends are dead already.

"She's about half a klick aft of us," says Phil, "in the shadow of Juji Station."

So she's using the derelict station for cover from the Trog cruisers higher in orbit. Just like us. "What's the status of her ship?"

Jablonsky answers, "She says one-hundred-percent."

"There's a formation of three more ships coming in," says Phil.

With the mess of so many pieces of so many broken ships orbiting the earth, with my ship's grav field pulsing through plates bent or destroyed by Trog fire, I'm not able to clearly sense the gravity fields of those vessels.

"They've all got Korean captains," says Jablonsky. "One with a Korean MSS colonel. He's the one who's making noise about being in charge."

"What do they want?" I ask.

"They're joining us," answers Jablonsky.

No shit?

"Brave," mutters Phil. "They're disobeying an order from Pyongyang. They'll be executed when they get back on the ground."

Penny laughs. "Don't be such an optimist, Adverb. They're gonna die up here like the rest of us."

"Five ships is enough," I tell them. "Phil, do you have my vector?" No more time to screw around.

"Yep," he answers.

"The Korean colonel says he's in command," says Jablonsky, apparently unsure of how to reply to him.

"Phil," I say, "send our attack path to the other ships. Jablonsky, patch me through to the other captains."

He complies.

"Captains, my grav officer has sent you our attack path. Form up on me." I'm telling, not asking. The Koreans will bristle, but I hope it works. Like every uniformed functionary in a totalitarian system, following orders comes so naturally to them, I might get away with it. "Come in tight in two formations—three in front, two following. Max grav in ten seconds."

"Wait!" I hear a Korean accent in that one syllable.

Dammit! So much for the stereotype in my mind about their degree of subservience.

"Koreans first," he tells me. "Americans second."

I want to curse, however, I've already decided it doesn't matter. Whoever goes in first, it'll be American grunts that'll do the bleeding once we board that Trog cruiser.

Still, he hasn't objected to my plan.

"Of course," I tell him in quick words. By disobeying his orders, his day can only end with dying. The least I can do is allow him to save face. "You have the attack path. You lead. We follow. Cluster tight on impact, so our soldiers can support each other when they leave the ship. Hit as close to the bridge as you can. We're taking that cruiser."

The colonel shouts something in Korean I don't understand, maybe a war cry, maybe the name of his own dead son for whom he needs vengeance.

As much as I despise the North Korean-uniformed mannequins, I know the Grays, with no regard for our artificial nationalities, have sacrificed a whole generation of their young as well to feed the war's boundless appetite.

"Max grav on my count!" I shout. "Five. Four. Three. Two."

Our ship hums and creaks under the strain of acceleration. My battle suit squeaks as it compensates for the fluctuation in our internal grav bubble. The walls and floor glow blue and brilliant. Field lines scintillate as they crawl across every surface.

"Coming around Juji!" shouts Penny.

And we all feel the ship make the turn.

"Lenox," I call, "strap in."

I find myself an empty seat as well.

The g's inside the cabin are starting to build.

The ship was designed to make 1.5 light speed, but in order to do that, most of the power needs to be fed into a set of plates in the drive array that creates a bubble of warped space. The drive array pushes that wave, and the ship surfs it to reach translational speeds exceeding the speed of light while never breaking Einstein's equations within our localized bubble.

Theoretical physics—nobody gives a shit about it as long as the ship is fast.

For sub-light acceleration, every grav-drive ship—the ones the Grays use, hence the ones humans use, and the ones the Trogs fly—needs massive objects like planets and moons to push and pull against. The push-and-pull is determined by the reversible polarity of the ship's grav fields. The stronger the ambient field, the faster a ship can accelerate.

In a way, gravity for these vessels works like the wind did for sailing ships back when those wooden hulks were the height of man's technological ability to slaughter one another. However, where sailing across a wind was the best way to reach the highest speed in a sailing ship, running directly into or out of a gravity well is the best way to maximize acceleration with grav-drive technology.

Bottom line on all this crap, Phil calculated the best attack path is not one where we shoot straight across space, curve around earth, and hit the Trog cruisers broadside. Instead, we're following a parabolic arc away from the earth. Once we come over the top of the arc several thousand miles up, we'll be on a collision path with our prey coming down from above.

Raptors diving on a pigeon.

I like that image.

"We're burning twelve g's!" shouts Penny over the comm, theoretically our max sub-light acceleration.

The ship is straining, but in seconds, we'll be going so fast any shots from the Trog cruisers in the area will hit us only through luck.

Brice is shouting into the platoon comm.

The platoon joins in a chant, loud and strong.

I can't make out what they're saying. Did I miss some kind of morale module in all that simulator training?

Brice is psyching them up, girding their strength for what's to come.

"Forming up," Penny tells me over the bridge comm. "Three Koreans in front. Our two about a klick behind."

With grav plates pushing so much g, I sense the other four careening ships. All other grav fields are a dim blur.

We're climbing the up-bound leg of our parabolic attack arc and it'll look to all of those Trogs onboard every ship in the area like we're maxing acceleration for escape velocity, running for the safety of the moon.

Like he's reading my mind, Phil says, "They're ignoring us. No one's shooting."

"Parabolic peak in twenty seconds," Penny tells us.

It's going to be a short, hard trip, thankfully. No time for skittishness.

Between the chanted words, Sergeant Brice tells the troops to ready their weapons and hold on tight, just in case the bridge dumbasses fuck up the grav bubble inside the platoon compartment.

Everybody laughs—the kind of laugh that sounds forced through a torrent of other emotions. Yet Brice isn't making a joke for humor's sake, he's bonding the platoon, gluing them with the cement of shared emotion.

I need to pay more attention to him if I want to learn how to lead soldiers.

The blue grav fields flash a blinding intensity, the ship shakes violently, and we all grumble as the internal bubble fails to fully compensate.

An instant later, things stabilize again.

"On the way down," Penny yells at us. "Impact in fifty seconds!"

Chapter 29

The ship is hurtling toward the earth.

The current is reversed in our drive array's grav plates, and so is the polarity of the fields. The earth is pulling the ship closer, and the planet is moving in the most imperceptibly minuscule smidgen of a degree toward us.

The mutually attractive hug of gravity. Physics again.

Far below us, I see our targets in my mind, glowing fiery-brilliant grav signatures from their megaton masses. Multiple fusion reactors pump gigawatts of power through their drive arrays, sending blue field lines pulsing over their hulls like giant jellyfish tentacles.

Each of the kilometer-long ships is shaped like a sleek leopard shark without fins, with a crest of bristling railguns down the back, and two more along the lower edge on port and starboard. It has a roughly triangular cross-section so the three rows of guns can shoot at the three hundred and sixty degrees of space surrounding the ship. Each crest is lined on both sides by rows of grav plates huge enough to handle the load of maneuvering the megaton monster through the solar system.

Despite all that strength, like our cruisers, those Trog ships max at four g's acceleration.

They can't escape.

At least not at sub-light speeds.

We're halfway down the descent leg of our parabolic arc when the Trogs realize what's happening. It's not something they expected.

Some of their dorsal guns start to fire.

The three Trog ships are cruising in a line with ten-kilometer gaps between them, yet their order is dissolving as each maneuvers tentatively.

Nothing they can do will make a difference now.

No ship in existence has the power to move a megaton mass out of our way in the short seconds left.

"Slowing to ramming speed!" Penny shouts over the comm.

God she's got to be the bravest of us, flying headlong into a collision we'll only survive if our secret weapon works as planned.

"Redirecting all power to the grav lens," Phil tells us.

The sky fills with railgun slugs from all three ships.

The Trogs' squirmy brains have deduced all the doubt out of their guess as to the flavor of shit that's screaming in their direction. Their fears have awakened.

I see their grav fields as clear as the sun.

All five of our ships are heading toward one of theirs, and it's maxing its starboard grav plates to get out of our way.

"Ten seconds," Phil warns.

All of the grunts tense.

Then the grav picture unexpectedly shifts.

"Shit!" shouts Phil.

Chapter 30

Ramming anything at the speeds we're moving would be suicide if it weren't for gravity technology.

As it is, even nestled in the grav bubble protecting the crew, if our ship collided with an alien vessel at several thousand miles per hour, both ships would be obliterated, and there'd be nothing left of our bodies but a haze of complex molecules.

The ramming tactic depends on something besides speed, and that's the strength and polarity of the target ship's gravity defense. The plates in their hull that help it maneuver and create artificial gravity inside—just like ours—serve double duty to create a repulsive exterior field that can deflect kinetic weaponry: bullets, railgun slugs, meteors, shit like that. That's the primary means of defense these ships have.

It sounds simple but it's not.

Too much incoming fire will overwhelm the deflective field. A poorly shaped field will repulse less efficiently than an optimally shaped one. Fire from multiple directions makes effective field shaping nearly impossible. At least with standard brainpower.

A big enough computer might work such a problem out in real time with a thousand tons of hyper-velocity steel bearing down from three directions, but there's nearly no computing power in our ships. Wherever the hell the Grays came from they never invented computers, and they don't trust ours.

All that aside, nobody's ever taken three hundred tons of steel momentum, used a grav lens to focus it down to the diameter of a pencil, and speared it through the defensive fields on one of these cruisers. Because the genius human engineers conceived, lab-tested, designed, and built these ships so quickly—no sarcasm intended—there was no time to field test or calibrate any of it.

That's just the way things are when you're losing a war. You do what you can with what you've got.

So, we have to depend on the pilot and the gravity officer in each ship to calculate the collision speed and angle correctly, first time, and every time.

Makes you wonder if the Wright brother who stayed on the ground was the one who won the coin toss.

"They're changing the grav field intensity!" shouts Phil, talking about the Trog ship.

"Goddammit!" yells Penny. "The Koreans are slamming the brakes too hard."

"Blow by!" I order. "Pass them! Ram that fat pigeon!"

Did I say I liked that image?

We don't pass the Korean ships. They're too far ahead.

And too slow.

The Trogs' defensive grav deflects them in quick succession, sending each careening toward the ground.

All three reverse polarity on their drive arrays and max grav to avoid burning through earth's atmosphere and burrowing into the Arizona desert.

"Reverse our drive array polarity!" I shout.

"But—" Phil protests.

"Do it now, dammit!"

He does.

Now, the Trog ship's gravitational mass and all of the power it's pouring into its deflection field suck us in, instead of pushing us away.

We can't miss.

"Max grav bubble!" shouts Phil on the ship comm.

The cabin burns bright blue like it did at the top of the arc. I feel squeezed from every direction.

"Ramming!"

A flash of blue nearly blinds me as the power sent to the grav lens surges.

Through my seat, I feel metal break, screech, and bend. We're in vacuum, so the collision happens in silence.

One of the assault doors blows in and smashes two grunts to mush. Flaming atmosphere from the Trog ship flashes through the platoon compartment.

Our battle suits protect us.

The blue disappears with the fire and the sound of metal turning to wreckage rips through the air.

And stops.

Everything goes silent for half a second.

We lived through it.

The ship quakes again under the sound of wrenching metal, different this time. Not close.

I hope it's the impact of Jill's ship.

"Go!" Sergeant Brice shouts. He's already unstrapped and out of his seat. "Get out there and kill 'em while they're stunned."

Grunts are slow to move. Most are shaken, or busy thanking God for the breath they just inhaled.

I'm on my feet, wobbly but moving to an exit. Lenox is beside me, and together we pull on the thick iron handles of a door. It grinds on rusty gears.

"Up, up, up!" Brice shouts. "Go, go!"

"Careful when you egress," I announce to the platoon. "You'll need your suit grav."

The door I'm working on with Lenox rolls fully open. Outside, across the opening, is a girder as thick as a man's torso. Cables, bent steel, and shredded composite debris make it seem like we're blocked in.

We're not.

Through gaps in the wreckage, I see the Trog ship's cavernous interior, all the way to the stern.

"Set up a machine gun here," I order. It'll give the grunts inside good cover with a wide field of fire.

Taking a quick glance around the platoon compartment, I see four assault doors are open. Grunts are lining up, but no one is yet out the door.

Brice is readying his squad, and he's not too happy about how slowly they're doing it.

I rush toward an open door with no debris blocking it from the outside.

I try to get a picture of what's surrounding the ship using my perception of gravity, although all I see is psychedelic noise. Too many grav plates shifting fields in too many directions, too much mass bent every which way.

I shout into the bridge comm, "Penny, keep the ship safe. Phil, keep me apprised."

Feeling like we've wasted too many seconds of our surprise, I push past a soldier hesitating at an open door. I take a fast glance at the situation outside and jump as I holler, "Follow me!"

Chapter 31

I'm in a howling wind carrying me toward a crack in the cruiser's hull.

Our ship smashed its way into the cruiser's central hangar bay, a warehouse space a hundred meters wide, and more than half a kilometer long. All the air in the void is being sucked into space, and I'm caught in it.

"Wait! Don't go!" I shout over the comm. Barely anyone in my platoon can control their suit well enough to be out here. "Stay inside!"

I'm maxing power to my suit grav to fight the gusts rushing past me.

Plumes of fire ghost into existence where hydrogen and oxygen from ruptured tanks mix in the presence of sparking metal. Fortunately, space's vacuum kills the flames as soon as they form.

"Close the assault doors," I shout. The air that rushed into the ship when we collided might now drag my troops back out again.

A tornado starts to form in the vast hangar as air swirls out through the holes in the hull.

I fly away from the vortex.

Debris, railgun slugs—the size of a fist, thousands of them—are in the air. More slugs, the size of cars, bounce and roll in the fluctuating grav and high winds.

Trogs, some stripped of their clothing by the powerful gusts, are bouncing off the floors and beams as shards of steel tear through them.

The tornado is writhing and jumping in the turbulence.

Feeling unsafe, I grav drive deeper into the Trog cruiser.

And then I realize I'm the first soldier ever to see the inside of one of these monsters. At least no other human has lived to tell about it. I spin in the air to get the lay of the land. Indeed, it does look just like one of ours.

I see Jill's ship is protruding through the hull, about two-thirds deep, just like mine. None of her assault doors are open.

"Situation?" Brice calls to me over the comm.

"The Trog's internal air supply," I tell him. "Give it another minute to blow into space, or we'll lose half our platoon when they exit."

The tornado is already dying. The gaps in the hull are huge, and there's only so much air inside.

Within the hangar space, the gravity is axial, the same way we set it inside our assault ship. However, this cruiser is so huge, Trogs can walk normally on any of the exterior walls as if they were floors. Right now, none of them are walking. Some are still tumbling in the wind. The rest are holding onto anything they can get their arms around.

Futile.

They're all going to suffocate when the last of the air is sucked into space.

The ship shudders and the gravity fields jiggle.

We destroyed hundreds of the big ship's grav plates during the collision, and the Trogs on the bridge can't stabilize the internal field. Thanks to the alien bug, I see the gravity shifts in stunning visual clarity, and it makes everything I see seem momentarily under the surface of a wavy pool.

I look toward the bow. The first tenth of the ship in that direction is walled off from the hangar bay. In our fleet's cruisers, that's the Gray zone. Only those pencil-necked little bastards and their North Korean toadies are up there, segregated from the lowly humans who do the sweating and the bleeding.

In the Gray zone, they've got communal rooms, cafeterias, pods where the Grays sleep, and dorms for the North Koreans, everything they need to live life separately from the grunts in the rest of the ship. The bridge is that way, right at the bow. The railgun targeting centers are also located up there, remotely aiming each of the gun emplacements along the ship's three spines. A Gray or a Korean with a bug in his head does that work.

You've got to have an intimate relationship with gravity if you want to aim a long-range railgun with any accuracy.

The expansive central hangar section houses giant hoppers, magazines for the slugs that feed the railguns, storage racks for the projectiles, and crane mechanisms for moving them from rack to hopper. The guns appear to be loaded manually, one shot at a time—both labor-intensive and slow. There are so many railguns down each spine, they can collectively pour out tons of projectiles every second.

All of the facilities for housing the Trogs' gun crews are in a gridwork of structures built in a layer along the three flat sides of the ship.

Suspended on the ship's long axis, connected to the sides by a web of thick supports and conduit, are a trio of fusion reactors, each separated by a hundred meters. They're the three beating hearts of this monster.

The aft quarter of the ship is walled off, just like the bow section. In our ships, that's the barracks. Ten thousand SDF soldiers are bunked back there in cubbyholes for sleeping quarters. There are also gyms, storerooms, infirmaries, latrines, and ready-rooms, each adjacent to a large door that opens to the outside. I guess there has to be ten thousand Trog soldiers in those quarters, recovering from the surprise of the impact and putting on their space suits so they can come and kill us.

This cruiser is the apparent galactic standard in ship design. It's made to bombard its targets from orbit, then land to let a contingent of soldiers mop up any who resist.

Everything about this ship is built for the kind of war the Grays fight—giant capital ships, pounding one another with railguns, fluctuating their grav fields for defense. It's like a game of chess where a punch in the face hides behind every bad move.

An unlikely form of war, evolved through a long history where the Grays and their adversaries have the same goals, because they value the same things.

They want to control solar systems with planets like earth, with hospitable atmospheres, non-toxic chemical compositions, and tolerable gravity. They like moderate temperatures with liquid water and not too many voracious microbes.

Most of all, they want to possess planets with large populations of technologically backward creatures that can be put to use constructing navies to fight their inevitable wars, building orbital battle stations to defend habitable planets, and to provide muscle and sweat for thousand-year projects building donut-shaped space stations ten thousand miles across, artificial ring-worlds, Eden bliss for a billion of their kind.

And why stop at one?

Earth's solar system is full of raw materials, and breathing human bodies are cheap—we just can't stop making more of ourselves.

Earth is a prize worth fighting for.

The gravity in the hangar bay is stabilizing.

Trogs are scattered like goldfish out of water on the decks above and below, and half a kilometer aft to the barracks.

Their mouths are opening and closing, gulping for breath in air too thin to sustain life.

Thousands of them dying, and I don't feel an iota of pity because of why they're here—to enslave me and every generation of humans from now until God gets tired of playing dollhouse with his shitty little universe and flushes it down a black hole.

It's time to do some killing.

Chapter 32

We're close enough now for suit-to-suit comm with the other assault ship, so I open a connection with Jill Rafferty. "Status?"

"Bumpy ride," she answers immediately. "We're all good. Glad you made it, cowboy."

Like our platoon, hers has three crew-served railguns that fire slugs the size of fifty-caliber machine gun rounds at speeds near 7k. "Leave three fire teams on board or near your ship. They need to be in a spot where they can fire on the barracks at the aft end of the cruiser. Start shooting as soon as they're set up. Punch holes in the barracks wall in the back of the ship until the Trogs start to come out, then pin them in the doorways if you can.

"But," Jill pauses, "why shoot the walls?"

"Vacuum," I remind her. "Any Trogs not suited up inside will suffocate when the air goes."

"Shoulder-fired rockets would sure come in handy for that."

"I'll file a complaint with the MSS," I tell her, a grim smile on my face, because she's right. With a half-dozen decent anti-tank rockets from any old rotting warehouse on a military base left over from before the siege, we could punch enough big holes in the forward and aft sections that most of the Trogs on the ship would die before we had to deal with them head on. "Hold another squad back for reserve and send the other two forward."

"Send?" she asks me. "I'm leading them."

I'd prefer she stayed with her ship to manage our rear defense, however, I've known her long enough to know there's nothing I can talk her out of once she sets her mind. "Leave a good sergeant, then."

"Will do."

"We took nearly thirty percent casualties coming up, including noncoms and officers," I tell her.

"Legit casualties?" She's asking if it was enemy fire or the mutiny that killed them.

"Legit plus a few," I tell her. "I've got two sergeants, and me. I'll take two squads forward and leave three fire teams on my ship for defense. Tell your sergeant guarding our rear to keep tabs on them."

I switch to my platoon's command comm. "Brice, Lenox, it's time to go."

A blistering red trail of machine gun fire traces a line from Jill's ship down the length of the Trog cruiser. Rounds pierce the barracks wall with so much energy metal explodes.

Another machine gun joins the first. A third opens up.

Maybe rockets aren't needed, after all.

I set my comm to loop in with Jill, Brice, and Lenox. I add in the grunts in Brice's squad since I'll be going in with them. It's not the optimal command solution for the battle, so I've got to earn respect from the grunt level on up, which means I need to do grunt work with a gun in my hand and dead Trogs under my feet.

"Jill, we're moving now."

"I'll race you to the bridge."

Soldiers in their dirty orange suits bounce out of Jill's ship and start running across the cluttered deck.

I hit my grav and fly toward the bow. "You better hurry."

Chapter 33

I accelerate as I fly, aiming toward one of the three closed doorways that'll allow us access to the Trog cruiser's forward command section. "Brice, bring the squad to me."

"Yes, sir." I hear him and the others over the comm as they make their leaps from the open assault doors into emptiness in the Trog ship's main hangar. They're flying for real, and doing so in a surreal environment as different from anything they're likely ever to see or feel.

Lenox's squad is jumping down to the decks, running, bouncing, or falling depending on their skills. They're using auto-grav full time, so their suits will always orient gravity toward whatever the feet are standing on.

Halfway to my target door and just beginning my deceleration, I see a pair of odd shadows in the jumble of strewn railgun slugs on the deck below. The shadows move enough like humans, so I don't need a full view to know they're Trogs—the jet-black concerns me. Trogs always wear suits that were once white when manufactured, but now are weathered, gray, and finger-painted in primitive symbols and designs.

Ghosts. The Trog elite.

The ones who wear black are their generals and captains. At least when they're among the Trog hordes.

The Trogs clad in crisp ebony who move about on their own are the killers. The best of the Trogs.

They need to be dealt with. "Brice," I say, "I've got ghosts up here."

"Trogs in black?" He asks without hesitation.

"Roger that," I tell him as I glance back at our ship and see him standing in an assault door hustling the last member of our squad out.

"Location?"

I point.

Lenox says, "My squad can take 'em."

"Be careful," Brice tells her. "You've got the numbers, use that to your advantage."

"Will do." Flying above her troops, Lenox divides her squad into fire teams, guiding them into deadly crossfire positions as they proceed toward the pair of ghosts. Some of the troops move like soldiers. Others straggle, just trying to maintain pace and direction.

The dying will start soon.

I hope some of us will live to leave this ship.

Taking a glance toward Jill's cruiser, I see her two squads running across the deck, bouncing, and some flying. She's apparently left her squads mixed.

I make a note to tell her about the way we've separated ours. Experience with grav control is the major factor in troop mobility, and maybe combat effectiveness. Units of mixed skill level only serve to drag the entire squad down. At least that's the assumption we're working under in my platoon.

However, the middle of a battle is not the time for those kinds of instructions, so I keep them to myself, and turn to see how close—

I slam into the wall and bounce off.

I hit the floor and rebound, going high and into a slow roll.

Dammit!

I'd stopped paying attention to where I was.

Good thing I'd engaged my suit's automatic defense. It creates an anti-grav field around my body to deflect incoming fire. Fortunately, it also works like an invisible fat suit to soften the impact of collisions, like the one I just had with the wall.

Just as I start to hope the mistake went unnoticed, a few women in my squad giggle.

"Silva? Mostyn?" I ask, and the giggling stops. "If you'll forget you saw that, we can negotiate a bribe later."

They laugh some more.

Clearly, they don't agree.

I switch my suit to auto-grav and orient my feet beneath me. All the time I spent in the zero-g room back home in Breck is paying off. Using the suit's controls is second nature to me.

I take one of the two C4 charges off my utility belt, attach it to the door, and tell my squad, "Explosive set!" Translation: Hurry the hell up.

The door is inset into the wall by eighteen inches, which works out perfectly for what's about to happen. I jump away from the door and take six quick steps before stopping to put my back against the steel.

I won't catch any shrapnel, and I should be far enough away not to be hurt by the blast. I amp up my defensive grav just in case, and take a few more steps.

Brice hits the wall beside me, followed quickly by Silva, Mostyn, Bautista, Mendez, and Hastings. All are women except Mendez.

It's an unexpected mix of genders that makes me wonder about the procrastination habits of the two. Maybe when the girls were hard at work with their sims, the boys distracted themselves with salacious videos. A thought for another time.

What really distracts me at a moment when I have a hundred more important things on my mind is Silva's smile. I can't put into words what it is about a woman's smile when it's just right, only that it opens a trap I happily fall into.

The smile wisps away in an instant.

Silva is back to business. I am, too.

My squad arranges itself flat against the wall.

I raise my arm so I can see my d-pad. There's nothing on the touchscreen but one big red dot. I push it to detonate the C4.

I feel the shock through my back and hear it through my helmet because it's pressed against the wall.

Over the command comm, I tell them, "Going in."

Chapter 34

Like me, Mostyn has only seen simulated battle, but she's already pulling an explosive charge off her belt and jumping around me for a peek past the doors we just destroyed. "It's an airlock," she tells us. "Inner doors intact."

"Blow 'em," I say.

She disappears through the outer doors' splinters.

Silva bounces around me, weapon up. "I'll cover."

I see Lenox's squad firing into a sunken walkway sixty or seventy meters away.

A ghost in black jumps out of another walkway. Scarily fast, he comes up behind a grunt on the flank of the formation.

Lenox yells a warning.

It's not enough.

The ghost swings a blade-shaped weapon with blue parallel lines glowing down its length. The blade cuts through the soldier's ribcage all the way to the spine, and then, as if the movement was planned, the ghost spins with his momentum and hops back into another walkway.

"Lenox?" I call.

"We got this," she tells me. "Keep *your* squad alive."

She's right. It'll be my grunts dying if I try to micromanage the other squads.

"Trogs coming out of the barracks!" Jill calls over the command comm.

"Does Sergeant Bruckert have it under control?" I ask. Bruckert is the man she left in charge of our rear defense.

"I'll tell you when he doesn't."

Silva and Mostyn come bouncing back out of the damaged airlock. "Ready?" Silva asks.

I give her the nod.

She winks at me and pushes the glowing red dot on her d-pad.

The charge blows.

Again, the walls and floor shudder.

A spray of metal shards rides a blast of wind out of the airlock as the ship's forward section depressurizes.

Pieces of one or two Trogs in black suits blow past us. It's hard to guess the count when the parts aren't sinewed together anymore.

A Gray flies by, missing an arm, head split, amber blood spraying out.

A Gray?

My squad congratulates themselves.

"Bow section breached," I call over the comm for Jill and my other squad leaders.

My grunts have their weapons up, and they're off the wall, forming up to move inside once the depressurization finishes, and I'm thinking we've not proven ourselves yet, but so far the simulator training hasn't produced a bad result.

I take point, knowing it's a terrible place for a commander.

Brice grabs my shoulder to stop me and shakes his head.

I can't get past the respect necessity even if it is all in my mind. "I need to. At least for today."

The walls and floor shudder again, and I glance toward Jill's squad. They've just blown their airlock's outer door.

The howl of wind out of our doors diminishes.

Any second now.

Lenox comms in. "Ghosts down. We're on the way."

Good news.

I step through broken metal doors and lead my squad inside.

Most of the lights down the hall are working. Most of those nearby are broken.

The white walls and floor are scorched by the blast, however, anything not built in is gone, blown out in the decompression blast.

Except—

I kneel quickly and grab the handle of a sword-like Trog weapon stuck in a crag of door metal. The parallel rows of blue light activate as soon as my palm wraps around the handle.

"How 'bout that?" utters Silva.

"Yeah." I'm thinking, how about that? Trog weapons are powered just like ours.

"You hold onto that," says Brice. "Damn things are deadly as hell."

"I got Trogs!" calls Lenox. "Coming out of the third set of bow doors."

The only door of the three we're not assaulting. "Ghosts or regular?" I ask.

"Regular," she tells me. "We'll take 'em."

Brice says, "Send a fire team in to cover our rear as soon as you can spare them."

"Will do," answers Lenox. Whereas our squad has five soldiers—not counting Brice and me—Lenox's squad has fourteen. The downside of separating them by skill level.

The walls and floor shudder again.

"Breach!" calls Jill.

I reach my ghost Trog weapon over my back and feel it clink against one of the magnet mounts on my integrated backpack. It sticks.

In we go, four of us on one wall, three on the opposite side.

It's easy to hurry. We have no obstacles.

At twenty meters, we pause as we arrive at a wide cross hall.

So far everything in the Trog ship's layout has been an exact match with our cruisers. That means to the left, at the end of that hall, are the residential quarters for the forward crew. To the right, down a short corridor, stands a pair of doors leading to a long bay running parallel to one of the gun spines. It's where all of the weapons-targeting personnel sit, aiming the railguns.

"On the corners," Brice orders the squad. "Cover both doors. Let's blow them simultaneously."

Silva runs toward the barracks door. Mendez sprints toward the other, each readying a C4 charge.

The rest of the squad aims their weapons down the halls.

I keep an eye up the main corridor in front of us, but glance back to see a fire team from Lenox's squad just outside the doors we blew to get in.

A blast of wind explodes from the main corridor.

The wind tunnel force nearly knocks me off my feet, but I increase auto-grav to keep my boots stuck to the floor.

Two of my squad slide down the hall, dragged by the wind.

"Increase grav!" I holler at them as I ready my weapon to shoot.

Everything is happening fast, and something I'm seeing down the hall doesn't make sense. It takes a frantic fraction of a second for me to understand. Two black shadows are riding the wind, coming impossibly fast. "Ghosts!"

Panic trips my trigger finger, and I fire on full-auto.

My rounds spread spears of red all through the hall.

The ghosts are bouncing off the walls, ceiling, and floor.

Brice is shooting, too.

The rounds whiz past the ghosts, deflected off their blue pulsing anti-grav fields. Suddenly, my brand new superior firepower 6k, two-hundred-rounds-a-minute, recoil-compensated, state-of-the-art, grav-drive Trog-killing rifle doesn't seem like it's worth its own weight in dog shit.

It's clear to me, the single-shot weapons our troops have been using so far in this war against Trog armies numbering in the hundreds of thousands is one of the big reasons we're losing.

Only a heartbeat or two has passed.

Still, I fire.

As the Trog in front moves closer, more of my rounds find their mark, and the blue anti-grav deflection field shimmers non-stop, overloads, and lets some slugs through.

The Trog's body takes a shot through the shoulder and he tumbles in the wind, still swinging his blue-lined blade.

Blood is spewing from his wound.

And he's on us.

He slashes his blade.

Bautista's head spins away from her body as her neck still squirts blood to feed a brain no longer integrated into the system.

The wounded ghost Trog is past us in a flash and slams into Lenox's grunts back at the blasted door.

Somebody shouts.

There's still one coming.

Chapter 35

I'm not sure how frustration turned to inspiration and then to action so fast. It's clear to me these ghost Trogs' black suits have an extra helping of defensive magic built in.

I let go of my rifle to dangle from its harness and I reach back for the ghost Trog blade I just acquired. Its pattern of lines glow blue with the power from my suit's fusion reactor.

The theory that only has microseconds to gel in my mind tells me these ghost Trogs in their special suits must think they're the most badass killers in this part of the galaxy and they'd likely want to carry weapons they could use to kill the meanest, deadliest bullies on the block—each other.

I step to a good spot just off center in the hall so I can put some power into my swing as the second Trog bounces off the wall, off the ceiling, and heads right toward me.

Brice and a few others are still shooting at the Trog.

At the very last moment, I kneel as I swing, and max the auto-grav in my suit to hold my boots against the floor.

The Trog didn't expect that move, and his blade cuts a path through the air where my neck was just a moment before.

My blade comes up with all my strength at his torso.

The blade's blue lines pulse intensely, and the Trog's defensive grav field flashes bright, but doesn't deflect.

The blade cuts through black suit, bone, and muscle, cleaving the Trog's body in two, sending a spray of blood and split organs into the wind blasting at Lenox's troops down the hall.

I understand immediately what the blue lines on the blade are for, and I know instantly our scientists on earth haven't invented anything new with the gravity lens on my assault ship. They simply came up with a new application for a technology that already existed in these Trog blades, a grav field focused to a fine edge, capable of cutting through deflective fields and enemy bodies.

"You all right, sir?" Brice is at my side, tugging at my arm.

I look at him through my red-spattered faceplate and realize I'm covered in blood that's just starting to boil as the air thins to vacuum. Not bothering to answer his question, I say. "Bautista bought it. Anybody else?"

"Mostyn and Hastings are banged up," he answers. "They'll live."

Outside in the hangar, two ghost Trogs are dead, at the cost of at least one grunt's life.

We killed two more in the hall at the cost of another.

We can't afford two for one. That angers me.

My desire to kill is giving me visions of genocidal slaughter.

Dammit, I barely knew Bautista's name and face, but being in my squad, her loss feels acutely personal. "Blow those damn doors and get this fuckin' show on the road."

"Mendez, Silva," Brice calls over the comm, "set those charges. Move it! We got killin' to do."

Good. We're all on the same page.

Chapter 36

"We've got Trogs in the hall," says Jill over a crackly comm channel. Now that we're in the bowels of the ship with lots of walls and whatnot between us, the signal is having trouble getting through. "Thirty, maybe forty."

"Stay safe," I tell her. "And keep them busy. Our path to the bridge is clear for the moment." I hail Lenox. "How are things out there?"

"Holding our own," she answers. "God, there's a lot of them."

"Kane," Jill calls, "Bruckert is under pressure back at the assault ships. He won't be able to hold them for long."

"Retreat to the airlock," I tell her. "Keep those Trogs in your access hall pinned, and send a squad back to help Bruckert." Taking one of the two bridge assault teams off the table is a risk to our objective, however, I need to make sure my platoons have a way to escape once this mess starts to go south. And it *will* go south. Though we killed several thousand Trogs when we rammed the cruiser, it's looking like there are plenty enough left to overwhelm us once they're organized. "Lenox," I call again, "be prepared to go where you're needed."

"Roger dodger, General."

Where did that come from?

"Ready to blow the doors!" Brice tells me.

I put my back to a wall. "Do it."

"Grav tight!" Brice tells the squad. He wants boots on high-g holding us to the floor when the doors go. We don't need to have more troops tumbling down the hall in the depressurization blast. "Three. Two. One!"

The ship shudders again.

The wind comes, carrying metal fragments and spindly gray bodies, broken and whole, dozens of them, eyes wide and black, showing no expression at all. Waving arms and grasping hands belie their desperation.

Everything alive fears death.

"Where the hell did all the Grays come from?" Brice spits as the bodies fly past.

"Kill any that are alive." It's no answer, just pragmatism. I point down the main corridor. "We need to move. We're running out of time."

Brice wrangles the squad. "Let's go."

We're running fast, weapons ready.

As I sprint, I wonder about those Grays. It doesn't make sense they'd be on the ship, unless they're Trog prisoners. But then, why have them targeting the cruiser's railguns? Could they be Trog slaves?

We reach the end of the corridor.

Four conduits, wide enough for a Trog or a human to stand inside, run toward the central axis of the cruiser, passing each level on the way to the bridge. They're the in-ship version of elevators, with grav plates set to keep each tube in zero-g. All one need do is step inside and push off, and then step out at the destination floor.

I peek inside and look up past exits to three levels to see the top of the tube sealed shut. "They've closed the hatch to the bridge."

Grunts in the squad confirm the other three are closed as well.

No problem.

"Silva," I point up my tube. "Get up there as quick as you can, plant your last C4 charge on that door and then hustle back down here."

"Gimme two seconds." Silva jumps in, and she's gone.

My thoughts wander. Why did I select Silva? Why is her pretty face stuck in my thoughts?

Brice tells the others, "Grenades up the other tubes as soon as Silva is out!"

Three soldiers pull pins and reach their grenades into each of the empty tubes.

Just as promised, Silva is back.

"Damn, that was quick." I give her a nod of approval, then glance at the others.

Brice says, "Grenades first. As soon as they detonate and discourage Trogs on the other levels—Silva, you blow the charge on the bridge hatch. Once it goes, follow me up. I'll lead."

"Follow *us* up," I tell her, nodding at Brice. "You behind *me*."

He shrugs.

The grenades go.

We all step away to a safe distance.

As I wait the two seconds for the explosions, I feel vibrations through the floor. The fighting elsewhere is growing intense. I hear Jill talking to Sergeant Bruckert. I hear Lenox ordering a fire team to support the rear defense. I've committed nearly half our strength to the defense of the assault ships. Jill's squad is fully engaged with a platoon-sized bunch of regular Trogs and Lenox is weakening her position to support the rest of us.

If the Trogs attack our little squad from the rear, we'll be in trouble.

Or if more of the black-suited ghost Trogs come at us...

The grenades detonate.

Silva sets off her C4 in a bigger explosion.

With the shock of the blast still tingling my senses, and with no rush of released atmosphere from above, I hop into the lift tube and take off. "Max grav!"

Brice is literally on my heels.

Chapter 37

The trip up passes in an eye blink, and I'm decelerating desperately to avoid breaking my neck in a collision when I reach the top.

I twist and crouch just before my shoulder impacts the ceiling through the cushion of my deflective grav. On the rebound, I luck my way into landing on my feet beside the blown hatch.

I'm all adrenaline and wide eyes, scanning for threats.

It looks like three pods of Grays, eighteen of them, manning the bridge. Most have been knocked to the floor by the explosion. Others are looking at me, and I read surprise into their expressionless, flat faces.

Parts of a ghost Trog are scattered outward from the tube entrance.

Wrong place, wrong time for you, buddy.

An ebony Trog is slinking along the back wall of the bridge, thinking I don't see him there. Another ghost already has his attack planned, and he's sprinting toward me from the far end of the bridge.

Disruptor time.

And my pistol.

I don't expect pistol slugs to penetrate ghost Trog shields, but each of those bullets packs a punch of momentum, and Newton's third law guarantees energy will impart a hard enough thump to throw a Trog off-balance long enough for me to kill him.

In theory.

I jump to my right, hoping to put a waist-high instrument console between me and the sprinting Trog, a little defense to help offset its power.

Then it occurs to me—I'm alone.

Brice, Silva, or one of the others should already be on the bridge with me. Nobody's popped out of the damaged grav tube.

Shit!

No time to ask questions, no time to wonder what happened. I don't have backup. I'm on my own.

New plan!

I skirt the instrument console and rush the Trog coming at me.

Its boots skid on the deck, and it waves an arm to catch its balance. It didn't expect me to attack.

I'm firing my pistol at its chest to press my tenuous advantage to gain another critical half-second.

The Trog's grav field sizzles blue from my pistol slug's impacts.

And then I'm close enough.

I swing the disruptor down and hack off his arm.

Bright-red blood and suit air explode out of the wound, shooting the arm across the bridge in one direction and knocking the Trog to the deck in the other.

I leap over him and move out of range of his disruptor in case he's able to muster a few more seconds of fight before the vacuum sucks out the rest of his life's blood.

I scan the bridge for the other Trog.

Where the hell is he?

And where's my damn squad?

I don't see the Trog.

I spin around, swinging my disruptor blade as I go, and I spot it. He's trying to come around behind me.

I realize, almost fatally late, these ghost Trogs are a lot faster than I ever suspected. Where Trogs in general like to keep their feet on the ground using auto-grav, these ghost Trogs use suit grav in three dimensions like they were born to it. And they probably were.

I pelt the Trog with a stream of pistol fire, aiming at his legs, hoping to trip him up as I run at him.

It works, almost.

I swing my disruptor down at his head to split his helmet. In quick defense, he moves his disruptor up to block me. For the first time since I picked up the alien weapon, I find something that can stop it—another disruptor.

I push down.

He pushes up.

Two soldiers, fighting face-to-face to kill one another, the age-old story.

Through his faceplate I see him looking at me from under thick, boney brows beneath a severely sloping forehead. He has a wide, flat nose, with a mouth full of broad, yellow teeth that look like they were built to grind through coconut husks. And he's smiling, like he thinks he's got me, like he's full of Neanderthal smugness from having killed a dozen—maybe a hundred—frail humans just like me.

And that pisses me off.

"Fuck you, Trog!" I shove my pistol up under the neck ring of his suit, inside deflective grav range, and I fire.

Just like the North Korean officer I killed when my mutiny started, the Trog's thick-boned head comes to pieces inside his helmet. A spray of blood vaporizes as the vacuum sucks it out the holes my slugs left in his suit's neck.

The Trog drops.

I slap my disruptor onto my back, attach my pistol to a magnetic mount, and raise my rifle. I pull the trigger and spin as I spray the whole bridge. Grays' heads explode. Others duck as rounds ricochet. I focus most of my fire on the giant wall of windows, giving the bridge a view out the front of the ship, the earth, a busted battle station, and the debris from countless other vessels.

There's plenty of blackness out there in space, and I want to make sure there's no ebony-clad ghost Trog standing in front of the glass, using that sky for camouflage.

I find none.

I take a breath and—

An explosion shakes the deck and sends hunks of shrapnel clattering in every direction. Some of it impacts my defensive grav field and the momentum sends me flying across the bridge to bounce off a waist-high console.

Damn Newton again with his fucking laws.

Luckily, my suit's defensive field saves me from injury.

I'm back on my feet in two seconds, shaking stars out of my vision and pointing my rifle at a bank of grav tubes on the far side of the bridge.

A grunt pops out, ready to shoot.

Another comes through a second later.

They're not mine.

"Jill?" I ask. "Is this your squad?"

A third soldier pops onto the bridge. It turns out to be Jill. "We cleaned up those Trogs in the hall," she says. "Just the regular kind. Not those ghost Trogs you dealt with." She's looking around and sees the bodies of the two I just killed. "Where's the rest of your squad?"

"Don't know." However, I've got a chance now to find out. I comm back to my people. "Brice? Status?"

"Dammit," he curses. "I was ambushed by a Trog a level down from the bridge."

"You okay?" I ask.

"It's dead," he answers. "But Hastings came up the tube after us, max gravved, got herself cockeyed somehow, and jammed her body in there. Clogged the tube."

"Body?" I ask. That's ominous.

"She's dead."

Another casualty. Something I need to get used to but can't imagine what that state of mind even feels like.

"Check those Grays," Jill tells her squad. "Kill them, or make sure they're dead." She's coming my way and gives one of the dead ghost Trogs a kick. "You're a badass grunt now?"

We're all bloodied. We're victorious. "*Now* we're all badass grunts."

Chapter 38

Brice pops out of the grav tube I came through. In a series as steady as metronome clicks, Silva, Mostyn, and Mendez emerge, my squad of six turned to four.

"What now, Chief?" asks Brice.

Jill looks at me with the same question on her face.

We have our objective, yet I know our victory won't last. Talking to Jill, I ask, "How long can Bruckert hold?"

"Minutes."

We don't even know how many more Trogs are in the stern barracks, or in the forward section for that matter. There might be hundreds massing on the other floors we didn't check. An attack could be coming. If that happens, we won't be able to hold the bridge.

We needed a lot more than two ships to ram the Trog cruiser for capture to be a realistic outcome.

Even though we have control of the ship for the moment, we need another way to capitalize on our victory. I hurry over to the helm and give it a quick glance. It's familiar to me. It's the same Gray design we use in our cruisers, with the same controls used on our assault ships. Only scaled up. A lot.

I know I'm no expert, but I've been through the basic flight simulators. I think I can fly this thing.

Jill cuts her eyes toward me. "What are you thinking?"

"It's time we give these dumbass Trogs a hard lesson in what war with unchained humans is like."

"What's that mean?" asks Brice.

"We don't need to control the whole ship," I tell him. "We just need the bridge. Jill, move your platoon back to your assault ship, dislodge it, and move it out of here. Brice, same for our squad. Lenox, can you hear me?"

"Loud and clear," answers Lenox.

"Don't take any more casualties. Load everybody back on board the assault ships. Do it fast."

"We're retreating?" asks Brice. He's mortified.

"You're not coming with us?" Jill asks, having guessed my intentions.

"No," I tell her. "I'm staying on the bridge."

She's not pleased. "Whatever suicidal—"

"I'm staying here," I snap, "but I'm not suicidal. Get your platoon moving. You've got two minutes. That's it." I lay my hands on the ship's helm and open a line to Penny. "Once you're away from this cruiser, don't go far. I'll grav my ass the hell out of here, and I'll need you to pick me up outside."

"Yes, sir." She's not happy, either.

Jill starts to move away as she orders her squad back into the grav tube.

I point to the bank of windows. "Anybody know if our C4 charges can break that glass?"

Brice shakes his head. "That glass is built to withstand railgun fire from other cruisers. C4 won't even scratch it."

"Then I'll have to do this the hard way." I look at him and put on a comforting little smile. "Don't worry. I'll make it out. Just make sure Penny doesn't leave me. Now, get moving!"

Brice doesn't. "You don't still have the kill switch set, do you?"

I shake my head as I laugh.

He laughs in that dark way he does. "I'm moving the squad out. We'll look for you outside. Good luck."

Chapter 39

Alone on the bridge, the moments are ticking down.

I'm monitoring the comm links as I familiarize myself with the Trog cruiser's internal grav controls. I don't want to do anything with interior grav until my people are loaded up. I do, however, try to set up a repulsive grav field in the tubes leading to the bridge. It won't lock Trogs out—it'll just slow down those that decide they need to stop in for a visit.

At least that's the idea. Unlike my assault ship, with one console to control the ship's grav functions, the cruiser has a bank of consoles and was manned by a dozen Grays. The longer I stare at the panels, the more certain I am that I'm not going to be able to do anything.

I check the time on my d-pad, then gaze out through the windows at a view the likes of which I've only ever seen in fictional movies and old space documentaries.

The world is spinning slowly below me as I look down on swirls of cloud, patterns of snow-capped mountains, evergreen forest, and gray cities.

Earth's massive battle stations, each constructed in hollowed-out asteroids towed in from the belt, orbit on their basketweave of paths. As I watch, one station seems to come toward me, but I know it'll pass overhead. I hope. I have no way of telling what my altitude is. Two stations closer to my course are way out in front.

Juji Station, dead and venting gases, is far ahead, slowly receding as it moves farther and farther away.

South of me, at the edge of the planet's curve, I see Trog cruisers, twelve or fourteen of them, hammering another station that's sending a storm of fire back. Railgun slugs, hot from the compression of gravity pushing them from standstill speeds up to six or seven thousand miles an hour glow bright yellow and red as they cut paths through the vacuum.

Assault ships, broken in pieces and shattered into bits, are floating in every direction.

Pieces of metal and the bodies of SDF soldiers flame bright as they streak into the atmosphere.

A cruiser, terribly damaged, jetting flame from a dozen fires, is sliding sideways far below me. It's starting to glow hot as earth's thick atmosphere drags across its hull.

I check the time on my d-pad again. Thirty seconds.

The two-minute mark was arbitrary. However, I had to draw the line somewhere. My plan will disintegrate the more time it takes to develop. I just have no way of knowing how long that time will be.

Penny comms in. "Where the hell are you?"

"I told you, I'd meet you outside."

"That's stupid," she tells me. "Get to the ship."

"Is everyone on board?" I ask.

"Everyone but you."

"Don't wait," I tell her.

Penny and I have been friends for a very long time. She's angry. "Don't go hero on me."

"Don't go Adverb on me," I shoot back. "This isn't a suicide mission. Seriously, look for me outside. I'll come out of the hole the ship's going to leave once you back it out."

"And you really think we'll find you in all the debris out there?" she argues.

"I'll max my suit's deflective grav once I'm outside. Phil sees gravity better than he sees internet porn. To him, I'll be glowing like a supernova."

Phil cuts in. "You wish."

Penny adds, "You know Phil's still mad at you about—"

I laugh, if for no other reason than to get back on topic. "I trust you, all of you. Now don't fuck it up. I don't want to be orbiting the planet forever." If I live through what I've planned, if I make it out of the ship, orbiting forever will be my only choice if they don't find me. My suit can generate a grav field, yet there's no way its micro-fusion reactor can sustain enough power to de-orbit me in any survivable way. "Now, move it, and stay focused. Things are going to get messy."

"Suit yourself. Penny out."

Jill comms in. "We're pulling out now. It was nice knowing you, Dylan Kane. I'd say more, but my mom always told me, 'never get in a man's way when he's got stupid on his mind.'"

"See you outside, Jill." I check my watch. Time's up.

I feel the Trog cruiser lurch as the two assault ships power up grav fields strong enough to disengage.

I drop into the tiny pilot's seat, made for Gray butts, not humans.

Is this a Trog ship then? A Gray ship?

I focus on the gravity fields of all the massive objects around me and see the other two Trog cruisers still raining railgun slugs down on Arizona and still shooting at assault ships lucky enough to make it up through the atmosphere. The three cruisers are in a line as we follow the spin of the planet below. Mine is first, the second follows me ten klicks back, and the third is another ten further.

They're holding their position against earth's pull.

Neither is doing anything to change that. Neither is reacting to the ship I control. Whether they don't know or won't accept that a stupid human monkey just captured one of their beautiful mechanical leviathans is irrelevant to me, as long as they don't change their minds for another minute or two. Then, the unmerciful and unchangeable laws of physics will be in control of their fates.

I attempt to kill power to all my ship's interior systems, and screw something up. Internal gravity starts to fluctuate.

Nonetheless, something worked right.

My console tells me I have more power available I can direct to the propulsion and maneuver plates—more power than those grav plates can sustain, actually. In short bursts, a grav plate can consume more electricity than it's rated for. It generates a stronger field for a short time—maybe seconds, maybe minutes—and then the plate's titanium housing superheats, frying its innards and rupturing. Then the unit turns to junk.

That's okay with me. I'm not interested in the resale value of this heap. I only want minutes.

I push the power flow and over-grav every plate in the ship as I jam it into reverse.

Blue grav fields glow, and field lines spray in every direction.

Every piece of metal framework in the ship strains as two million tons of composite and steel try to change direction. The deck rumbles.

Interior grav disappears completely and alarms sound on one of the consoles. Now every Trog on board, every personal item in every berth, and the loose tonnage of railgun slugs and wreckage in the main hangar tumble forward, smashing interior walls and crushing bulkheads.

A smile slowly creeps across my face. It strikes me as bizarrely funny that four or five years of labor by thousands of Trogs went into constructing this cruiser and it won't last ten more minutes under the abuse I'm heaping on it.

It won't have to.

The bridge crews piloting the other two ships—I guess now not Trogs but Grays—with their hypersensitivity to gravity, have to be stunned by the intensity of what just happened inside my ship. I hope they're speculating and making bad guesses, like maybe a catastrophic reactor failure, or perhaps an impact by another of the humans' tiny assault ships.

All I need is another thirty or forty seconds of dithering conjecture from them.

Once megaton masses start lumbering on a collision course, there reaches a point where nothing can be done to tease the physics of the situation toward any outcome but disaster.

The seconds tick.

Grav plates rupture and pop in my hull, shaking the entire ship with each burst.

The distance between my cruiser's stern and the bridge of the following ship has halved, and that ship responds.

Its grav plates plume blue energy as it veers. Railguns still firing at distant targets start sending slugs skipping across the atmosphere and off into space.

Now I know for sure, the Grays driving the other ship reacted too late and didn't respond drastically enough. At this point they couldn't, not without making the hard choice to over-grav their plates and ruin their ship in order to save it.

Tough shit for them.

The last satisfying seconds pass.

My cruiser's stern smashes into the second cruiser's bridge, and I steer away just as the collision starts. I don't want a direct hit, but a glancing blow, just enough to destroy the other ship's bridge, kill the command crew, and rip away enough of the forward section to expose its expansive hanger bay to the deadly vacuum of space.

My ship is shuddering around me. Every piece of metal feels like it's going to break welds and shear rivets as four million tons of reinforced hull and payload in the two giant ships deform and break.

Still, I pour every amp of power my redlining reactors generate to over-grav my plates.

My ship is accelerating as my hull rips along the other cruiser's side.

A huge rocket of air is blasting out of the tear in my victim's main hangar bay, pushing it to list hard to starboard and roll onto its back. Its grav plates—those with power—are thrusting the ship with nothing controlling them.

Our ships separate.

I'm still flying.

The other is lurching toward the atmosphere and a fiery death for every murderous Trog onboard.

"Ha!" I shout. "That's what war feels like, bitches!"

I turn my attention to the last of the three cruisers.

I already know I'm going to succeed in killing it.

It's slowing cautiously, trying to process what just happened. Maybe the Grays think it's an accident—one damaged ship losing guidance and colliding unfortunately with a second. Maybe they're trying to hang close to pick up survivors.

Maybe the little Gray masters of our universe are indecisive.

Perhaps that's the flaw of the hive mind. All those big heads filled with orange brain-goo, arguing telepathically while their placid black eyes cast dirty looks at one another, are unable to reach a decision as fast as a stupid human monkey like me. It might be the key to their downfall.

It certainly is working today.

The last cruiser casually veers.

It chooses left.

Any direction besides left would have increased its odds of survival. However, at this point, over-grav acceleration is the only tiny chance it has.

They do me the favor of not selecting that option.

Still moving faster, I take aim with my smashed stern, my ram.

Expectedly, they finally get it, and their grav fields erupt in brilliant blue.

Unfortunately for them, it's one-hundred-percent too late.

I laugh.

I brace myself.

My stern smashes into the other ship's flank, just aft of the command section. Steel framework drives through composite hull as both ships start to disintegrate.

It's time for me to go.

I jump out of my seat and fly using my suit's grav.

I'm across the bridge and into a clear grav tube in seconds, blazing at a dangerous speed, curving hard in a burst of blue as I make the turn out the bottom of the tube and move into the main corridor back to the hangar bay.

I see Trogs ahead—three of them—using auto-grav to stick to the buckling floor. They have to know catastrophe is unfolding around them, yet they're unsure how to react.

My rifle is in my hands, and I trigger a long burst of full-auto slugs as I max power to my deflective field and put the rest into acceleration. I drive right at them.

Hoping.

Praying.

I don't care if I hit them. I only need a gap.

No collision.

I flash past the Trogs, out of the hall and into the hangar bay, wondering how I managed to miss them.

The stern of my ship is a half-kilometer down from me, collapsing in slow destruction, with geysers of flame searing through the vacuum and disappearing as soon as they form. Explosions of sparks burst in sprays a hundred meters across.

Cracks run all up and down my hull.

Giant support ribs buckle.

I have to find a hole in the hull big enough to use for escape.

I'm all eyes and panic, knowing the heartbeats left in my life are small in number.

And there it is, the ragged hole left by Jill's ship after it wrenched free.

I adjust my grav field and push toward the opening. It's deforming as the hull bends.

A gravity pulse pushes me off course.

Grav plates on two massive ships are maxing current and bending space—one to avert, one to cause the disaster already destroying them—and the chaos of attraction and repulsion is making it damn hard to stay on a straight line.

A metal support the size of a railroad car rips loose and spins through the hangar bay, tearing up every structure in its way.

I swerve and push.

I see empty space through the collapsing hole and play the only card I have. I over-grav my suit plates for a punch of acceleration.

Suddenly, unbelievably, I'm out.

The earth's daylight surface is below me, a million scraps of metal are careening in every direction, and the black void of space stretches out to forever above me.

"Hell, yeah!"

I back off my suit grav to save my plates.

I need to get away from the cruisers while avoiding any hunk of metal big enough to kill me.

I scan around for my assault ship's gravity signature. Instead, I see in the distance my first victim starting to break up in the atmosphere.

The two ships above me are still merging, as blue snakes of grav field lines swim all over the crunching wreckage.

"Penny!" I call into my comm. "Penny!"

"Searching," Phil answers.

As promised, I max power to my suit's deflective field. "I'm about half a klick below the bow, earth side."

"Dammit!" yells Phil. "You're gonna hit atmosphere if you keep going!"

"Well, then come save me, goddammit." I'm giddy as I speak, because I just avoided a brush with death that should have killed me. "Wasn't I clear on that part of the plan?"

"I see you," says Phil.

"Headed your way," Penny tells me.

I veer left, bursting blue with grav wash to avoid a huge section of ship's hull that just blew off.

Out of the blackness, growing impossibly fast, I see my assault ship coming right at me.

The grav field dissipates suddenly, and the ship matches my vector. It effortlessly maneuvers up beside me.

I'm impressed. "Good driving, Penny."

Brice opens one of the assault doors, reaches out, and drags me inside. "He's in!"

"Hold tight," Penny calls back. "Max grav!"

I grab a handhold and put my butt in a seat.

The platoon compartment is full of battered grunts looking at me in awe. Actually, full is the wrong word. Half the seats are empty now. Half my platoon is already dead. That puts a hollow in my gut I think I might fall into.

Penny pours on the speed.

Space flexes for a microsecond as one of the colliding cruiser's fusion reactors loses containment and blows both ships apart in a nuclear blast.

Chapter 40

I'm on the bridge with Brice, Lenox, and the rest of the bridge crew.

Phil is jabbering on because he can't contain his excitement. "That's not the kind of thing that happens, not in a fusion reactor. The old fission ones might melt down, but to see a runaway cascade? No, that's fission. But fusion? That collision had to do something just right. Know what I mean? Just right. Or maybe it *is* a fission reactor. Do Trogs use fission?"

"Why don't you be quiet," asks Penny "and let me drive?"

Phil huffs. He likes to pout. He usually wallows in it until somebody caves in and comforts him.

"While you boys were out having your fun," says Penny, "I talked with Jill's pilot. We're going back to Juji Station to see if anyone else from our company made it."

"Anything on the ship-to-ship from them?" I ask.

"Nothing," answers Jablonsky.

"They might be there," says Phil, finding his voice earlier than expected, making it clear his feelings are still bruised.

"Yeah." I don't agree. I think they're dead. Dying's apparently an easy thing to do up here. "Phil, what's the status of our ship?"

"A few more dings," he tells me, losing a little of his act now that he has something else to think about. "Nothing major since the first salvo when we were coming up."

"Systems are stable?" I ask.

"Yes."

"How are we set for fuel?"

"Including what we burned off and what leaked out from punctured tanks, we have about sixty percent of our hydrogen left."

"Grav plates?" I ask.

"Seven percent compromised or dead," he answers. "All of those are hull plates we use for our defensive field and the inertial bubble. The drive array is fine."

"Can we bubble jump?" I ask.

In one of the more advanced training modules, I learned that jumping to light speed and beyond is mostly about generating a sufficiently enormous power surge and dumping it through a specially configured plate array in the rear of the ship constructed around the reactor. The surge spikes an intense and localized grav field that punches the space-time fabric so forcefully it produces a circular three-dimensional wave.

Did I say I love this kind of techno-shit?

A simplistic, but illustrative way to picture it is like a wave on the ocean.

The counterintuitive but important point is though a powerful wave—a tsunami—might travel across the ocean at four or five hundred miles an hour, it's not the water flowing, it's the wave moving through the water.

Just as a submarine could never hope to generate enough power to move at several hundred miles an hour underwater, a surfer on a board could theoretically ride the wave at full speed across the ocean. Of course, the analogy breaks down on so many technical levels it's useless from an engineering perspective.

The major difference is that the space-time wave would dissipate almost instantly if not sustained by a power source in the spacecraft that first generated it. By using the grav array to create the wave, a ship can then feed the warp with a lower energy output to create a standing wave that exists within a three-dimensional space around the ship. A bubble.

The size of the bubble and the amplitude of the wave are determined mostly by the power the ship can generate to sustain it. The taller the wave, the bigger the bubble, the faster the wave moves through space. The faster the ship moves surfing it.

Theoretically, there's no limit to how fast the wave can move, so likewise, there's no limit to how fast the ship can travel. From outside the bubble, the ship seems to move faster than the speed of light. However, Einstein's equations aren't violated, because inside the bubble, the ship isn't exceeding the universal speed limit, it's stationary relative to the wave of warped space.

It all sounds easy, but it's not.

The first big obstacle to going any distance is power—a lot of it—and power ain't free.

Fusion-drive ships turn pairs of hydrogen atoms into helium, and because the curve of binding energy has an advantageous shape with respect to that type of atomic reaction, scads of energy is thrown off, snorted up by the mechanical systems of the fusion reactor. The smaller reactors, at least with the designs we've inherited from the Grays, are less efficient at converting hydrogen to usable power. Little ships like ours have to bring along a crap-load of hydrogen to get where they're going and have enough to bubble jump back again.

Run out of hydrogen somewhere along the way, and the bubble disappears, the wave dissipates, and the ship falls below light speed. If that happens on a jump between planets, maybe you get lucky, and you fly along at five or ten thousand miles an hour until the gravity of some planet catches you and hauls you in. Maybe you are picked up by a salvage crew, and you have a great story to tell your friends at the bar about how your ship went ballistic in deep space and yet here you are, still alive.

Run out of hydro on an interstellar trip ten trillion miles from nowhere, and you might as well just shoot yourself, because eventually, you'll run out of food, water, or air, and die. That's it. You'll never reach a planet, and no one will ever find you. The void is just too damn big.

The other critical aspect of bubbling is navigation. Thanks to our friendly Gray masters, there's precious little computer power built into our ships. Those little Gray fuckers, with their naturally evolved gravity-tuned sensory systems in their funky-big heads, can stand on the bridge of a cruiser, look at a star twenty light years away, eyeball a vector, and bubble jump right to it.

It's one of a thousand reasons Grays are easy to hate. They're naturally better at something than we are.

Any human endeavor to jump from star to star or even planet to planet would need to run on the precision of a computerized navigation system. What we have instead is Phil with an alien bug in his head and grav skills honed from working twelve years on the line at the factory.

Penny and me are the backup systems.

So we'll be making our jumps in hops—a few long ones, and some short ones. It's like playing croquet and trying to knock your ball closer and closer to a wicket, hoping to make it through before something bad happens, like running out of hydrogen because you keep missing the mark.

Oh, and if there's even the tiniest imperfection in the alignment of the grav drive array relative the ship's central axis, forget about it. You might as well email your mother one last time and fly into the sun, because your life will end badly.

And they say bubble jumping isn't fun.

Chapter 41

"How fast will this thing go?" asks Phil. "Rumor I heard from one of the pilots in the fitting hangar was 1.5c."

"C?" asks Lenox.

"Engineer slang for the speed of light?" answers Penny.

I know the answer, and it's not as rosy as any of them would like to hear. Unfortunately, they need to be told. "If we can make the jump to light speed the ship might do 1.5c."

"If?" asks Phil, pumping about ten groans of trepidation into that one syllable.

"This ship is new." I drag my hand across the wall to help with my point. Paint flakes off. Flecks swirl in the light-g and turbulence left by the passing of my hand. "I think they skipped some quality steps when they rushed these things through production."

"Quality?" Phil asks, as his voice finds one of its emphatic, higher octaves. "Quality? This ship is a rusty piece of shit!"

"It flies," Penny tells him. "It'll pull twelve g's." She glances quickly at me and the others who rode in the platoon compartment through the roughest parts of the battle. "Without too much discomfort."

"We're not talking about bull-dyke-gas-pedal-pushing through low earth orbits," Phil argues.

"Hey," says Brice, giving Phil a stern look.

I didn't expect Brice to stand up for Penny. I wonder what that's about.

"Jumping to light speed," Phil continues, as though Brice has said nothing, "isn't about pulling g's, it's about precision—super precision. Every plate in your drive array has to be perfectly configured. Perfectly. Do you know what that means? In a ship this size, the geometrical position of every plate has to be relatively aligned exactly with the axis of the ship."

Penny says, "They've been building drive arrays at the Arizona shipyard since you were still wishing you'd grow up to be a man."

Phil's on his stump, and when he's up there, everybody else is ignored. "The capacitors storing the power that produces the electrical surge have to be exactly timed to fire—not just at the same time, but the electricity also has to arrive at the grav plates at the simultaneously. If any moron in the factory mis-measured the wire length, put in a dead capacitor, ran out of shielded wire and threw in a length of some crap they found at an old, abandoned Home Depot, then we won't hit light speed. Worse, we will, but our grav wave won't be perpendicular to the axis of the ship, and instead of flying in the direction the ship is pointed, we'll skew off one way or the other and smash into the moon."

"The grav wave will flow around the moon," says Penny, and then in a spiteful tone, she says, "Basic grav dynamics. Even us *bull dykes* know that."

Phil slumps in his chair. He's out of steam for the moment. "If our ship flies a tight turn around a gravitational mass when we're moving at light speed, our inertial bubble won't save us. We'll all be mashed to jelly inside these shitty secondhand suits."

Everyone's awkwardly silent for a minute. Penny and I have all seen Phil ride the wave of his little tantrums on countless occasions, over anything from the watery gruel served at the factory cafeteria to the inherent injustice of North Korea's favored status with the Grays.

"You're a moody bitch sometimes," observes Brice. He's talking to Phil.

Phil stares sheepishly at his hands in his lap. "I know." He turns to Penny and says, "Sorry about the dyke remark."

"You know I love you, Adverb." Penny smiles sweetly. "But don't hate me because I like *real* men."

Everybody laughs.

Everybody but Phil. He brings it on himself.

It's time to refocus. I say, "Now that you kids are through, Phil's not entirely wrong. The SDF has been hush-hush about everything having to do with these ships." I pause because I'm reluctant to tell them the truth of the situation we're in. Still, if it were me, I'd want to know. "My contact with the Free Army says one in twenty of these ships disintegrates the first time they make the jump to light speed."

That stuns everyone on the bridge.

"Can you trust this guy?" asks Brice.

"I already bet my life on it." That's a true, and hopefully sufficient, answer. "Some of these ships barely made light speed when they tested them. Some of them will do the full 1.5."

"So they've all been tested?" asks Penny. "You mean the ones that blew up already blew up, and we're good, right?"

I shake my head. "They tested the first ships off the line. There's no way they could have tested them all without attracting Trog attention."

"Oh, holy shit!" Phil gets it. "This is absolutely the first time this ship has ever flown—now, today."

"You got it." It's a crappy truth, but it needs to be out there.

"If we don't blow up," Phil is putting sarcasm to use, "that'll make navigation a breeze."

"You'll figure it out," I tell him. "You're *good* at that sort of thing." I make it sound sarcastic, but it's true.

He mutters a response only he can understand.

"Phil, Jablonsky," I say, "I need to know what's going on out there. Penny, get us to Juji Station if that's where we're going. Brice, Lenox, get me a casualty count. My damn d-pad still tells me everyone's fine."

Chapter 42

Penny is steering the ship through the debris field surrounding Juji Station.

"Jesus, they beat the hell out of this place," says Phil.

"Any radio traffic from Juji?" I ask.

"No," says Jablonsky. "I've hailed them, asking for anyone. I receive no response on any channel."

"That's the way they do it," says Brice. He's talking about the Trogs. "If they don't land an army to take it, they keep pounding long after defensive fire ceases. They want to kill everything, reduce the base to rubble."

"Why?" asks Phil. He can't believe the brutality of it.

"So they won't have to fight the same battle again when they come back," answers Brice.

"It might get bumpy," says Penny. "Gases are venting through the fissures. You want me to pull farther away?"

"No," I answer. "Down here in the debris no one is likely to think we're a target worth wasting fire on."

"That's not a problem," says Jablonsky. "The Trogs are withdrawing. I'm picking up chatter about it now."

Phil stares off at seemingly nothing for a moment. "I see them." He's using his finely tuned sense of gravity. "They're all bubble jumping out."

"Going back to reload," says Brice. "It takes the Trogs about a week to fill one of those cruisers with a full supply of railgun slugs. They have bases scattered in the asteroid belt and out in the Kuiper Belt."

"They're not going to different bases," says Phil. "They're all hopping down the same vector."

"They don't even respect us enough to hide it," mutters Penny.

"Arrogant bastards," agrees Brice.

"Maybe," I say. "Maybe not. Nothing's to say they're not hopping a billion miles out of the orbital plane and redirecting from there."

"Only they're not," says Phil. He plays around with the computer on his console for a minute. "They're headed out to Ceres."

Brice shakes his head.

"What?" I ask.

"Trogs took Ceres about six months ago." Brice looks angry, like there's something he's not saying.

"I thought we still had Ceres," says Lenox. Everybody knows it's the largest object in the asteroid belt, nearly half the size of Pluto. We have a huge base there. "I saw the video of —"

"I saw that video, too," Brice tells her. "They made it look like some kind of San-Juan-Hill-*Remember the-Alamo*-hero-gasm. Pretty good video if it wasn't ninety-proof Hollywood bullshit. We were slaughtered there. I lost a lot of guys that should have lived." Brice looks around the bridge like he's wrestling with what to say next. "Command bugged out. Left us there."

"What do you mean, command bugged out?" I ask.

"Exactly what it sounds like," says Brice. "Morale was bad. We were short on everything because the Trogs had been blockading us for months. Everybody figured we'd already lost the war. Once the assault started, most of the field grade officers jumped in a ship and bubble jumped the fuck out of there."

"You're kidding?" Mostly, I just don't want to believe it.

"MSS went first," says Brice. "One minute, North Koreans are around every corner, sneaking and trying to catch you doing something wrong—you know how they are." Brice looks at each of us. We all know exactly what he means. "Then they were gone. The rumor spread over the base they were 'called back to the moon.' Yeah, fuckin' right."

Knowing nods. The MSS doesn't play by the same rules as the rest of us. It doesn't need to be said.

"Two or three hours later," says Brice, "you'd be lucky if you could find a lieutenant. By then, the Trog cruisers were pounding the hell out of us, and half our railguns were unmanned because crews were busy making their way to the hangars to catch a ride on the last ship out. That sealed it."

"How'd *you* get out?" asks Phil, it comes out like an accusation, but he probably didn't mean it that way. That's just Phil.

Brice bristles and gives Phil a look like he's thinking about unloading a magazine into his pudgy gut. And then his tone comes out icy and dark. "I don't answer to you, donut-junky."

"Be cool," I tell, Brice. "Phil's a harmless idiot. You'll figure that out soon enough." But that doesn't seem like enough to defuse the situation.

Brice is still glaring.

Phil is squirming in his seat and probably pissing in his suit.

I need them both. Phil is talented with gravity like nobody I've ever met. I don't know how Brice got off Ceres, and I don't care. Everything I've learned about him in a single day tells me he's exactly what he seems to be—a good soldier. And then, intuition comes to my aid. "Was Milliken there?" I ask. "On Ceres?"

That takes Brice off-guard. He redirects his attention from Phil and looks at me. "How'd you know?"

It was a guess, but I say, "Is that the beef you had with him?"

"He was never a good officer," says Brice, "but he had a goddamn duty."

"Did you file a complaint when you got back to earth?" asks Lenox. "Charges? Those officers were guilty of desertion, right?"

Brice shakes his head. "You've got a lot to learn about the world, honey."

"The SDF couldn't file charges against its officers," I deduce, "because the MSS deserted first. If the officers were guilty, then so was the MSS."

"If I'd have made a peep about it," says Brice, "it would have been *me* they hanged." He takes a long slow breath. "So I end up back with my unit on earth—the officers and just a few of us enlisted men—only a handful out of a whole company. Over a hundred are dead up there on Ceres."

"Jesus," says Phil.

"So I didn't say anything," says Brice. "I waited because I knew they'd send us up again."

"And today was your chance?" I ask, as though the answer isn't obvious.

Brice nods again, and in his eyes, despite his seeming certainty, I can see he's conflicted about what he did.

I say, "Duty is more about following your heart than following the rules."

Chapter 43

"How organized is the SDF right now?" I ask.

Jablonsky looks at me, wide-eyed. "You asking me?"

"You're on the ship-to-ship radio. You hear what's going on. You'd know better than anyone."

"Sounds like a mess," he guesses. "Nobody knows who's in charge. We're hearing conflicting orders from a division commander still on the ground in Arizona, different instructions from some North Korean Colonel up here—I think the same one we went on our attack run with—and Pyongyang is still squawking."

"Confusion?" I ask, summing the situation up to a single word.

"Yes," Jablonsky answers definitively.

"Okay." I turn to Penny. "Get us down on the surface close to the deepest hole you can find."

"What's with the change of plan?" asks Brice.

"Our supply rooms are empty," I tell him, as I look around the bridge. I'm not yet sure everyone's aware. "The generals sent us up here with what we have on our backs—three days' power, three days' rations." I glance down at my d-pad and see that I have barely enough hydrogen to power my suit for six more hours. "They didn't expect any of us to live long enough for resupply."

Brice guesses first where I'm going. "I can take a squad inside, and see what we can find."

"Lenox," I say. "You take one, too."

"Can do," she answers.

"Don't wander too far," I tell them. "Scrounge what you can, as quick as you can. "My guess is we'll have twenty or thirty minutes. We don't want to push it. I want to be away from earth before anybody downstairs has time to figure out we're not one of the derelicts out here junking up the orbits.

"Okay," says Penny. "I think I've got one." She confers on a private comm link with Phil to coordinate.

Brice and Lenox exit the bridge and head for the platoon compartment.

"And medical supplies," I call after them. "Whatever we need for the wounded."

Brice stops and turns back to face me. "None of the wounded made it."

"What?"

He guesses I'm still running on earth intuition. "Most of the time the wounded don't make it. Sealing the suit after a wound only buys you some time. The only way you have a chance is to move them into a pressurized environment."

I feel a little bit like a scolded schoolboy for having Brice remind me of our earlier conversation. "If you happen across a portable welding rig we can use to patch the holes in the hull, pick it up."

"That reminds me." Brice looks up the length of the hall. "Lieutenant Holt is stowed in the supply room."

I'd forgotten about Holt. I nearly laugh at the callousness of it, but excuse myself. I've been busy. "I don't know what to do with him." I make the first guess that comes to mine. "Prisoner of war?"

Brice shakes his head. "In my experience, we always run short on H or calories, something. Keeping useless bodies alive is expensive."

Many have died at my hands, yet none were murdered in cold blood. I don't feel a thing one way or another about those deaths. The thought of killing Holt bothers me. It would be murder. Murder in the in service of the revolution, but still murder.

Brice, reading my face, comes to my rescue. "I can't murder him either."

I purse my lips and draw a sharp breath. I'm the commander. I can't ask Brice to do what I'm not willing to do myself.

"I don't think we should kill him."

My jaw drops. "Honestly, the idea of a dead Lieutenant Holt doesn't bother me. The thought of killing him for the crime of being a moronic asshole doesn't appeal to me. What do you have in mind?"

"Something stupid."

"We've been through some shit today." I think Brice is wary because he's still not sure what to think of me. "You had my back. I've got yours. You don't need to worry about me putting a knife in it. Just say what's on your mind."

Shaking his head, because he can't come up with a decent solution, Brice says, "We leave him on Juji. He'll get picked up by a rescue party in a few days and put back into circulation." Brice chuckles. "He'll be dead five minutes into his next deployment anyway."

Brice's solution is a relief, also a new burden. It worries me. "He's a witness to what we did."

"If the MSSW gets their hands on us," concludes Brice, "we'll hang for what we're doing whether we kill him or not."

"Leave him here, then. I'll unlock his suit when we take off."

With a relieved smile, Brice nods and heads up the hall.

Chapter 44

Looking out through one of the small, thick windows, I see an assault ship slowly weaving its way through the debris field. "Is that Jill?"

"Yes," Phil answers.

Having expected Jablonsky to respond, I turn toward them with the question apparent on my face.

"Gravity signature," says Phil.

I look back through the window and see gravity fields fluxing off the plates of Jill's ship. Nothing appears unique to me. "Hmm."

Phil says, "Maybe now you can apologize for calling me an idiot."

"Phil," I resist, as I watch Jill's ship come in, "you were doing that thing you do. You're going to get yourself in trouble one day and I won't be there to pull you out."

"I don't need you to help me out of trouble."

"I know, Phil." Sarcasm is such a wonderful thing. "Any word from the platoon?" Brice and Lenox have been down inside the station for ten minutes and tons of metallic asteroid ore lay between us. My suit comm isn't powerful enough to send or receive with them.

"A lot of static in the line," says Jablonsky, "but they've found something."

"Ammo? Hydro?" I ask. "Cal packs?"

"Can't say," answers Jablonsky. "I relayed the information on to Lieutenant Rafferty, though."

"Jill's coming to resupply, too?" I ask.

"Yes," Jablonsky confirms.

"Thanks for passing our plan along to them," I tell him. "Let her know we're on a short deadline here. Our top priority needs to be getting these ships to the Free Army's base."

"Are you ready to share that location with us, yet?" asks Phil.

"Location?" I shake my head. "Nothing against you, Jablonsky, but I'll keep that info to myself until we're well away from the earth. Phil, you two coordinate a rendezvous point with Jill somewhere a long way from here. Once we bubble out, we'll meet up there, and I'll pass along the coordinates."

"Yes, sir," answers Phil, just like any snotty junior high kid would say it.

"Is there really a Free Army base?" asks Jablonsky.

"Yes," I tell him. "Don't worry, this rebellion is bigger than just two ships."

"Honestly?"

"Of course." Honestly, that's my worry, too, and it'll stay that way until I see the base with my own eyes. "You two get to work."

"A word?" asks Penny.

"You don't need to ask permission to talk," I say.

Andrea shrugs. "I wasn't sure how military we were going to be with Phil calling you 'sir' and all."

"Do you have a question, Penny?"

"Grays," she says simply.

"Yes?" I prompt for more.

"Why were there Grays on the bridge of that other ship?" asks Phil, turning away from his task.

"Are you done finding us a rendezvous?" I ask.

"Sure," he answers. "I just gave the coordinates to Jablonsky. He's radioing them to Jill's ship."

I roll my eyes.

"It doesn't take that long to pick a random point in space," says Phil. "Most of it's empty."

"Why were the Grays there?" asks Penny.

"Not just there on the bridge," clarifies Phil, "but commanding the ship and targeting the weapons, just like they do on our cruisers."

"Not exactly," I answer. "On our ships, the Grays are mostly on the bridge, and Korean bug-heads handle the targeting."

"That's not the point," argues Phil. "We're supposed to be at war with the Trogs. Why are we fighting Grays?"

That's the question that's been nagging me since I stormed the bridge of the Trog cruiser and saw all those Grays there.

"Maybe we've been fighting them all along?" suggests Phil.

Penny says, "Despite what the news tells us, people say the SDF has never captured a single Trog cruiser. They could have been there all along and we wouldn't know it. Phil might be right."

"Maybe the Trogs are just like us," says Phil. "Gray slaves."

"You think this is a war between two Gray factions?" I ask. It's a plausible theory. More than plausible.

"Why not?" asks Phil. "Humans fight each other all the time. Why wouldn't Grays do the same?"

"What if the Grays are Trog slaves?" asks Penny.

That brings the conversation to a halt. Something neither Phil nor I have considered.

Is that possible?

"There wasn't a Trog—" I drop the thought before I finish it.

"What?" asks Phil.

"I was going to say there weren't any Trogs on the bridge when I got there, but of course there were. Three ghost Trogs were up there, and more were in the halls."

"Lenox told me you guys came across five or six of them in the forward section," says Penny.

I nod.

"That's a lot, if they're just some kind of ninja assassins," says Phil. "You never hear about more than one or two. I mean, when you hear stories about them at all."

"Or maybe they're allies," I guess. "Trogs and Grays. We don't know anything about their relationship, right?"

"Except the regular Trogs do the fighting and dying," says Phil.

"Just like us," I conclude the comparison.

"By the millions," finishes Penny. "You've never seen a video with a thousand Gray bodies laying on the ground. Only humans and Trogs."

Chapter 45

It's been a long day of pitfalls and fuckups, so when we get the platoon back on board and blast far enough away from earth's gravity well to make our bubble jump and it all goes as planned, I'm surprised.

I'm sitting at the front of the platoon compartment in the blue glow of our ship's inertial bubble, looking down the tube between two rows of facing seats. Brice is on one side of me. Lenox is on the other. I'm wrestling with how I should feel about the empties.

The empties!

I realize immediately my mind is trying to dehumanize the loss of half my platoon, protecting itself from indulging too much pain for the casualties of my choices. I tell myself I shouldn't grieve over people whose names I don't know, whose faces I can't pick out of a lineup.

I was their commander.

I have to feel something. However, at the same time, I know I can't let their deaths paralyze me into impotence. What kind of officer would I be, then? Definitely the kind that would get the rest of the platoon killed.

I turn to analytics, a path to rationalizations I can depend on.

Most of our losses for the day were suffered while taking the Trog cruiser we rammed. That was an expensive venture, but my God, the payoff. What general wouldn't trade a handful of lives for so many of his enemy's?

How many could it have been?

Thirty thousand?

Forty thousand?

Grays and ghost Trogs among them.

Three cruisers.

Hell, they were killing my SDF comrades every moment they floated there in space over the Arizona shipyard, taking potshots at the grunts trying to board ships far below.

Whatever guilt I have for the mistakes I made—

No, not guilt.

I've got nothing to feel guilty for.

Interrupting my thoughts, Brice asks, "Are you worrying over whether I'm going to frag you?"

I don't know how to answer, because in fact, it is a lingering worry.

Brice laughs. He finds humor in other people's discomfort. But who doesn't?

"Sir?" Lenox nudges me. "You okay?"

I glance at Lenox and smile, then turn to look at Brice. "Are you thinking about fragging me?"

He gives it some thought. "Probably not."

I cock my head toward the partially empty platoon compartment. "A lot of casualties."

Brice shakes his head. "This is nothing." His face turns pained. "SDF troops get mauled every time we face the Trogs. This is the norm."

Lenox says, "Makes me think my odds of seeing my next birthday aren't very good."

"Shitty," Brice tells her. "Look at me, I've lost count of how many actions I've seen. At least a couple dozen. Some, like the battle for the moon, went on for nearly a month. That was the only one we won, and I'm still here."

"Are you that lucky?" I ask. "Or that good?"

Brice shrugs. "At first, mostly lucky." His voice sounds a bit melancholy when he adds, "We're all alive by the grace of luck, no matter how good we are."

Lenox leans forward to look past me and finds a direct line of sight to Brice. "Do you really believe that? Can't a well-trained, disciplined grunt make good choices and live?"

"There's always an element of luck," says Brice. He looks up at the glow of our inertial bubble. "This ship could have broken up when we went to light speed. We all talked about that on the bridge. Nothing you could have done about it. Bad luck."

Lenox leans back in her seat.

"You can swing the odds in your favor," says Brice, "but there'll always be things beyond your control. Hell, this day's been full of 'em."

"That's the truth." It sounds like a nothing phrase, however, it's a truth sinking in with me as I realize how many times I tempted fate and won.

The pleasant glow of the inertial bubble flickers out, and the platoon compartment turns back to dim, yellow light splattered over steel and rust. We've just finished another jump—our fourth, though we'd only planned for one.

Phil links through the comm to tell me something I already know. "Kane, we're coming out of jump, and we're finally where we're supposed to be."

"Is Jill here?" I ask, hoping her ship wasn't one of the unlucky ones that fell apart while powering up for light speed.

"She's been here three or four minutes," says Phil. "Quick guess is her ship will do the full 1.5. We barely made it over the hump. That screwed up our navigation."

"As long as we can make light speed," I tell him. "It's not like we're flying out to another star. Everything else okay?"

"The ship handled the jumps fine," says Penny. "It looks like she doesn't fly straight, though. Maybe a degree or two off."

"So Jill's ship works just fine, and she made it to the right place in one jump?" I ask.

"Yeah," says Phil. "That's about the size of it."

"I see." I'm a tad jealous. "Penny, can you correct for the imperfection on future jumps?"

"Mostly," she answers. "Probably. On a long jump, I can't make any promises."

"Noted," I tell her. "Phil, I assume we're alone out here?"

"Nobody but us, and Jill," he answers. "Everything going as planned."

I hate that he said that. Maybe down deep, I'm a superstitious believer in bad luck. Maybe it's the weight of all those empty seats. I key in the orbital coordinates of the Free Army's base and send them to Penny. "After it decrypts, share it with Phil."

"Asteroid belt." A moment later, Phil says it like he knew it all along.

Maybe he did. With the asteroids in that belt traveling a solar orbit one and a half billion miles around, and with one or two million of the rocks big enough to build a base on, Phil's guess is still pretty worthless. I keep that to myself, though. "Forward those coordinates over to Jill's bridge crew. Sounds like she'll be there ahead of us. Tell her to save me a place at the bar."

"You think they have a bar?"

"I hope so." In truth, I don't care. Mostly, I want to hook up with the Free Army so I can feel the security of knowing I didn't drag two platoons of grunts into a rebellion that's already fizzled out.

Chapter 46

Brice opens a private comm between us. Everyone else in the platoon compartment is asleep or trying to. "Penny tells me you slept with Phil's wife."

I didn't expect that to come up, especially not from Brice. I deflect. "You and Penny getting pretty chummy over the comm?"

"We hit it off," he admits. "Nice girl."

I feel a twinge of jealousy. Still, I've got no claim on Penny. She's got none on me. No matter what carnal thoughts she and I have teased through our imaginations over the years, we never moved past friendship. "That's not an answer."

"More than you gave me," Brice chides.

"Yeah."

Brice waits a moment and says, "If it's something you don't want to talk about."

Yes, it's not something I want to talk about.

I start to explain, but stop myself. What does it matter? "Yes, I did sleep with Phil's wife."

Brice nods slowly as he takes that in. "You and Phil, you've been friends a long time, right?"

I rise to my defense. "Don't make it sleazier than it already sounds. Sometimes fucked-up things just happen."

Brice's dark laugh taunts me with how much it shames me. "You ever wonder if that's a common thing, coming up with tidy excuses so you don't have to feel guilty?"

"You think that's what it is?"

"I don't know, Kane." Brice reaches his hand up clumsily and hits his faceplate. He chuckles. "You'd think after all the time I've spent in one of these suits, I'd remember I can't scratch my nose."

I chuckle. "I miss scratching."

"Not as much as you're gonna," says Brice. "Seems it peaks around day three. After that, you lose the urge. You get used to it. Go back to Earth, though, take off the suit, and the next time you're in it, it starts all over again." He looks at me, truly curious. "I wonder why that is."

The urge to rub my eyes suddenly seems too much to bear.

"Do you feel guilty about what you did?"

Ugh. I hoped we were off that subject. "I suppose."

"You and Phil," says Brice. "Seems like he hasn't gotten past it."

"Probably not." I nod my head aft, toward the bridge where Phil is working his navigation magic with Penny at the helm to bounce us all over the solar system. "Phil doesn't let go of things. He carries shit around a long time."

"How long?" asks Brice. "Years?"

"Maybe forever," I laugh. "I'm trying to think of the last thing I know of that Phil actually stopped whining about."

"Stopped whining?" asks Brice. "Over infidelity? Kinda cheapens it, right? No big deal?"

"You're judging me," I suggest. "Maybe I'm too harsh on Phil."

"Is that why you did it?"

I laugh some more. "Are you trying to be a dick?"

"Maybe a little bit." Brice smiles. "Comes natural sometimes." He sighs. "I can't count the number of times I told a soldier to do a thing and do it now, only to have him choose something stupid, like ask why, or wait and think about it, or choose to do something else. Then they die. Makes you wonder if being nice is worth it."

"Nice?" I'm not sure 'nice' is the right word.

Seemingly resigned to it, Brice says, "It wears a man down."

We let that sit for a moment. I don't have anything to add, no advice to give. I'm still the novice leading people into war.

When Brice becomes bored again, he looks at me with an obvious question.

I know which one, so I tell him. "Phil and me go way back. We grew up together. And no, that's not why I did what I did." I rearrange myself in my seat, turning to face Brice. "You want to hear this story?"

"There's no inflight movie. How else am I going to pass the time? Everybody else is asleep."

"You need to lay off the stimulants," I tell him. "Too much of that shit will fuck up your head."

"Suit Juice?" asks Brice. "It's not addictive."

"You know the fact that the MSS tells us Suit Juice isn't addicting pretty much guarantees it is, right?"

Despite the artificial stimulants in his blood, Brice suddenly seems a little worn down. "I've been doing this a long time, Kane. I know what I'm doing. I know what I need. Suit Juice sharpens my focus when I'm in the shit. Might be the reason I'm still alive." His laugh comes back. "I'd rather be a live addict than a clean corpse."

I don't know if that's funny, but I laugh anyway.

"What about you?" he asks. "You juice much, yet?"

"A little," I tell him. "I don't think I get any focus out of it. Focus is something that comes naturally to me—hyper-focus, almost."

"When the slugs were flying and Trogs were dying," Brice flattens a hand and gestures down an imaginary straight line in front of him, "you were 110% in the game. It's like you turned into a war machine back on that Trog ship. You don't see many guys who can do that."

"Thanks?" I think it's a compliment.

He reaches over and raps his knuckles on my helmet. "I read an old news article once from before the siege."

"You're a history buff?" That surprises me.

"After I joined the SDF," says Brice, "I started reading any old military literature I could get my hands on. Figured I could learn something that might keep me alive."

"Did you?"

"Yeah, some stuff," says Brice. "This particular article I read, it was about this helmet they developed at some warfare science lab they had back then. I don't remember what it was called." Brice spreads his fingers and drags them down over his head. "This helmet was full of wires and little magnetic electrodes or whatever the right word is."

"What did it do?" I ask, as I try to envision what Brice is describing.

"This whole research program was about trying to understand the human brain to make better soldiers."

"And?" I ask again, prodding Brice toward the point.

"This woman goes into a battle simulator. A big thing, it filled a whole room." Brice spreads his hands in a wide gesture. "Video screens on all the walls. Big enough to make you think you're really in the situation."

"Sounds like a pretty cool simulator." I wish the ones we'd trained on had been something along that scale.

"The woman had never fired a rifle before and had never been in a simulator before," says Brice. "The simulator starts running, sending dozens of enemy soldiers to kill her, shooting and such. She's overwhelmed. There are so many and she can't kill them all. She's frustrated. She fails."

"It happens." I'm thinking, that's why we train.

"The point is," says Brice, "it was her first time. Nobody expected her to do well. The second time through, they put the helmet on her. They turn it on and run her through the simulator again. Same simulator. Same situation. Same overwhelming number of attackers."

"What happened?" I ask.

"She kills all of the bad guys," says Brice. "Every single one. Afterward, she can't believe it was the same simulation. She thought they'd made it easier. They didn't. It only seemed easier because the thing on her head sharpened her focus, made all her mental distractions go away. Made her a killer. A damned efficient one."

Interesting story. I put my hands on my helmet as I imagine having such a device. "You think they have that kind of technology built into these?"

Shaking his head and pointing at our sleeping troops, Brice says, "You saw how they behaved in combat. Some of them did well. Most are lucky to be alive. No, I think that bug in your head does that the same thing to your brain that the helmet did to that woman. It makes you into a stone-cold killer when you need to be one."

I wonder if Brice is right about that.

Chapter 47

"You still didn't tell me about this thing with Phil's wife," says Brice.

"You're the one who got off on the subject of brainwave helmets."

"Why don't you stop evading and just get it off your chest."

I huff. "I don't need to get it off my chest. It was a mistake. I made my peace with it. Besides, it's not as interesting as you seem to think it's going to be."

"Try me."

Where to start? "They're twins, Claire and Sydney, his wife and mine. Back when Phil and I met them, you could barely tell them apart."

"This has the makings of a good comedy," says Brice.

"Are you going to heckle me?"

"A little." Brice gestures at the rusty tube we're riding. "Entertainment on these long flights is hard to come by. A man's got to do what a man's got to do."

"It's not a comedy."

"Drama is fine. I like those, too."

I refocus on my story and say, "I think somewhere back when Sydney and Claire were still sipping make-believe tea and mashing mud pies, Claire lost one too many games of checkers and Sydney decided she was maybe a little better than Claire."

"It's going to be a psychological drama," guesses Brice.

"Are you going to let me tell it?"

"Please do," says Brice. "I'm riveted already. But first, which one were you married to?"

"Claire?"

"And Sydney, she's the one you... you know." Brice makes a rude gesture.

"Sydney was Phil's wife." Steering the conversation back toward Brice, I say, "I thought you were Mister All-Business. What's with the teenager routine all of a sudden?"

"I am who I need to be," says Brice. "Right now, I'm just a passenger on a ship. My platoon is asleep. This is my off-time. Get on with the story."

"I think Claire developed some kind of complex about Sydney being better than her. The two competed at everything. Eventually, Claire was tired of losing, and gave up on most things. That made Sydney push harder."

"You're talking about more important stuff than checkers," deduced Brice.

"Sydney made good enough grades to go to high school," I tell him. "She eventually became an accountant. Not a bad job. Like most folks, Claire went into the labor pool after sixth grade. She worked on a factory line."

"That is big stuff," concludes Brice.

"Yeah," I agree, already knowing where the story is going, "the big stuff." I pick up my place in the story. "Phil and me met Claire and Sydney at an MSS social function."

"Never went to one of those," says Brice. "By the time I was old enough, I'd signed up for space construction and I was off-world when my first required function came up on the calendar."

"Free food and free beer," I tell him. "Besides that, a waste of time."

"Except you met your wife there."

"By accident, really, but that's outside the scope of this story."

"Getting technical?" laughs Brice.

I nod. "Me and Claire got married. I was happy on that day, maybe the happiest I've ever been. Claire glowed like an angel, prettier than I'd ever seen her before or since. The memory still shines in my mind. I can't reconcile that memory with the one of the shrew who eventually got out of bed one morning and never moved out.

"Phil and Sydney married soon after we did. I didn't question it at the time. It didn't seem unusual, just a bit lucky, two best friends marrying twin sisters. It wasn't until months, maybe years later when I was trying to figure out why the glue that held Claire and me together didn't feel like love, I realized I was only a mark on the scoreboard between her and Sydney. I worked at the grav fab, a good job that afforded me a lot of privilege. Because of the bug in my head, but you know that."

"You're saying Claire married you to one-up her sister?"

"I think so," I answer. "I think Claire was trying to beat Sydney in the game they'd been playing their whole lives. I think after we met, she played the role of best girlfriend ever, being everything I wanted her to be so she could cross the matrimonial line first. I think when the sun came up the morning after our honeymoon, it occurred to her that winning had a price."

"She was stuck with you," says Brice, "because to back out, to divorce you, would invalidate the win?"

"That's right," I confirm. "We rung up a few years of pretending we were happy. Even smiling for real sometimes. Eventually, I realized she had no love for me." I look at Brice when I say it, because it's embarrassing. "I loved her. It broke my heart."

Brice reaches around and pats my back. "Everyone deals with it, eventually."

"To her credit, Claire tried," I say. "She was dutiful. Committed. We even had that *us against the world thing* from time to time. Maybe most of the time. One of the sad aspects of her personality that grew out of all those years of losing to Sydney was an unrealistic idea she was always being cheated by everyone.

"I fell in with it. Not wittingly, not at first. Hell, back in the early days, I did anything to earn love that was never going to come. I was her champion. I got into fights. I cursed my neighbors. I berated people at the commissary. I went after anyone who pissed-off my sweet Claire."

"Sour," comments Brice.

Again, I nod. "Funny thing is, I saw Sydney treating Phil the same way as Claire treated me. Actually, worse. But I never saw the mirror of it. Claire saw plenty there, though. In the privacy of our house, she always talked about what an ugly man Phil was. He was a slob. He smelled bad. He'd never make Sydney happy. Divorce was in their future. They'd never have kids. None of us ever did, by the way.

"That was all just Claire telling herself that her grav fab bug-head was a better catch that Sydney's. She was looking for the decisive win." I shake my head and laugh. "I can only imagine the conversations Claire and Sydney must have had about me and Phil when we weren't around."

"I don't think you'd want to hear any of that," suggests Brice.

"As the years passed," I say, "Phil put on more weight, spent more time with his hobbies, and talked incessantly about Sydney, whom he worshipped, though she seemed to ignore him more and more as she spent all of her time hiking in the mountains and going to an old gym that for some reason was still open in Breck. It's like she was trying to work the imperfections out of her body. Or trying to punish herself for marrying Phil. I don't know.

"Claire didn't have any remarkable habits, except that she was slowly morphing into a brittle, flavorless reflection of the girl I married. Her anger was always lurking behind a veil, unashamed when anyone saw it. She started to overeat, something hardly possible for regular people these days."

"Ain't that the truth," agrees Brice.

"In the bug-head community," I say, "we had privileges, and one of those was plenty to eat. I don't know if the eating was the competition again, or a symptom of Claire giving up. She got a little doughy, not so much that she couldn't cover it up with a slack dress or baggy shirt. She was still pretty and when she turned on that pearly smile, it didn't matter, I was still her stupid puppy.

"For my part, it's hard to say how I passed the years. In a way they were a blur of things I wanted to forget. I felt trapped in a marriage I was afraid to get out of. I was stuck at the grav factory because that's where the Grays put me. I used to read a lot of history with my mom when I was a kid. I started doing that again. I watched a ton of old videos from when the ticks arrived and conquered the earth. I longed for those older days. It was a romantic view of humanity's past. Not to say it was all roses and sunshine, I hid all the dirty parts of our history from myself because I think I needed to love something.

"Everybody does that kind of shit," says Brice. "Healthy self-deception. It's a good thing."

I go on, "The precarious mess of our lives finally collapsed on my birthday a few years back. Sydney and Phil came over to our house. Phil brought buffalo steaks, a rare treat, expensive as hell. I grilled them in the backyard while we drank on the deck. Phil and I talked about work. Claire and Sydney traded barbs.

"We had dinner, drank, played cards, and drank some more. We were all a little drunk, at least. Phil checked out early and went home. We had work the next day and he'd had too many tardies at work already and couldn't risk another. Sydney and Claire found a weird place in their inebriation where they were able to get past their animosity and share nostalgic stories of their childhood.

"It was weird. They were sitting on the couch looking at old pictures, closer than I'd ever seen them before, smiling, and even crying. I trundled myself upstairs to go to bed. I was drunk enough that I knew when I got up in the morning for my shift, I'd still be buzzed.

"I don't remember actually settling into bed but I remember waking up in the dark with a woman's hands on my skin and a pair of lips breathing alcohol breath into my mouth. She smelled like Claire. Tasted like Claire. In the dark, she even looked like Claire. But she didn't feel like Claire. She was lean and tight, not soft and comfortable.

"With alcohol excuses all queued up and impaired logic brushing right past any question of getting caught, I let myself go with it. The blankets were kicked off the bed with the last of our clothes, and we went at it like a couple of teenagers discovering sex for the first time.

"When the bedroom light blinked on, Sydney was on top of me, facing the bedroom door and making enough noise to wake the neighbors, enough to wake Claire from her stupor.

"Sydney stopped what she was doing and sat up straight, showing off the perfect sculpture of her body and blocking my view of the bedroom door.

"I prayed and panicked, hoping I'd been so drunk that I hadn't noticed the light was on when I got in bed, or maybe it was morning and I'd just lost track of time, or maybe I was so drunk any behavior was excusable, even mistaking my wife for her sister. Anything that would save me from the wrath I knew was only a heartbeat away.

"Claire called Sydney a slutty bitch. Shouted it through angry tears. She told Sydney to finish getting me off, and flicked out the light. I was seeing spots in my vision when

Claire slammed the door and wailed as she ran down the stairs, stomping each one so hard I caught myself wishing she'd break one, fall, and die of a broken neck as she rolled to the bottom. Anything so I wouldn't have to face my shame.

"Sydney lifted a leg high in the air to get off me, so high it seemed awkward, rude even, like she was trying to avoid stepping in something she didn't want on her feet, like something about me was so disgusting she couldn't bear to have me touch her skin.

"She deftly rolled off the bed and scooped her clothes off the floor. Covering her breasts with her shirt, I saw only a shadow over her pubic region and a line of moonlight cutting across her face. Everything sweet and flirtatious was gone. She'd turned just as icy cold as Claire. She said, 'Proud of yourself?' She wasn't asking a question. She was stapling the blame to my forehead.

"She left the room and closed the door casually behind.

"I waited to hear her feet going down the stairs, to hear the detonation when she made it to the bottom. I listened for Claire to tear into her, to hear the front door slamming, or maybe the police coming because I knew it *could* get that bad.

"There was nothing.

"Only Claire's sobs drifted up through the dark house.

"It was as if Sydney dissolved into the night, a succubus, pleased her carnage was sewn, flitting into the void."

"What happened after that?" asks Brice.

"I admit," I say, "I was a pussy. I was afraid to go downstairs and face Claire.

"I told myself I'd let her cry herself out and then I'd go down. I spun up a hundred different excuses that all blamed the alcohol. Hell, I even figured I could play dumb, pretend I had no recollection of it. An alcoholic blackout. How could I be blamed for something I didn't know I'd done? Hell, how could I even be sure her accusation was real and not just a drunken dream in her own head?

"I dozed off, and slept hard.

"I woke the next morning feeling like a smashed bug, still afraid to go downstairs.

"I was late for work before I'd even looked at the clock for the first time.

"Regardless, I needed to get my ass to the plant. The ticks weren't forgiving when it came to slowing their production.

"I showered, brushed my teeth, got dressed, and rushed downstairs, with a promise on my lips ready to tell Claire I loved her, and we'd have to talk about it when I got home from work.

"She was gone already.

"Everything downstairs was clean. It was as if there had been no party the night before.

"I took a perfunctory look around the house, hoping I wouldn't find her, then I rushed off to work.

"It was when I got home that evening I found her sitting at the dining room table. She didn't look at me. She didn't yell. She simply said she'd told Phil about it and she'd volunteered us to host a Gray hatchling."

"Shit," says Brice. "You're kidding. She took on a hatchling?"

I nod. "A five-year commitment to raise a tick from hatching to maturity, a commitment to give herself to it. Everybody knows what that means. She knew it would age an extra twenty or thirty years out of her and likely as not leave her dead. She knew the surviving family would get a big enough stack of money to leave them well-fed for a generation.

"Claire got her revenge for what I'd done and she'd committed herself to something that would make me feel shitty every day for the rest of my life.

"Later that night, Phil kicked Sydney out of his house and she came to live in our basement, making it easier for Claire to shove her revenge in the face of the two people she hated most.

"Two weeks after that, the tick moved in and Claire started to shrivel away."

"Goddamn," says Brice. "That's some shit."

Chapter 48

Seven jumps, and we're out again. I've dozed through three.

Most of the grunts are asleep. I've lost track of how many hours we've been trying to reach a destination we should theoretically have made in about forty-five minutes.

"Lived through another one," announces Phil over the bridge comm.

At least there's that. Our ship hasn't blown up, yet. I ask, "Are we any closer this time?"

"Don't be an ass," Penny tells me.

I didn't think my tone carried any inflection of hidden meaning, but I suppose she's getting as frustrated as the rest of us.

"There's a wonkiness to the drive array that's—"

"It's okay, Penny," I tell her. She's explained it to us a few times already.

"throwing us off course by—what, Phil—as much as thirty degrees in each jump?"

"Thirty-two's the most so far," he clarifies.

"And we don't know which direction we're going to go."

Phil says, "At least the hyper-light speed is consistent on each jump, so we're developing a cone of probability on our calculations as to where we'll end up."

Lenox shakes her head and pretends to punch herself in the face and looks at me with a silent question, "How many times do we need to hear this?"

"We understand," I tell them. "When we get to the base, maybe we can fix the ship. They have to have maintenance guys there, right?" That's only a hope. I know nothing about where we're going except it's an asteroid.

"We're three thousand miles out," Phil tells us. "The asteroid at the orbital coordinates looks to be a little more than two kilometers long."

"That's pretty close," says Brice. "Too close to be coming out of bubble jump, right?"

Crap. I don't need Penny and Phil more defensive about this than they already are, but Brice is right. Coming in or out of jump near a massive object can lead to trouble, the Russian-roulette kind. Maybe you come out just fine and laugh your good fortune in fate's face, or maybe you're atomized so quickly you don't even have a millisecond to think *"Oh, shit!"* right before you die.

"Yeah," Phil agrees, flatly. "Looks like that consistent speed thing I just mentioned is off the table, too."

Brice pats the bulkhead beside his seat. "Fantastic!" Then he leans over and catches Lenox's attention. "Luck."

She chooses not to respond.

"Two assault ships are already here," Phil tells us. "They're not directly on the other side of the asteroid. I can see them above the horizon. And Jupiter is huge. I can tell you one thing, we're a lot closer to Jupiter out here than to the asteroid belt."

"Jablonsky," I call, "find out which ships those are."

"Aye, Captain."

Really?

Brice laughs.

I decide Phil must be infecting the bridge crew with his pushy cynicism.

"How fast do you want to get there?" asks Penny. "We could pull some g's and arrive in five minutes if you want. If there's no hurry, we can take it slow and cruise on over in an hour or two."

"Hydrogen?" I ask. That's the variable on which the question depends. Heavy g acceleration and deceleration will burn through more of our H than if we take it slow. In fact, if we had a day to spare, we could give the grav plates a tiny bump and then frictionlessly coast the distance.

"We're down to just over half in our tanks," answers Penny. "Depending on where we go after this, we need to start thinking about getting a refill."

"We need it either way," I tell her. "That's the standing order. Wherever we go from here, make sure our flight plan includes enough hydrogen to make it back to earth."

"The standing order?" asks Phil, in a vague tone. He doesn't have that much overt aggression in him. He likes to chip away with snide comments. "Are we still in the SDF?"

"Adverb," says Penny, "don't start."

"He already started," says Brice.

It seems Brice is starting to feel comfortable with the social dynamic of our grav factory clique.

"Phil," I take a breath, "this isn't the—"

"Oh, crap!" he shouts.

"What?" I ask.

"They're under attack!" he shouts back. "Someone's shooting at them!"

Chapter 49

Minutes burn away along with our diminishing hydrogen stocks. We pick up speed and the platoon compartment flutters blue. Our inertial bubble is earning its pay today.

Rather then driving right at the asteroid, Penny has us riding an arc on a path that'll curve us around to the other side of the asteroid at high speed.

"Both ships are dead," Phil tells us, petulant inflections absent from his voice now that the war has fallen back into our laps. "They concentrated fire on the reactors in the stern of each one."

"Are the ships damaged otherwise?" I ask.

"No grav field emanates from either ship," Phil answers. "Otherwise, the forward sections are intact."

"Are the Trogs still shooting at them?" I ask.

"No," says Phil. "They've stopped."

"Prisoners?" speculates Penny. "The Trogs want to take them prisoner."

I'm willing to go with that guess, however, there's another possibility I want to keep to myself. What if it's not Trogs on that asteroid? What if we've been set up by the MSS in a sting operation to weed out disloyal bug-heads just like us? What if the MSS wants to collect live traitors to feed into their interrogation system so they can find more of us?

Granted, I can't think of a reason why we wouldn't have been arrested before we ever had a chance to board our ship.

A lifetime under Gray rule has left me with a healthy sense of paranoia.

"There's nothing we can do for them," Phil tells us.

"You want to leave your fellow grunts out there to die?" Brice spits into the comm.

"We don't have any armaments," Phil shoots back. "In case you haven't noticed, this rusty turd was built to harpoon those big Trog cruisers. How are we supposed to attack an asteroid base?"

"Phil," I tell him, "cut the chatter. Keep an eye on what's happening. I need to know everything I can about this place."

Jablonsky says, "I can set the computer up to record the feed from the exterior cameras."

"How quickly?" I ask.

"Doing it now."

That makes my next choice for me. "Penny, when you swing around that asteroid don't slow down. Bring us in close and fast. I want a good picture of what's on the ground. As soon as we're past, I want to jump."

"Bubble jump?" Brice asks. "That's dangerously close to the asteroid."

"Where to?" asks Phil. "I need a vector."

"The asteroid's gravity field will affect us," argues Brice, his voice calm and slow. He wants to make sure I understand what I'm asking.

I don't need the reminder of the danger, but I don't have time to weigh the pros and cons. "We're not going anywhere," I tell them all. "I just want the Trogs on the surface to see us make the jump. They need to think we're bubbling out to save our asses. I want them to believe we're not coming back." Same thing if it's the MSS down there.

"Gotcha," says Brice. Back to business. He understands. Whoever has control of the base on the other side of the asteroid, our one dinky ship and half-strength platoon can't take them in a frontal assault.

"Five or six seconds at light speed is all we need," I tell them. "That'll put us a million miles away, far enough they might not notice us pop back out again."

"Hey," says Phil, getting a little excited. "Two ships are coming up off the surface."

I try to see the gravity picture in my mind. I see a blurry image of the asteroid, a halo of smaller rocks randomly floating nearby, and the Rusty Turd's grav plates distorting everything.

Damn, Phil is good.

I admit, "I can't make them out."

"Give it a sec," says Phil. "Another second."

"Grav lifts," Penny tells us. "Just like the ones we rode to the shipyard."

"They're definitely going for the ships," I deduce out loud. "Penny—"

"Got it," she says.

I feel the ship's course alter slightly, and I know she understands what I want her to do.

We're accelerating again. I only have one suggestion. "If you can nail them both."

Blue waves burst over the bulkheads. Our inertial bubble strains and we all feel gravity buffet us with pulsing fluxes.

Phil is jabbering, trying to help Penny line up on our targets.

"I got it, Phil. I got it," she tells him.

Phil powers up the grav lens and brilliant blue fills the platoon compartment.

The ship shudders.

"They're lined up!" shouts Phil.

"Everybody hold on," Penny tells us. "Shifting power."

"Hold tight," Brice tells the grunts.

They're already tense in their seats.

"They see us!" shouts Phil.

"Nowhere to run, now." I hear a vicious smile in Penny's voice.

The ship lurches to a blinding flash of blue.

We've shattered the first shuttle.

Another flash follows as our grav lens obliterates the second vessel.

Bent steel and broken Trogs are thrown into space. The gravity field around our ship is in chaos.

"Got 'em!" shouts Penny.

"Jump!" I order.

"They're shooting," shouts Phil.

The ground guns are trying to hit us.

The ship shudders so hard I think it's going to come apart.

Electric blue light strobes through the cabin in waves as bright as when we hit the Trog cruiser in the battle over earth.

Voices are screaming over the comm, and the grav in the cabin is ratcheting up past two g's, then five.

Oh, no.

Without warning, the blue blinks away and we're suddenly surrounded by nothing but dead rust and the sick yellow glow of the cabin's weak bulbs.

The Rusty Turd is quiet, seemingly motionless.

We're in zero-g.

"We're out of bubble jump," says Penny.

Damn, that was quick.

"Nearly a million miles," confirms Phil, sounding proud. "Nine hundred and seventy-three thousand."

"And we're alive," says Brice, because he wants to make the point it wasn't a foregone conclusion.

He's right, but we did what we had to do. I glance right and left, and say, "To the bridge. We have an assault to plan."

CHAPTER 50

I'm starting to feel like I'm stuck in a déjà vu cycle: go to the bridge and make a plan, strap into a seat, ram something, go to the bridge and make a plan, strap into a seat…

Ugh.

Is this what glorious revolution really is? Repetitive tedium punctuated by frenetic moments of fighting to stay alive?

I kick things off. "Jablonsky, tell me we got good pics on our flyby."

He's looking at his monitor, scrolling frame by frame through a video of the asteroid's surface. "Once we hit the lifts, debris flew everywhere."

"Can you composite the good frames to give us a complete picture?" I ask.

"That's what I'm working on."

"We should wait a few minutes and then go back," suggests Phil. "If they send up more lifts, we can take those out, too."

"No," says Brice, as he comes through the doorway to the bridge. He glances at me. "No, sir. I disagree."

"So do I," I tell him.

"Why?" asks Phil.

Phil is great with gravity, but he doesn't have a good mind for war. Brice knows the answer, so I give him the nod.

"If we go back and attack," says Brice, "in the same way we just did, maybe we'll succeed. Maybe there's nothing they can do about it. However, if they *can* do something about it, they will. They won't be surprised like that again."

"So," I tell them all, "we need to surprise them a different way." I look at Brice for the next part because I suspect he won't like it. "We have to wait long enough they'll think we're gone for good."

"That's okay," says Brice. "I know why you're looking at me."

"Then you know if we go back too soon," I say, "they'll be waiting for us."

"Who's to say they won't be waiting for us anyway?" argues Phil.

"They will," Brice tells him. "The longer we wait, the more complacent they'll become."

"Or they'll kill more assault ships that come to the base and fall into their trap," says Phil.

"Unfortunately, that's right," I tell him. I look around at the others. "Those two ships they were firing on weren't burning hard to escape. They were hovering over the base, probably looking for a spot to land, and the Trogs on the ground opened up on them. Unfortunately, we can't just rush in. We're probably outnumbered. We know we're outgunned."

"So what, then?" asks Phil.

"That's what we need to figure out," says Brice.

"First things first," I turn to Phil. "There are plenty of smaller asteroids in the space near that big one."

"It had to be a mining operation," Brice tells us. "That's what they do. They put a base on some big rock and while they work on mining it for ore, they send out a tug or two to bring smaller asteroids and claim them for later."

"I don't understand," says Lenox. "I thought the base was in the asteroid belt. Aren't asteroids everywhere?"

"It's not like the movies," I tell her. "Asteroids out here are something like a half-million miles apart."

"The bigger ones," says Phil. "You could fly through the belt a thousand times looking out the window and never even know you were in it."

"Really?" she asks.

"Yeah," answers Phil.

"Around some of the bigger mining colonies," says Brice, "they might have a few hundred smaller asteroids corralled. Those places are like the asteroid belts you see in the movies with big hunks of rock everywhere you look."

I turn to Phil. "I want you to pick one of the bigger asteroids and plot a course for Penny to bring us around so we'll be flying in behind the smaller adjacent one. If we do it right, the Grays in that mining colony on the bigger rock won't be able to see us coming."

"They'll detect our grav signature," says Phil as he shakes his head.

He's almost right about that. Grays see gravity—hence mass—better then humans see light. "If we bubble jump, the grav shadow of that small asteroid won't hide us. However, like we already agreed, we have time. We'll come in at sub-light speeds, starting with an acceleration way out here where they're not likely to notice, and then slide in, decelerating very slowly when we get close."

"Okay, okay," says Phil, looking toward Penny. "We can do that."

"No problem," she agrees, "we'll use more hydrogen than you'll want to. I think it will work."

"Hydrogen's not a problem," I tell her. "Attacking this base will either get us all killed, or we'll find some miraculous way to succeed. Either we won't need the hydrogen because we'll all be dead, or there'll be plenty available from the colony's stores."

"That's my kind of optimism," says Brice.

Chapter 51

"I've pieced together a map," says Jablonsky. "If we were back on earth, and I had my computer, I could have put together a 3D rendering, but with what I have here..."

The ship is rife with shortcomings. I say, "We're lucky the Rusty Turd has any onboard computer systems at all."

"They spared every expense," agrees Brice.

Jablonsky says, "I'm sending a copy to each of your d-pads."

"Wait," Penny stops us as she laughs and pats the console. "The Rusty Turd. That's the name you're giving this beauty?"

"Fits," Phil mutters.

And that settles it.

Aside from the smallish monitors on the control consoles, the ship has no large screen we can all stand around and gawk at. Certainly no spiffy, three-dimensional, animated, full-color hologram like spaceships have in some of the old movies. I guess back in those days, with no constraint but the imagination, the realm of the future's possibilities was as expansive as the universe itself. Unfortunately, the future we wound up with gave us hyper-light travel, yet did so in a Spartan iron tube.

But I exaggerate.

It's salvaged steel and titanium. Iron would be too brittle.

Looking at his d-pad, Brice says, "I see lots of blurry spots on my map."

"I had to extrapolate," explains Jablonsky. "We were ramming through two lifts when we made our pass."

"Got it," answers Brice.

Pointing at the map, Jablonsky says, "The asteroid is oblong, around two kilometers in length, and three quarters of a kilometer at its widest. It's shaped like a big gnarly potato."

I'm examining the photo on my d-pad, as is everyone on the bridge. The first thing I notice is a canyon gouged erratically down the asteroid's long axis.

"They must have hauled out a shit-ton of this rock's ore already," mutters Phil, as he scrutinizes the image.

I notice the canyon's walls are too neatly cut for it to be natural. Then I spot mining equipment in the hole, and try to make a guess as to how many people it took to keep the mine producing. I don't have any idea.

Down at one end of the canyon, I see most of the colony's permanent structures. Dozens of habitat domes and industrial buildings rooted into the asteroid, no telling how deep. A couple of large hangar-style structures stand among the others, I guess housing equipment for separating the ore from the tailings, or whatever it is mining operations on asteroids do with the material they dig up before sending it back to earth.

The roofs of the hangars look sturdy and need to be so. They're piled with layers of crumbled stone a few meters thick. The roofs out here in the belt aren't like those back on earth, protecting from rain and hail, instead providing protection from gamma rays, micrometeors, and high-velocity space trash. Nobody wants to get a sub-light screwdriver through their skull while topping off the hydraulic fluid on a surface excavator.

A single mining tug is parked in a well-worn area near the center of the community. I can't tell whether it's operational. I have no reason to suspect it's not. With a drive array a quarter the size of the ones they put on the big Trog cruisers, it looks strong enough to push a good size asteroid at light speed, but not nearly big enough to move the rock it's parked on anywhere fast.

I spot three more grav lifts that I guess are functional. They've all been beat to hell. I've never seen one that wasn't. Workhorses of the human space industry, used for moving anything and everything from the surface up into space and back again, they've been produced on earth by the millions and they never seem to wear out.

I notice rows of equipment lined up in the bottom of the mining pit. Zooming in, I'm surprised. "In the floor of the pit, just where it starts to angle away from the colony, do you guys see what I see?"

"Ships?" says Brice, fingers scrolling on the screen on his arm.

Inside her helmet, Penny is nodding. "Look closely."

I'm looking at that part of the image, too. "They look like assault ships. Kind of like ours, but smaller."

"First-generation vessels?" suggests Brice. "Prototypes?"

"Fuck me," Phil nearly shouts. "There's got to be…" he's tapping the space above his screen as he counts, "fourteen ships?"

"That's what I see," Penny confirms.

"Keep zooming," says Brice. "See that one on the bottom of the image, closest to the wall? It's on its side. Look at what's painted by the airlock door."

Phil's fingering his d-pad and then freezes. He gasps.

I see it, too, a red flag with a big gold star in the corner and four smaller ones bordering it. The People's Republic of China.

"What the hell?" whines Phil.

What the hell, indeed.

Chapter 52

"They're all damaged," says Penny.

"This doesn't make sense," says Brice.

Phil takes a closer look. "Why are these ships here? I thought *we* were getting the first assault ships."

"Looks like maybe China got the first ones," I conclude. "Whatever else you're thinkin', that much is obvious."

"This is all bullshit," whines Phil. He stands up. "You all see that, don't you?"

Nobody responds.

Phil focuses on me. "This whole conspiracy thing, it's a trap. This whole thing about getting us out here to the asteroid belt, they're going to destroy us just like they did these other ships. It stinks so much I can't believe we fell for it." Phil is right in front of me. "Your contact with the Free Army was a spy. This whole thing is a ruse to weed out dissidents. That's what this is. I'll bet this whole war is some kind of bullshit scheme the Grays are using to manipulate their slaves to kill each other."

"That doesn't make any sense," argues Penny.

"Sure it does!" shouts Phil. "Don't you see? The Grays are trying to kill off the parts of the population that are a danger to them. Hell, maybe they think there are enough of them now that they don't need us, and they're using us to exterminate each other."

That theory shuts everybody up.

Could that be true?

Lenox is shaking her head and backing away. Whether it is true or not, the idea frightens her.

"I can't accept that," says Brice, though it's the weakest I've heard his voice yet.

"Think about it." Phil taps a finger on his helmet. "It makes sense, right?"

"It's a guess," I say. "A theory." I don't want to believe it, and I see Brice's expression through his faceplate and I can see the idea is slowly pushing him to rage. He's lost a lot of friends. He's seen them fight for the survival of the earth and he's seen them die.

Could it all be a waste?

"You've never told us who your contact with the Free Army is," says Phil. "All of us at the grav factory trusted you on that. You said it had to stay secret. I think it's time you tell us."

"Why?" asks Penny. "We're a half-billion miles from earth. What good will the information do you?"

"Maybe we know him," Phil pushes.

"You don't," I tell him.

"Maybe we can contact him. Beam a message back. Get some answers."

"You can't." I try to make it sound final.

"Our communication equipment's not that good," says Penny.

"Then we should go back!" shouts Phil. "We've been gone a long time, and that battle was a nightmare. We can show back up and tell them some bullshit about chasing a Trog cruiser. Hell, we took out those other three—"

"We?" asks Brice. "I don't remember a lot of you in that '*we*'."

"We," I tell him. "We all had our part to play."

"Who the hell cares?" Phil's escalating. "If we go back, we'll be heroes. Nobody's going to question us if we say we went chasing Trogs across the solar system." He looks around to gauge our mood, but doesn't realize that in typical Phil fashion, he's incapable of reading other people. "We find your contact with the Free Army and get some answers, or kill him, because it looks to me like he fucked us."

"You can't kill him." I see where this is going.

"Don't tell me he's not real," says Phil.

"Is he real?" asks Brice, looking for a place to focus a rage building inside.

"He was real," I tell them. "Now he's dead."

"Dead?" Phil nearly explodes.

"How?" shouts Penny, matching Phil's volume.

Lenox drops into a seat. "I think I'm going to be sick."

"The MSS arrested him this morning," I pause. Was it this morning? "Yesterday morning? I don't even know what day it is. I do know they arrested him, and you can be sure they've beaten every bit of information out he can give, and you can be sure he's dead."

Brice is nodding silently because he knows it's true.

"And you led us into this shit anyway?" shouts Phil. "Even though you knew the MSS would be after us."

"We all committed," I tell them. "We all agreed. No turning back."

"That's when I thought we'd still have a chance," yells Phil. "That's before I knew we'd be stepping into a trap, a trap we were doomed to fall into before we even left earth." Tears are brimming around Phil's eyes in the light-g, not rolling down his cheeks like they would be on earth. He's past anger and moving into despair. "I've known you my whole life and all you ever talked about was one day being a free man, like that's something—something better than the life we had. Well I followed you and I went along and I let you have your secrets and now I've let you drag me into this, to get me killed.

Dylan Kane, you fucked my wife and you fucked up my life. You toxic prick, you've murdered us all!"

"Phil," I say as he seats himself back in his chair and stares at the floor. "I don't know if any of that is true. Maybe some of it is. Maybe all of it. It doesn't matter. Whatever the Grays' reasons for doing what they're doing, they're sending us to the slaughter—not just us, but millions of us, maybe more than a billion." I point to Brice. "He's seen it firsthand." I look around at the rest of those on bridge. "We've all seen the pirated videos. We've watched our towns empty out—first, all the twenty-year-olds, then most of those in their thirties, then the teenaged boys and girls. They're all being murdered by this war. And before that, in space, killed in zero-g construction accidents or brain cancer from too much time out in the vacuum with nothing but these shitty orange suits to protect them from solar radiation. We're being used up."

I stop for a breather and try to put my rising anger aside. "That asteroid base with those Chinese ships, those other two ships we saw shot out of the sky, it doesn't change anything. If this is an ambush, I don't care. It doesn't change my mind one single bit. I put on this fucking shitty suit today and climbed into this rusty turd of an assault ship because I chose a long time ago I wasn't going to be a slave, and decided I'm not going to die for a bunch of Grays no matter what reason they have for it. I'll die for you, Phil. I'll die for Penny, and Brice and Lenox. I'll die for every grunt on this ship and I'll die for every human scattered on every asteroid and broken spaceship from here to earth and back again. I'll die if I have to, because goddammit, if nothing else, we're going to die anyway. Why do it for those little gray fucks? Let's die for each other, for our children, and for humanity."

I look around.

They're all speechless.

Still no standing ovation, though.

"The way I see it," I tell them, "is if we can figure some way to take that asteroid base, and there are more ships coming this way, we might not save the first few to arrive, but we can save the rest. And if we do that, then we have our Free Army. We all saw what we did today with our small army of two assault ships. If we can get six or ten or twenty, we can win this war. If we can win this war, we go back to earth and deal with our Gray masters."

Brice is the first one to speak. "I'll sign up for that."

"I've always been with you," says Penny, though she sounds like she's reading it from a script.

"I'm in," says Jablonsky.

I look at Lenox. She nods.

And, of course, Phil is last. He despondently nods.

"Phil," I say, "I'm proud of you."

He says, "That makes me feel wonderful."

It's a great day for sarcasm.

Chapter 53

We're all looking at the images on our d-pads again.

"On the edge of the pit," says Brice. "Right where it bends. Zoom in and tell me what you see."

"I noticed those, too," says Penny. "The dust on the surface around each of them has been disturbed."

I'm zooming and scrolling to get a look at the top edge of the canyon wall. I see it almost immediately. A perfect circle, roughly the color of the asteroid, but with an odd texture. Easily missed at a glance. It clearly doesn't belong. In the center of the circle is a small dark-colored hole. I've seen these before. This one looks like the railgun emplacements the Grays built on the moon all those years ago.

Brice concludes the same thing. "Railguns."

"Easy to miss if you're not looking for them," says Penny.

"Seven," counts Lenox. "That's how many I see. Some along the edge of the mine pit. Others among the colony buildings."

"I saw those when I was stitching the pictures together." Jablonsky apologizes, "I thought they were part of the mining operation."

Brice glances at Jablonsky. "Don't sweat it, that's why we're planning this together."

I zoom out to get a bird's-eye view, and the gun emplacements turn almost invisible. "Jill never had a chance."

"Anybody have any suggestions?" asks Penny.

I start. "Phil, given we want to return to the base without being seen and without bubbling all the way there, how long until we get back?"

"Twenty, maybe twenty-two hours," he answers. "Any faster and I think we'll create too big of a gravity flare and any Grays looking our way will spot us."

"Twenty-two it is." I look around at the others again. "That gives us plenty of time to put together our plan, rest up, and top off our hydro and cal packs."

"And load up our magazines," adds Lenox. "We found plenty of ammo on Juji. It's all for the single-shot rifles. We need to stuff our magazines with those slugs so we can fire on automatic."

"Get everyone to work on that," I tell her. "Let's all get some rest for a few hours and meet back here. We'll figure something out, then take that asteroid."

CHAPTER 54

Scooping up dark gray dust by the handful, I powder myself, working it into the composite fabric. Probably not good for the longevity of the suit, but what the hell do I care? Like the sarge who gave it to me said, I probably won't live long.

Especially with what I'm about to do.

The Rusty Turd is lying on the surface of the small asteroid, just behind me. We came in on the dark side of a stadium-sized hunk of rock, keeping the mass of oxidized nickel and iron ore between us and the potato-shaped asteroid on which the mining colony sits.

Now only a few miles of vacuum stands between us and our objective, and surprise is still with us.

As far as we can tell.

My squad of fliers is out here with me—Brice, of course, Silva, Mostyn, and Hastings—the only four left after we commandeered the Trog cruiser. Each of us is dusting ourselves in the asteroid's gray-brown powder, camouflaging our orange suits.

Hopefully, it's enough.

"What you've need to remember," says Brice, talking to the squad, "is Trog suits aren't that different. They've got a defensive grav field like ours. If you don't shoot them from the side or behind, your round will deflect." He pats the center of his chest. "They've got a big grav plate right here.

Our suits don't have those. When they power it up, nearly any shot aimed right at their chest won't make it through."

"What about those ghost Trogs?" asks Silva. "Seems like you couldn't hit 'em anywhere."

"They have more grav plates in their suits," guesses Brice. "Or they're more powerful. Nobody's ever gotten their hands on a dead ghost Trog to find out. Once that happens, we can cut the suit open and see what the defensive plate configuration is. Until then," Brice pats his weapon, "overwhelming fire is all you've got."

Silva pulls a Trog blade off her back and the intricate lines on its face glow blue. "These do the trick."

Brice looks at me, like it's my fault Silva is carrying a Trog disruptor, yet he's got one, too. "Don't depend on that thing. One-on-one, sure, why not? If you like even odds. What we saw on that ship—that was unusual. When they attack, they always come in big numbers."

"Maybe we need to stop waiting to be attacked," argues Silva.

That quiets everyone down for a second.

Brice takes it to heart. "Maybe. Maybe you're right."

"When we get over there," I tell them, "use your grenades when you can. We need to catch them in a crossfire when we can, so at least some of us are shooting at their flanks. Then we can kill them."

"If everything goes to shit," says Brice, "we meet back here and wait for pickup."

Nods all around.

"Everybody ready?" I ask.

Nods again.

"Let's go."

Using auto-grav set just strong enough to keep us on the surface, we skip away from our ship and slowly work across the asteroid.

Everyone's quiet while we move. We'll be fighting the Trogs again, and as a platoon, we lost half our number last time out. Like me, they're probably thinking about the randomness of war and hoping a railgun slug or a Trog blade doesn't come their way.

We make our way over the curve of the asteroid's horizon and stay between rocky protrusions twenty and thirty feet tall, giving us good cover.

Finally, Brice says, "I think this is as good a spot as any."

I look up. The potato-shaped asteroid is above us, with its narrowest end pointing toward the spot where we stand.

"When you kick off," I say, "be gentle with the grav. We don't want to arouse any Grays up there."

"Turn off your auto-grav before you go," says Brice, with a chuckle. "Or you'll fall back down."

A few of them laugh, imagining the embarrassment.

"On me." I jump, and I'm suddenly moving at escape velocity for the asteroid's micro-gravity. At least I hope so. Going into orbit around the rock isn't in my plan.

Brice, Mostyn, Hastings, and Silva follow.

It's hard to gauge my speed, though we're moving slowly.

I look around and feel a twinge of panic. The sun is several hundred million miles away and is bright, but tiny. Jupiter is ahead and off to the left, a three-quarter crescent of orange, tan, and gray stripes filling a large swath of sky. Many of its moons are easy to spot. Twinkles from the sun glinting off other asteroids spread into the distance, almost like the faint bones of a rainbow.

Everywhere else I see black, and billions of pinpricks of light, stars, and galaxies, all so far away—too far away.

Never have I felt so small, so unmoored.

"This isn't fun," says Hastings, I guess feeling it, too.

"Keep your eyes on the Potato," says Brice.

Good advice. I look forward.

We're on course toward the tip of the asteroid far from the mining colony. I'm hoping the massive rock's gravity will help pull us toward it, so if our aim is off a bit, it should self-correct.

I take a quick glance to make sure the others are coming along behind me.

Mostyn appears to be drifting off, separating.

"Mostyn," I say, "are you okay?"

"Yes, sir."

"Outer space can be disorienting." Yeah, sage advice I'm just figuring out for myself.

"I'm fine," she says, "I pushed off a little too hard with my left foot, I think."

"Don't use your gravity to correct, yet," I tell her. "Wait until we're closer. Heck, it might be the rest of us who are off course."

They laugh.

Good.

We're loosening up. I think we're ready for the fight to come but we're not obsessing about it.

"Look at Jupiter," says Silva. "My god, there's so much out here and we're fighting over one planet."

Despite Phil's theory about extermination, I say, "It's not the real estate, it's the slave labor they want—*us*."

"Most beautiful thing I've ever seen," says Mostyn. She's still gazing at Jupiter.

Turning back toward the asteroid we left, and then looking at the Potato, I guess we're halfway across. "I think we all need to adjust a little."

The women each take their looks and make their estimates.

"I think we'll all overshoot," says Mostyn.

"Very small grav corrections only," says Brice. "We don't want to alert them to our presence."

I nudge my suit with a tiny push, then look forward and back again. I think I'm on course.

A quick glance at the others tells me we're all moving in the same direction.

The potato is starting to loom large above, and I feel like I'm falling headfirst. "Don't panic," I tell my grunts as much as I tell myself. "Don't hit your grav to decelerate yet. Remember, we're coming in with the same velocity we kicked off the other asteroid with. When we get close, use your suit's grav to get yourselves oriented feet-down. It shouldn't hurt."

"Unless you land face-first," laughs Silva.

"I'll land better than you," says Hastings, and I guess the two of them must have some private joke about it.

Within fifty yards of the surface, we're not in a direct line of sight to anywhere along the top or bottom of the Potato. With all the stone and metal ores between us and our enemies, we're at a point where we can do pretty much anything with our suit grav and it won't be seen by Trogs or Grays.

Over the command comm, I notify the ship. "We're coming in on the surface. Give us five or ten and—"

"Jesus!" shouts Phil into the comm. "You see that?"

I look around and see nothing except black and stars. I spin myself around.

"I see it," says Penny.

I'm getting anxious. I still don't see it. I'm coming down on what looks like rough ground, and I need to keep an eye out where I land so I don't twist an ankle.

I hit, bend my knees, lose my balance, and fall.

My suit's deflective grav cushions my landing, and I bounce right back up.

"Nicely done," laughs Silva, just ten feet away, on her feet, rifle at the ready.

Brice is on the ground, looking at the sky. He heard Phil's warning, too. "Into that crater over there." He's directing the squad to a hole the size of a basement, and motioning them to take up positions facing outward to cover every direction.

"Phil," I'm still looking while I head toward the impact crater. "Tell me what's up."

"About twenty thousand clicks out," he says, barely able to contain himself. "On the other side of the Potato. Coming this way."

I try to get a sense of what's on the other side. It's like looking at the ground and trying to see into it. I'm good at working with g up close, but distant stuff is not my forte.

"It's a cruiser," Phil tells us. "It just phased out of bubble jump and it's burning heavy g's this way."

Chapter 55

Losers die when plans go awry.

I'm not going to be a dead loser.

I evaluate my choices, and select my path while my four Grunts in the impact crater cast anxious glances at me, talk among themselves, and keep an eye on their sectors.

They all know what's on the table.

Our lives.

But that's the way of it. I'm the officer.

Desertion has been an option for disheartened soldiers all through earth's history. Out here in space, it's not a choice. As enlisted personnel, their choices boil down to *trust me and follow*, or *frag me*.

Over the command comm, I tell Phil, Penny, Brice, and Lenox the plan. I don't ask for objections. This isn't a situation where time for debate exists. If we want to live, we need to move.

I switch to my squad's comm. I inform them of how we're going to handle it. We'll use surprise and our technological advantage to face our foes.

They're enthusiastic, having killed three Trog cruisers already. I think they believe in me, and they believe in each other. I hope that's enough.

We set out across the asteroid's surface, taking turns to move quickly from cover to cover.

Almost immediately, we divide into smaller fire teams. I take Silva to head up one side of the pit mine. Brice takes Mostyn and Hastings up the other.

Silva and I are leapfrogging, and moving too quickly for stealth. Time isn't a luxury we have.

"Maybe two more minutes," Penny tells me over the command comm.

I look into the black space overhead. I see the cruiser up there, a pale blur, small but growing as it races toward the asteroid colony. Glancing back down to my d-pad, I check our position against the map Jablonsky shared. I look for landmarks along the edge of the mine, and then look forward to gauge my location. "We're on schedule here. Alert me when you're ready to go."

"Will do. Penny out."

I tell my grunts, "We need to move this along."

With Silva close by, I point along the ragged curve of the mine pit. "The first emplacement should be two or three hundred yards ahead. Keep your eyes open for anything else out there."

We move over the landscape like we were born to it, tuned to the asteroid's gravity, amplifying it enough for us to run and leap over obstacles, yet not enough to hinder mobility.

We cover the ground and move into position with twenty seconds to go.

Brice comms me. "We're ready."

"We just arrived," I answer. I'm maybe twenty feet from an emplacement. A quarter way around the pit's perimeter, Silva is positioned behind a pile of mining debris.

Chunks of rock are piled in a circle about fifteen feet across to mark the hole. A canopy the color of the asteroid is stretched in a frame over the top, leaving a gap of a few feet around the edge. Through the gap, standing in the center of the pit, I see the barrel of a railgun, and I know down inside,

Trogs are at the ready, or maybe lounging and waiting for orders.

Either way, I know they're down there.

"Are we on time?" I ask Penny.

"Ready," she tells me.

"On my mark." I look at my watch and count the seconds. We don't want to start our attack early and give the incoming cruiser any warning of what's coming, because the cruiser is the biggest danger.

I pull the pin on a hand grenade, one of the old-fashioned kind, chemical explosives and steel. "Five. Four. Three. Two. Go!"

Even through the small asteroid's dense mass, I sense my ship's gravity flare.

Penny just poured the ship's max reactor output through the plates.

I throw my grenade into the gap between the canopy and the edge of the short, rubble rampart, and roll behind a mound of stone. I hear Silva grunt as her rifle kicks. She's shooting. A Trog must have looked out of the hole when my grenade flew in.

The ground below me shudders a little as my grenade detonates. No sound, of course.

That's one of the dangers of using grenades in space. There isn't an audible explosion to let you know it's gone off. That, and the shrapnel has effectively infinite range.

I raise my rifle and leap out from behind my stone to see Silva coming to the ground near the far edge of the gun pit at the end of her own leap.

She's aiming into the hole through the torn canopy and firing.

By the time my feet hit the ground again, she tells me, "Clear!"

I train my weapon at the Trogs inside anyway, scanning from one to the next, looking for signs of life. All I see are eleven motionless bodies with gases and blood spewing from holes in their suits.

"Pit one, neutralized," I say into the comm, trying to keep the rush of excitement out of my voice.

"Pit two, down," says Brice. "On to three."

I hear the squad breathing hard as they take up a run to cross several hundred yards.

"We should go," Silva tells me.

I point into the pit. Worst case scenario. "Door."

Silva glances inside. She doesn't see it.

"Come around to this side. There, along the bottom edge." I'm pointing for her benefit, while looking above us to see how the plan is proceeding.

Streaking across the spangled black, my ship is engulfed in blue jellyfish tentacles produced by grav plates straining to push it at max acceleration.

Farther away but still visible is the cruiser, just starting to respond.

It shimmers in blue, and bursts star-bright as I watch.

"They're trying to get away."

If Penny's course is true, if Phil can puzzle through the complexities of the cruiser's defensive gravity pattern and its evasive maneuvers, the Trogs won't make it.

Railgun slugs glow bright as they shoot up from the surface. The gunners in the five remaining pits are quicker to react than I anticipated.

No time to worry about the door at the bottom of the gun pit. I unload a dozen rounds into the weapon's dedicated control mechanisms to disable it, and turn to Silva. "Fly with me." I adjust my suit grav and jump.

Chapter 56

I'm flying over the pit mine, taking a shortcut across a bend, pushing myself fast.

Silva is behind me, moving slower, struggling to keep the line. She's not doing too badly considering she can't see gravity fields the way I can.

I'm heading for the second gun pit. It's hurling slugs into space at an alarming rate considering the manual load technology of the Trog's guns.

I glance up as I near the wall of the canyon, just to check, and I see my ship's grav lens field blazing brilliant as it pierces the Trog cruiser's innermost gravity defenses, tearing a hole through the bridge and burying itself in steel as huge geysers of gas burst outward, exploding debris in every direction.

"They got it!" I shout over my squad comm.

I'm elated.

I need to focus.

That's only half the battle.

I aim my weapon at the pit and fire, trying to grav compensate for instability generated by my weapon's rounds as I send them into the Trog hole.

Hypervelocity projectiles hit the stony walls and smash into the railguns' sturdy tube, vaporizing into pure energy and exploding in a hail of glowing shrapnel into the pit and out through the canopy.

"Kane!" Silva shouts, zipping past below me.

I stop shooting as I see her make a landing forty meters from the pit, hitting the ground running, grenade in hand.

I'm several hundred meters off the surface of the asteroid, and I reverse my gravity field to drift back down, keeping my weapon trained on the gun emplacement. I decide I'm not going to land.

"Pit two neutralized," comes Brice's voice. "On to number three."

Damn, his team is quick.

Silva's grenade explodes in the gun pit and in a flash she's on the edge, firing down. "Two down on our side!" she tells me. "This one's got a door at the bottom, too."

Without a doubt, they're all connected by tunnels. Into the squad channel, I tell them, "Keep an eye out, they may come at us from behind!"

Changing course, I keep an altitude of a hundred meters above the asteroid, speeding toward a spot I've picked well above the next gun pit, which has stopped firing now that its target is buried in the bow of the cruiser.

"Look out!" Silva screams.

A blinding streak of lightning flashes my vision. I feel heat through my suit. I blink.

"Railgun!" Silva continues, "Shooting at you. Get down to the surface!"

I don't even look around to see which gun is trained on me, I juke hard in the first direction I can make my suit's grav take me, then I dive into the canyon.

Another searing round streaks through the vacuum near where I was just a second before.

Missed. Ha!

I'm between the walls of the mine pit and I'm reversing my grav again to keep from splattering myself into goo when I hit the bottom.

"On the way to that gun shooting at you," Brice tells me. "You okay?"

"They missed," I answer.

"We're taking Trog fire," Mostyn tells us calmly.

"I'm going wide," Hastings tells her.

"From the Trogs in the pit?" I ask, as I maneuver toward the canyon wall.

"Yes," answers Brice.

Good.

I think.

It's gunners defending themselves, not the garrison.

I glance again at the cruiser. Our ship is still locked in the hole it tore through the bridge. Blue gravity waves are pulsing wildly. Penny accomplished her mission and disabled the cruiser—it won't be flying again. The things are all built to Gray specifications, and that means no backup control system. It's all right there on the bridge.

However the little gray trolls evolved, they just never got that good at war.

"Trying to break free," Penny tells me. "Could use a little help with the grav, Phil."

"I'm trying!" Phil sounds frantic.

I dial back the command comm.

"Suppressing fire!" orders Brice.

"Got it," answers Mostyn.

They're coordinating an assault on their gun pit. With our automatic weapons, any two of us can maintain fire superiority over a few dozen Trogs. And that's if they all carried railguns, which they don't. Most prefer disruptors.

"I'm almost there," Silva tells me.

"I'm coming up over the edge of the canyon." I land my feet on the ground and sync my grav with the asteroid. My weapon is at my shoulder and I'm shooting at the pit as I take my first steps. A Trog too slow to react to my appearance is pierced by several hypervelocity slugs, and he's thrown back into the pit through an expanding haze of his own blood.

Half a second later, he's flying out of the hole again, as the air in his suit rockets through the punctures, propelling him away from the asteroid.

I don't pay him any attention. He's dead.

"I need a sec," Silva tells me as she runs up a small rise to find a better angle on the gun pit we're attacking.

I come to a stop as I listen to Brice, Mostyn, and Hastings coordinating their fight.

Glowing hot rounds spear bright across the asteroid's gray surface from Silva's position. They spall shards of hot metal off the gun's barrel, flying into space, and into the pit. "Go now," Silva tells me.

I jump up and run. When I'm a dozen long strides closer, she stops shooting.

In seconds, I'm at the edge of the pit, looking down through the shredded tarp, raking my rifle across the moving Trogs inside, not taking the time to decide whether they were busy dying or not. It's quicker to put enough slugs through their bodies to make double sure.

"Next one," I tell Silva.

"We're tied down here," says Brice. "We've got ten or twenty Trogs trying to flank us."

The colony's garrison is joining the fight.

"Can you handle them?" I ask. In the first version of the plan, we'd be calling in the ship to disembark the rest of the platoon by now. Unfortunately, they're stuck up there in the Trog cruiser.

"Got it so far," Brice answers.

"If you get in trouble, retreat."

"I'm not still alive because I'm a hero," he laughs.

I think that's a lie, but I laugh, too.

Chapter 57

The last gun emplacement is among the colony's surface buildings.

As I hurry toward it, I see it's directing fire toward the space in front of the crippled cruiser. They're not shooting close enough to hit anything, but I'm guessing they've already deduced our ship is trying to power itself free and back out.

If Penny gets the ship moving and that gun is still firing, they'll take a hit.

I yell, "Silva, we gotta do this fast!"

I comm Penny to warn her about the gun firing at them. I receive no response, only the crackle of static, interference from wrecked metal, chaotic grav fields, and electrical cables shorting out and sending currents in every direction.

I can only hope Phil senses the gravity of the rounds blazing past their stern before Penny wrestles the assault ship free.

Silva is moving at a run in bounding leaps past a big boxy tug that looks like it's spent a few rough decades moving asteroid-size hunks of rock around the solar system. She's heading toward the nearest building in the colony, some kind of structure housing mining machinery is my guess. It's a shed, a big one, not airtight. I see flashes from the rounds leaving the railgun emplacement through the gaps in the sheets of metal on the walls.

Past that, to the right, deeper into the village, I see a dimly glowing dome. It's made of smart glass. No other transparent material could hold up to the vacuum in pieces that large. Nothing else could stand the continual rain of micrometeors and solar radiation.

Out of an airlock on the side of the dome, five Trogs emerge, railguns in hand, looking for targets.

"Silva," I call, "you've got Trogs to your right, just past the tall shed you're running toward." Seeing the odds of the fight changing, I decide I don't have time to wait for the airlock to cycle again and burp another handful of Trogs onto the surface. And then another. There's no telling how many are down there. There's no guessing how many airlock exits the Trogs will be coming out of.

Things are going to turn a whole new flavor of shitty if we can't take that last anti-ship railgun out and transfer the rest of our platoon down here.

Time for bold moves.

I let go of my gun, yank two frag grenades, and pull the pins as I launch myself—Superman style—toward the collection of surface buildings.

Not risking altitude and the fire I'll take from Trogs with railguns on the other side of town, I take just as big a risk and skim the surface, seven or eight feet up, pushing my suit to accelerate between two buildings, setting myself on a course for that gun. I call to Silva. "Keep those Trogs busy for a moment."

She's nearing the shed as I whiz by.

I feel my speed as I pass the hangar and see a pair of mining vehicles, giant and spidery, parked in my path.

I swerve hard to avoid impaling myself, and cut back onto my course as I pass them. I see the gun emplacement just ahead.

A Trog spots me, too, and I see his eyes widen through the tint of his faceplate as I aim right for him.

Like any thinking animal with a survival instinct, with a high-velocity something coming at him, he ducks into the hole where he's standing, instinctively dodging out of harm's way.

In the half-second he spends figuring out what the thing is speeding toward him, I reach the edge of gun pit and throw the two frag grenades into the lookout hole where the Trog guard just disappeared.

I brake hard, with blue grav lines enveloping me as I spin to get my feet beneath me. A heartbeat later, I skid on the asteroid's gritty surface, coming down on my belly, pointing my rifle back toward the railgun hole, and I stop.

Thirty meters from the emplacement, I'm ready to fire.

The Trogs in the pit are probably just now realizing what fell in with them.

Another second is all I have to wait. I see a flash as the camo canopy shreds. Fragments of steel shoot into space.

I'm up and on my feet, rushing the hole.

Once at the edge, I fire even as I look, only caring to hit the bodies with blood already foaming out of the tears and wounds.

I stop. Evaluate.

Nothing alive.

"Silva, this one's done."

"I could use some help here!" she shouts back.

I fire a few dozen rounds into the railgun's targeting mechanisms and blast off again, taking the risk to fly low across the surface, knowing in the stark shadows and shades of gray and black, I might come upon a squat object and not identify it until it's too late to turn. "Silva, stop shooting. Take cover!"

I zip around the curve of the glass dome, tight and fast, seeing the handful of Trogs spreading out and moving toward Silva's position behind the shed. On full auto, I spray them from the back as I fly by, and don't see the Trogs just exiting the airlock until I'm on them.

We collide.

Suit to suit, body to body.

Everything is spinning, and I'm rolling across the surface, being pushed by my suit's grav fields that are compensating too late and too wrong.

I slam something hard that knocks the air out of my lungs, rattles my brain, and sends my eyes spinning in their sockets.

Chapter 58

My senses come back slowly, but when they do, I see Silva staring through my faceplate. She's panicky, yelling. "You okay? You okay?"

Seems like the kind of question that answers itself to the negative when there's no response.

She shakes me. "You okay?"

"Yeah?" I'm not sure. I feel like an elephant stepped on me. "Sure."

"Can you walk?"

How the hell would I know? I'm not entirely sure I'm even breathing.

Wait. Of course I am.

I know because it hurts when my chest expands.

"The Trogs," I remember. I turn my head to look around.

Oh, good. My neck works.

I move my fingers and toes.

Thank God. Not paralyzed.

"Can you walk?"

Silva turns her attention to my d-pad. She keys the medical alert button and my screen flashes to a diagnostic menu. I feel the suit's inner liner contract in places, testing resistance while biosensors measure pain. I know it's sampling my urine, checking my heart rate and blood pressure.

"You're not bleeding," she tells me. "The inner suit's intact."

"Really?"

Her expression turns to anger and she pounds the d-pad.

"Ouch."

"Sorry." She looks at me, frustration on her face. "Damn things says you're in perfect health for a twenty-two-year-old woman on her period."

I laugh. How could I not? Some things are just too funny. "At least I'm not pregnant."

Silva laughs, too.

I sit up. "Where are the Trogs?"

"You may have a concussion."

I shake my head. I don't feel concussed.

She's back to querying my d-pad. "The suit says you took an impact that could have caused a concussion."

"Just rattled my brains," I tell her, as I start to get to my feet.

"Don't." Her hand presses down on my shoulder to keep me in place.

"We need to get back in the fight." It hurts to breathe, but all my body parts seem to be working, my brain seems to be coming back online.

"You need a medic."

"I don't." I push past her restraint and stand up, shaky in the knees and feeling lightheaded. It's the adrenaline I tell myself. It's got to be just that. I reach down and take up my rifle.

"You're wobbling."

"Gravity."

Silva frowns.

It sounded like bullshit to me, too. I tell her, "It's passing. Where are the Trogs?"

Silva keys out of my medical evaluation screen. "I guess if you can stand, you're not going to die, at least not right now. You might have internal injuries."

"Then I'll die in a few hours," I tell her, looking around. "Nothing we can do about that unless we take this mining colony and they have a pressurized medical facility with a real live doctor."

"Or you'll injure yourself worse and bleed out through your ass."

"I'll just max power to my suit's recycler and I'll be fine."

"I didn't realize you were so full of shit." Silva's being very protective, and I can't figure out why.

I respond by being stubborn. "Let's get this done."

"Yes, sir." Full dose of sarcasm.

My kind of girl. Too bad I have a wife.

Silva turns and points to the airlock where the Trogs were coming out of the glass dome. "Mostyn tossed a grenade in. Maybe it'll discourage them from using that exit."

Glancing around, I see the bodies of ten Trogs scattered about. "How long was I dazed?"

"Unconscious."

"Whatever," I tell her. "How long?"

"A minute? Two? Three, maybe."

"Damn, you ladies work fast."

"Well, Mr. I'm Fine, if you had the sense to turn your comms back on, you'd know what the hell was going on."

I accept the rebuke without protest. "That gun Brice's team was attacking?"

"Out of action." She shakes her head. "That's why Mostyn was here to help with the airlock."

I smile and nod. *Good job.* I toggle on the squad comm and listen.

Brice's team has just killed another handful of Trogs outside a surface-level storage building. Looking at Silva, I say, "Lead the way."

With a sigh, she starts.

"Faster," I tell her. "I'm not that injured."

She picks up the pace, bounding across the rock, not as quickly as I saw her moving when she was on the attack, but not so fast as to leave me behind.

I'm slow. My head is swimming. A handful of aspirin and a few days on my back might be what I need. That'll only happen if we take this mining colony.

We round an outcrop of jagged rock and come upon the other three. They're arrayed outside a warehouse airlock. Trog bodies are on the ground around them. Helmets are scattered everywhere—not the misshapen Trog ones—but high-forehead human helmets.

Worse, down one side of the building, stacked like chopped wood and frozen in their death poses, are humans in militarized versions of orange construction suits.

I decide in that moment I don't care if the Trogs own the Grays, are their allies, or are slaves just like us. They're murderous pigs.

Chapter 59

I notice as I hurry toward the building's airlock, letting my anger run away with my judgment, the corpses piled against the wall are in their full suits, helmets included.

It doesn't make sense.

Where did the scattered helmets come from, then?

When I get close to the other three, I ask, "What's the plan?"

Brice is surprised I'm still alive. "What's *your* plan?"

I glance at the helmets on the ground. I'm hoping they came from prisoners and I'm guessing bodies are all we'll find. "We need to see what's inside."

Silva laughs, and so do Mostyn and Hastings. Silva says, "That's why he's the major."

"Let me finish," I tell them. "Brice, you wait out here with Mostyn and Hastings and keep guard. Me and Silva will go in."

Silva starts in, "You're in no shape—"

"No," Brice tells me. "You two stay out here." He turns to Hastings. "Stay with them. I'll take Mostyn. " Looking at me, he says, "If things get dicey inside, we need to be at one-hundred-percent."

"Fine." I turn to face the other buildings in the compound and raise my rifle as I drop to a knee among the field of helmets. More Trogs will be coming. "Make it quick."

Brice and Mostyn hurry to the door.

Silva takes the right flank. Hastings takes up a defensive position to my left. Each of us has a wide field of fire.

Brice is already opening the outer airlock door.

I drop down to my belly. When the Trogs come, I hope I'll look like a discarded helmet or a wayward corpse, until I surprise them with a hail of hypervelocity titanium-wrapped lead.

"I've got movement," says Silva.

That was quick. But then again, we are invading their little asteroid fortress.

I look. I don't see anything.

Silva is down on her belly as well. "Coming up past that outcrop."

Still looking. The rocks are blocking my view.

"We're inside the airlock," says Brice, "waiting for it to cycle."

"Tell me when you have them in sight," says Silva, talking to me. "Thirty, maybe a few more. Packed close like they do. A few are stalking along close to the rock."

"I see one peeking this way," I tell her. "We'll open fire when we can both target them."

I scan across what I can see of the compound, looking for other movement, knowing once the shooting starts, I'll likely not think to look for flanking Trogs, I'll be too busy trying to stay alive. "Hastings, anything?"

"Nothing on this side," she answers.

"Airlock at pressure," Brice tells us. "I'm ready to open the inner door. Ready, Mostyn?"

"Ready," she answers.

"You see the Trogs, yet?" asks Silva.

"Got 'em," I answer, and the abstraction of the number turns concrete and deadly. Odd, how the two things can feel so different. "Brice, Mostyn, keep your ears open. We might get into trouble out here."

Might? Inside my head, I'm laughing.

There's no might. Things are going to become interesting.

"Full auto, pray and spray," says Silva. "We'll start on the right, shoot down my line."

Good thinking.

If we double up our fire on the same targets, we can overwhelm their suits' grav deflectors. "I'm game. On three?"

"Three," she says, "two, one."

A light show of glowing metal flares out from our positions, sweeping back and forth across the line of Trogs, deflecting in every direction.

The Trogs have no time to react. They're falling and exploding—literally exploding—as suits and chests decompress through holes just torn. Arms are ripped away and more than one head spins off into space.

They're all down in moments.

Many are squirming.

Dying or knocked over?

I don't know.

Silva targets and fires single shots at those still moving.

I scan around for more Trogs, and catch one gawking from the edge of the rocky outcrop. I fire just a second too late. He's back behind cover. "At least one more behind the rocks."

"Many of these are still alive," says Silva.

I roll to my left, three or four times to shift my position. I'm still in the garden of white helmets. "Shift," I call to Silva as I move.

A second later, the Trog behind the outcrop pops out, aims his gun, and sends a hunk of metal right at the spot I just left. Shards of rock explode when the round hits, and the helmets tumble around.

"I thought they were all terrible shots," I tell the others.

"Most are," someone responds.

The Trog is working the bolt on his rifle to load another round as three more Trogs come running out from that side of the rock.

Moving targets are harder to hit, and I ignore them for a second—it's the one with the gun I want. "I've got four charging me!" I call into the comm. I fire.

The Trog with the railgun takes a glancing shot on his shoulder and spins away out of sight. A wound, but only for a moment. He'll decompress and die.

Silva is firing at the other three Trogs when I adjust my aim and help her finish them off.

Our automatic weapons make all the difference.

And just as that happy thought crosses my mind, the price for automatic fire comes due.

A beep sounds inside my helmet and a small red warning light flashes.

"What the hell?"

"What?" asks Silva, alarmed.

"Warning." I'm looking down at my suit, feeling around for holes, taking deep breaths, thinking I might be decompressing. "A beep. A red light."

"On the left edge of the faceplate?" asks Silva.

"Yeah."

"Hydrogen pack," she tells me. "You've burned through yours."

"What the hell? It's a fresh pack." And the damn yellow warning light never came on to tell me it was low.

"Brice told me the hydro level indicators don't work on half of them."

No wonder we're losing this fucking war!

I reach down for my backup pack strapped to my thigh.

Gone.

Shit!

Must have been knocked off in…

Oh hell, it doesn't matter where I lost it.

"Here," says Silva, "take mine." She's already removed it from its mount. She tosses it over.

Halfway across, it explodes as it's hit by a red-hot railgun round.

I can't believe it!

"That's the luckiest shot I've ever seen," says Silva.

Lucky because they were probably aiming at one of us.

Still, bad luck for me.

CHAPTER 60

Silva fires three more bursts. "Let me do the shooting unless there's a Trog on you."

That's not a solution.

"Hastings," she calls, "you got an extra hydro pack?"

"I only brought one with me," she answers. "I picked up a cal pack by mistake. Brice and Mostyn will be out soon. One of them might have some H."

Ugh.

"I can't raise them," says Silva.

"Me neither," says Hastings.

"It's probably the building that's interfering," I tell them, hoping they're not both already dead inside.

"It's okay," says Silva. "You've still got a few minutes."

The ubiquitous hum from my backpack suddenly stops. I notice it for its absence.

Now I know I have maybe five minutes.

"I've got Trogs!" says Silva. She fires.

"Some here, too," says Hastings. "I've got 'em!"

With no power, it's not just air I'll run out of. My suit will lose heat, and my weapon won't fire. I'm useless.

I look over my shoulder at the warehouse, willing the airlock door to swing open.

Is there atmosphere inside?

Are there Trogs in there?

I spot the feet of the bodies stacked along the outer wall—dead soldiers, all in their suits.

Glowing rounds streak past us, past the warehouse, and into space. They're not even close to hitting anything.

"I can't see where that fire is coming from," I say.

"Back toward the center of town," answers Silva.

That's too far away for most Trogs to hit a target.

I have to make a choice.

I slowly stand, careful not to push too hard. An excited jump might send me into orbit. Now, with no suit grav, I have to control my movements manually. I low-g skip to the side of the warehouse, round the corner, and I scoot back along the stacks of corpses, moving far from the line of fire. "I'm checking these bodies for a hydro cell," I tell Silva and Hastings, so they won't think I ran away.

Selecting one of the many suits, I stop and grab its hydro pack. I twist and tug until it's free. Two seconds later, I've popped off my empty and put the new cell in its place.

I wait.

Nothing happens.

No reactor hum.

No breath of fresh air.

Damn.

I try another pack, switch it out, same result.

I try a third and realize the mistake I'm making—all of these packs would have continued to burn through hydrogen until they ran out of juice. They wouldn't have stopped when the person in the suit died.

Two hundred bodies, and not one of them has a good hydro cell.

Think.

How many minutes before my suit's atmosphere turns bad. Will it be suffocation or hypothermia that kills me?

The suit already feels cool on my skin.

I call to Brice and Mostyn.

Still no answer.

At some point, I need to risk the airlock.

I scan up and down the pile of bodies. They're all Chinese SDF recruits from those older ships shot down and dumped in the mine pit. I don't see extra hydropacks strapped to their thighs, which means they didn't have the automatic weapons we did.

Still, there had to be a heavy weapon of some sort in each platoon—larger caliber, higher muzzle velocity, more energy to run. All of our SDF railguns are powered off our packs, and a heavy weapon would require extra hydro cells. I drop to my knees and start sorting through the maze of frozen legs.

Searching.

Scooting.

Searching.

Success.

I see a hydro pack wedged between two frozen legs and I start prying it out. "How's it going out there, Silva?"

No answer. Of course not, no power. Dead radio.

I seat my hydrogen pack in its cradle, and instantly feel the micro-reactor's familiar buzz.

Air flows in my suit.

"I'm good to go," I call over the comm." I'm already running. "I've got a full cell. How's it going out there, Silva?"

"Holding my own," she tells me. "They're massing back toward the town center. I'll be in trouble in a minute."

"How many?" I ask.

"One or two hundred?" she's guessing. That's the Trog's favorite tactic. Mass their troops—everyone they've got—and then bonsai charge.

"Brice! Mostyn!" I call into the comm. "I need you out here." Just in case they can hear.

No response.

Not good.

Not good at all.

"I can't raise them, either," says Silva, staying surprisingly calm, considering what she's facing.

"Hastings," I ask. "Can you help her?"

"I have a dozen at least," she answers, "among all those pieces of equipment over there."

She needs to protect our flank.

I try to raise the ship on the command comm. Static.

Partially exposed, I stop at the corner of the building and see the mass of Trogs back toward town.

They spot me, too.

Rounds fly in my direction.

I kneel and do a quick check for ammunition. One magazine in my rifle, nearly empty, and two more full mags to spare. One full magazine in my pistol. "How are you set for ammo?" I ask Silva.

"Enough," she answers.

"Brice? Mostyn?" I check again.

"Here," Brice answers.

"Where are you?"

"In the airlock," he answers. "Coming out. No signal inside the building."

"Careful," I tell him. "Trogs are massing a few hundred meters back toward the center of the base. They're shooting and they'll be coming this way."

"Are you up for this?" Brice asks. "You okay?"

"Bruised is all," I reply. "I'm good to go."

"The airlock is finished cycling," says Brice. "Let me know when it's safe to exit."

"Now's good!" shouts Silva.

I peek around the corner and see Brice and Mostyn run out of the airlock door. They take up prone positions among the empty helmets.

"This isn't a defensible spot," says Silva.

"That's okay," I tell her. "I know it. Hopefully, the Trogs know it, too. I have a plan."

I explain quickly.

Moments later, Brice and Mostyn start firing a slow, steady stream of rounds in the direction of the mob.

I'm running away and Silva is beside me.

We're in danger of being shot in the back, but the Trogs need to see us flee.

Chapter 61

"Don't be long," says Brice.

"Don't shoot us," I say, grinning as I leap and push power to my grav plates, flying off the asteroid's surface with Silva right behind me.

"It's time to see what this suit can do," I tell her as I accelerate and turn to follow the curve of the Potato.

Silva is straining to keep up, so I slow down. We don't have a lot of time to pull this together but we need to arrive at the same time. Probably.

In seconds, the mining colony is out of sight. The asteroid's surface is a few hundred feet below us and it feels like we're rocketing into the void with nothing but stars shining a hundred trillion miles away. We're aiming to power through a tight orbit around the narrow trunk of the asteroid.

"Holy Jesus!" shouts Silva.

"Thank God for catheters," I tell her as we pick up speed. "No wet pants!"

We're beneath the Potato, I think, on the opposite side of the asteroid from the mining colony.

"ETA?" asks Brice, barely audible over the crackling connection.

"Almost there." I call back.

Silva and I are burning hard. We come over the horizon to see the mining colony's building from the opposite side relative to where we left Brice, Mostyn, and Hastings.

"They've split and are attacking us from two directions," Brice tells me.

"We'll be behind them in ten seconds."

"I don't see you!" shouts Mostyn.

"I see your rounds," I call back. "We'll stay out of your line of fire."

Silva veers to the right and I swerve left. She's going to take one of the groups from the rear flank and I'm taking the other.

I keep my altitude, about a hundred meters up.

Silva heads for the ground. She doesn't feel comfortable enough yet with her suit's gravity to maintain stability while shooting her weapons.

I can fire from above with no problems, until the Trogs spot me. Then I'll be in trouble. There's nothing to hide behind up in the sky.

Below and ahead of me, Brice, Mostyn, and Hastings are still prone among the helmets. Hastings is covering the left flank, but Trogs are starting to gather in numbers among the pieces of equipment over there. She's picking them off, one by one. Soon they'll have enough numbers to feel confident, and they'll charge.

Silva is nearly in position.

I'm where I want to be. I say, "I'm going hot." I open fire on the Trogs from behind, where they're weak. I burn quickly through the partial magazine in my gun, while keeping myself stable enough for my slugs to land mostly among the Trogs below.

At least two dozen of them go down.

Mostyn is firing at the same group. She's switched to auto and is spraying them in quick bursts.

As I'm trading my magazines, the Trogs have stopped creeping forward and they're looking behind them and to the sides. I make the guess that these basic infantry types aren't as bright as the ones who'd manned the anti-ship emplacements. They're all thinking two-dimensionally and none—at least not one with a rifle—has thought to look up to see me.

That'll change as soon as I start firing again. A spray of glowing rounds leaving the barrel of my weapon will show them all exactly where I am.

I fire again.

They fall. Some of them come apart. Most of them don't look dead because of the air escaping through the holes in their suits, jerking their bodies back and forth.

The ones that turn to face me get it in the back from Mostyn—the ones that keep moving toward her get it in the back from me.

When I stop firing, some of the Trogs are running away. Most are dead or writhing.

"I've got this now," Mostyn tells me.

No doubt. Only mop-up work left on this flank.

"We could use some help," says Silva, coming back onto the comm.

I'm already zooming in her direction, and see the other half of the mob was mauled just as badly as the first half and Silva is gone.

"I've got these," Brice tells me, as I fly past.

A flash of red over by the equipment yard catches my eye and I see Silva standing atop a bulldozer, shooting into the gap beside it.

Before I arrive, she leaps and lands on a stack of conveyor sections.

She fires into another gap as railgun rounds sail past her from another direction. She doesn't see them.

"Behind you!" I yell.

She leaps again.

I come down on another stack of conveyor sections and point my rifle into the gap where the shots aimed at Silva just emerged. A handful of Trogs are down there, still looking in the other direction. Four are carrying disruptors. One has a rifle and I cut him in half with a burst through the back. His innards explode into the vacuum and splatter his comrades, who barely have time to react before I shred them, too.

It takes us several minutes to clean them up, at least all we can find, leaping from one piece of equipment to the next, and shooting down on the Trogs from above.

"Any more?" Brice asks.

Everyone responds to the negative.

"Everybody all right?" I ask.

"Good," answers Silva, though I can see her twenty meters from me, looking around for targets.

"I'm good," replies Mostyn.

"Bueno." says Brice.

"Me, too," adds Penny.

Penny?

"What?" I look up, finally having a second to take my mind off the battle on the asteroid's surface.

The Trog cruiser is drifting past the end of the Potato and smashing into one of the huge asteroids as atmosphere spews through the breaks in the hull and random blue grav fields slide across its surface.

Looking higher, I see our ship coming down toward us. I tell Penny, "We could use some reinforcements."

Chapter 62

We're standing in front of the warehouse looking at Hastings's body. A huge gash is cut down into her chest, starting where the shoulder meets the neck. Her heart stopped beating minutes ago, but the vacuum of space is still sucking blood out of the wound.

Mostyn sounds like she's choking back tears as she walks around in the garden of loose helmets, inexplicably collecting an armload of them.

"What gives?" asks Silva.

Brice provides the answer. "All these helmets out here on the ground, they belong to people inside."

"Alive?" Silva is shocked. "Inside?"

Brice answers with a nod.

"Wait," I tell Mostyn.

She immediately stops and turns to me for more instructions.

"More people?" I ask.

"SDF," answers Brice. "A hundred, maybe a hundred and fifty."

"Rebels, like us?" I push. "Or loyal SDF soldiers?"

He shrugs. "This is a Free Army base, right?"

I nod. I don't know why SDF troops would be here unless they were mutineers, like us.

Glowing blue and coming in fast, our ship arcs down toward a flat patch of rock behind the warehouse. I flinch back a step and everyone turns to see what I'm looking at. Dust and small rocks fly away, pushed by the ship's blue grav waves as it settles onto the asteroid's surface.

"Penny's getting a real feel for driving that ship," admires Brice.

"Yeah," I agree. "She's a real hotrod." Back to business. "Mostyn, come over here."

She does.

I raise my wrist and show her my d-pad. "Does yours function?"

"Yes," she answers, confused. She doesn't know what I'm driving at.

Brice looks at his.

I ask, "Can you pull up the regiment hierarchy?"

She shows me her load of helmets, as if to point out how silly my request is.

Brice taps his d-pad and brings up the screen I'm looking for.

I reach over and start pointing at the names of pilots, nav officers, and commissars. "These are the ones I know I can trust. If any of them are in there, give them helmets and bring them out first. The rest stay, for now."

Brice takes a moment to consider my request. "I understand."

To Mostyn he says, "Wait for me out here." Looking at me, he continues, "If none of them are in there, it'll be easier if I don't bring any helmets in with me." He heads toward the airlock.

Lenox and her squad, disembarked from the ship, come bounding around the corner of the warehouse.

"Sir?" she asks as she comes up.

"At the moment, we're clear up top," I tell her. I look around. "Or we're between attacks. Deploy your troops in a defensive perimeter around this warehouse. Make sure the machine guns have good fields of fire. This building is full of human prisoners."

Lenox looks at the helmets scattered everywhere. "Pretty ingenious way to keep them in, take their helmets and leave them inside. You don't even need to lock the door."

"Yeah." I point at Silva and Mostyn. "You two mind doing recon?"

Mostyn drops his load and nods. In the light-g, the helmets don't fall. Instead, they start to sink very slowly.

"Will do," says Silva. "Where do you want us?"

I look at the black sky. "A few hundred feet up, where you can see the whole colony. If Trogs pop out anywhere, don't shoot and give your position away, call in the troops."

"I'll go up, too," says Lenox. "It worked well back on the Trog cruiser we captured, with me controlling my squad from up there."

"Okay."

She turns to Mostyn and Silva. "I'll watch the area around my squad. You two keep an eye on the rest."

Moments later, they're all three off the ground and taking up positions overhead.

Brice emerges from the airlock. By the expression on his face, I can see he's pleased. "Jill Rafferty is in there."

"No shit!" That is good news.

"And some pushy MSS Colonel named Blair. She wants out first."

Chapter 63

Brice is back inside the warehouse, having gone in with two spare helmets—one for Jill, one for Blair.

I'm waiting for him to come back out, while formulating plans about what to do next as I make guesses about our enemies. I know there have to be more Trogs on this asteroid.

"Grays," says Phil, over the comm, tossing the comment into the silence on our link like it's barely worth a remark.

"Here?" I ask, surprised.

"Yeah," he tells me. "I can sense them."

"Do you know where?" I'm already spinning through guesses as to what the presence of Grays implies.

"Hard to tell, exactly," he answers. "Somewhere down inside the asteroid. If I got out of the ship and walked around—"

"No," I tell him. "You need to stay on the ship. Penny, you should probably get the ship off the ground, but stay close. If Grays are present, there are probably a lot more Trogs down in the subterranean levels."

"Will do," Penny tells me, and I see the ship lift off immediately.

"How many Grays are below?" I ask.

"A pod," answers Phil. "I don't think more than that."

Six Grays would be enough to target those defensive railguns we had to take out. That would explain the accuracy of the fire coming from those weapons.

The warehouse airlock opens and Brice comes out with Blair and Jill in tow.

"Kane?" says Blair, like she can't read the name off my chest.

I give her a nod and then turn to Jill. "Your crew? Your platoon?"

"Most of them are inside," she tells me.

"Your pilot?" I ask.

"He made it," she answers, uncertain why I'm asking.

Blair starts to say something, and I silence her with a raised hand. To Jill, I say, "Grab the helmets you need. Round up your crew and troops and free them as quickly as you can." I point to the mine operation's big tug. "See if your pilot can fly that thing. I need it in the air as soon as possible."

"What do you need him to do?" she questions.

I point toward the giant Trog cruiser shrinking in the distance as it drifts toward Jupiter. "Penny and Phil destroyed the bridge on that thing. It's not going to fly again. However, it's probably full of Trogs who are going to figure out soon enough their best chance of staying alive is to put on their suits and grav-drive themselves back here."

"We don't need it to be raining Trogs," Jill tells me. "You want us to ram it with the tug?" She grimaces. She knows the tug wasn't built for that kind of work.

"No." Pointing toward the gas giant so prominent in the sky, I explain, "If the tug has enough fuel, push the cruiser into orbit around Jupiter."

"We can shove it out of the orbital plane and accelerate fast enough so it'll never be a problem," suggests Jill, "and we'll be back here in an hour, instead."

"Not a bad idea." I look at the cruiser, weighing the pros and cons. "I hate to waste the ship. I'm hoping we can one day salvage it, if we leave it in orbit long enough for the Trogs onboard to die."

Nodding, Jill says, "Okay, I'm with you. I'll make it happen." She turns and scoops up an armful of helmets and heads for the airlock.

"I'll give her a hand," says Brice, turning to follow.

I finally give my attention to Blair.

"Good job," she tells me. "Mission accomplished. You made it here. You saved us."

I don't know what to say to any of that. I'm half-believing that this Free Army base was a trap all along and she's the one who put my neck in it. But I have no way of proving that one way or another. "How many of those inside are Free Army?"

"Most of them."

"How'd you get here?" I ask.

"I brought my assault ship."

"I thought you were on the command ship."

"I was."

"Division command is in there?" I can't help but glance at the airlock door. "This revolution goes that high up?"

Blair shakes her head. "Division command is dead."

"Dead?" I reply.

"All of them," she tells me.

"How?" I ask. "Did your ship take fire on the way up?"

"Kill switch." She's proud of her answer.

"The MSS gave you kill-switch authority over the division's top officers?" That's beyond belief.

"We have people in places where they need to be," says Blair. "I wasn't supposed to have kill-switch access over anybody but my commissars."

"When did you do it?" I ask.

"As soon as we took off." She doesn't seem to have any emotion attached to the murder.

Murder? Why does that unvoiced word seem to be the right one?

I don't know whether to admire her coldness or be afraid of it. Either way, I know now she's a lot more dangerous than I initially thought. "So, who was left on your ship?"

"Me," she answers. "The pilot, and the grav officer."

"Comm?" I ask.

"He was North Korean."

Dead, of course.

"We came straight here," she continues. "We were the first to arrive, the first to be ambushed." She nods at the warehouse. "In there ever since."

"So those really are our people in there?" I ask.

"As soon as we get them armed again," she tells me, "they're our army."

"Is this it?" I'm disappointed. "All of us?" God I hope not. A few hundred against an endless flow of Trogs, not to mention what's left of earth's armies who are loyal enough to the Grays to fight against us.

Blair shakes her head. "We have other bases, too."

"How many?"

"I can't tell you that."

"You better." A threat is veiled behind my words. "I'm not playing the secrecy games anymore. This isn't spy bullshit now. This is war. The Grays and North Koreans back home will figure out eventually what we've done and they're going to come after us. I'm okay with that. I've been planning for this a long time, but I've got men and women who are fighting and dying for me, for this rebellion. I need to be able to look them in the eye and tell them it's real, tell them there are enough of us that we have a chance to actually win."

"Let's move all these troops out of the warehouse," Blair tells me. "Put weapons in their hands and kill the rest of the Trogs on this base. We'll have plenty of time to talk afterwards. For now, I swear to you, this rebellion is real. It's bigger than just us on this little rock. We're not throwing our lives away on nothing. We can win this. We can free our people."

Free our people?

She's talking my language like she's reading my thoughts and using them to convince me. I can't argue, can't resist. That is my dream, to free my people.

Our war has begun.

Freedom!

THE BATTLE CONTINUES…

Freedom's Fury, Book 2 available now!

But wait...there's more. Keep reading.

There's a little more to the story...

(Okay, maybe a request for reviews wrapped in a fun story?)

"Dude," says Brice. "Do you feel that?"

"What?"

"That?"

"Are you high?" I ask. "Drunk? Too much Suit Juice? Brain tumor from too much solar radiation?"

"No," answers Brice. "Look around. Things are different."

I do look around. "Holy shit! Where'd everything go?"

"I think we transcended."

"We're dead?" I can't believe it. "After all the shit we just went through, now we're dead?"

"No" Brice is awed. "It's a weird limbo state. Purgatory. Not dead, but not alive."

"You're freakin' me out, man."

Brice closes his eyes and inhales deeply. "You feel that?"

"Are you asking me to touch..."

"No, dumbass." Brice points into the air at nothing I can see, just dark that's not really dark, gray that isn't gray, light that doesn't glow.

I shiver. "This place gives me the fuckin' creeps."

"Close your eyes," urges Brice. "Feel it."

"Fine." I do because I know how hardheaded he can be. I wait. I breathe. *I do feel it.*

"Holy shit!"

Brice grins. "See what I mean?"

"What the hell is that?" I'm looking around. "It feels like somebody's spying on me only I can't figure out where they are."

"You know what that is?"

If I did, I'd have guessed already. "Why don't you quit being cryptic and just tell me?"

"That's the reader."

"Bite me." I roll my eyes. "There's no such thing as readers."

"Man," says Brice. "How can you not believe in readers? Our whole existence depends on readers. In fact, they say that every instance of existence in our great two-dimensional plane proceeds at the whim of a reader sitting on some great cosmic couch, turning pages, sipping wine, and ignoring his kids in the other room."

I make a certain motion, exaggerating as I always do the size of my invisible tool.

"I'm totally serious," says Brice, he's getting excited, like maybe Santa Clause is nearby with a bag of surplus Christmas toys. "Here's the kicker, the reader controls time itself. Our moments flow from one to the next when she turns a page. When she's not turning, we're not—"

"Not what?" I interrupt. "Not alive?"

"Not that exactly." Brice says it calmly, not rising to my argument. "We're in a gooey nothing limbo land. Like this place. Not existing, really, just waiting for something to happen."

"That sounds like a shitty metaphysical system."

"Dude, you can't talk that way." Brice is mortified. "You'll offend people. They might put the book down and never pick it up again, and then you'll cease to exist."

"I did say, shitty, right?" I huff. "*Shitty!* I mean who wants to live in a world where they have no control over whether they live or die? Not me. I don't want anyone controlling my life any more than I want those damn Grays running it."

"Oh, it's worse than you think," Brice tells me.

"How could it be?"

"There's also an author?"

It all sounds like hokum to me. I try to come up with a gesture that'll express my derision more forcefully than that last juvenile hand motion.

"He's like a middleman between our world and the reader's world."

I sigh.

"Really. I'm serious."

Looking for a way to get through to Brice's rational side, I suggest, "Fine. Let's go talk to him."

"We can't."

"Of course." I laugh. It's mean. I want it to hurt. I want to embarrass Brice back to reality.

He doesn't take the bait. "The thing you need to know about authors is they tend to be antisocial. They hide in dark rooms and make shit up all day. And they don't like being around other people. So if they see you coming, they'll run away."

"Poplar at parties, I'll bet." I'm getting exasperated. "Why don't we make an appointment, or send this author dude an email or something?"

"That's the other thing," says Brice. "We can't. He lives in the three-dimensional world with the readers and exists in a separate temporal space."

I look around again at the ambiguous nothing of where we're floating and realize, not only is everything around me undefined, but I am too. I have no body. I'm just a disembodied voice. That scares me.

Brice senses my fear. "You're finally looking. You're feeling it, aren't you?"

I don't want to admit it, but the words slip out. "I'm worried."

"So you finally see what I'm talking about."

"Not really," I admit. "I don't like this place. Maybe the Grays and Trogs weren't so bad. I want to get back to our universe?"

"That's what I've been telling you," says Brice. "We're not in control. It's the author and the reader. Lots and lots of readers that control our fate."

"Can't we get off this shit?" I argue, "Do you really believe that we float here in the gray nothing until some reader comes along? We can't do anything to change our fate?"

"Well," says Brice. "There are theories."

"Lay them on me, man." The nothingness is getting to me. I'm willing to listen to any ideas.

"First off, the author is probably living under a bridge, eating rat-flavored ramen from the clearance bin, and drinking coffee brewed from used grounds filtered through a hobo's underwear. Life as an author is hard."

I shrug. "Sucks for him out there in three-dimensional-land. What's that got to do with us?"

"The only way the author's life can improve," says Brice, "the only way he can write more books is if readers take an active role in his welfare."

"This sounds like the beginning of a multi-level-marketing pitch. I'm out."

Brice laughs.

"What are you laughing at?"

"You said you were out. But you're still here, stuck in the limbo with me."

"Shit."

"Listen to me," says Brice. "It's not an MLM. All a reader has to do to make our lives full, and long, and eternal, is read the book and then go to a party, get drunk and dance on a table while shouting to everyone who can hear that this is the greatest book they ever read."

"Sounds like a commitment," I grumble. "Nobody's going to do that. Is there anything easier?"

"Well, they could tell their friends, I suppose. Maybe on Facebook or social media or something?"

"Facebook?" I ask. "What's social media?"

"It's what people do on the internet when they're stuck in a line somewhere and bored or when they're at home and they're tired of trying to play smoochy-smoochy with the wife."

"Ah," I say "So that's it. We're afterthoughts to their sex lives."

"Well, they could leave a review where the bought the book, just tick some stars and save it, or even say a few kind words, you know, like 'This book was a tolerable string of syllables that kept me distracted while I was waiting in the dentist's office. But seriously, buy it. It ROCKS!'"

"Okay. Is that it?"

"Not really?"

"What else?"

"Well," says Brice, "there's the email list. If readers sign up, the author can spam them from time to time when he as a new book out. Or maybe when his friend (or anybody who buys him lunch) has a new book out."

"Eh, I'm not sure I'd give up my email address just for a notification about a book."

"It's not just that," says Brice. "There's a free book in it."

"Tell me more," I'm interested. "Are we in it?"

"No," says Brice. "It's about the Grays' siege of the earth before we were born. Your dad's in it."

"My dad?" I ask. "He died in a mining accident before I was born."

"That's what you think," Brice reveals. "He was a sergeant in the assault force earth sent to attack the Grays on the moon."

"I thought they were all blown out of the sky."

Brice shakes his head. "That's what the MSS wants you to believe, dumbass. You can't trust those bastards."

"So, it's the story of my dad." I'm having a hard time believing it. "I'd like to read that."

"Sign up for the email list," Brice tells me. "And leave a review and tell your friends so the author can stop drinking hobo coffee and write some more books."

Reviews are awesome and a great way to bank some good Karma. Please visit the site where you purchased the book to leave a quick review, or just some stars if you liked it...many thanks!

And to learn more about Kane's dad, sign up for our we-hate-spam-too mailing list, and get Freedom's Siege, the free prequel to Freedom's Fire: http://smarturl.it/FreedomsSiege-Free

MORE ABOUT BOBBY'S OTHER BOOKS...

Slow Burn Series (9 books), a best-seller!

Slow Burn is Bobby's flagship post-apocalyptic zombie series, but so much more than a zombie book. Follow the adventures of Zed as he wakes up one morning to find that something's a little different in the world. As the world is going to shit, Zed meets up with Murphy, and they try to navigate their new reality through a world of the "slow burns" before they are completely consumed by the virus. Great reviews, with over a million books sold, readers LOVE this one.

The Last Survivors Series (6 books)

A collaborative series with fellow zombie author T.W. Piperbrook, this series has a little more of a Sci-Fi feel, popular with folks who like Game of Thrones. It explores what happens 300 years in the future after the apocalypse, when man has rebuilt and gone back to an almost medieval society.

Ebola K: A Terrorism Thriller (trilogy)

A really great terrorism thriller with awesome reviews. It focuses on the devastating Ebola outbreak and the possibility of weaponized Ebola by terrorist organizations and nationalized resources like blood with Ebola antibodies. A more in-depth and complex observation of the real world. This series follows an American college student teaching in Uganda as the country comes under attack from the deadly virus as he tries to make his way back to the safety of his family back in the United States.

It's also historically and medically accurate, so you'll learn a little about the history of the disease as well.

Black Rust, Black Virus (first two in a series)

A newer series from Bobby that also deals with a different post-apocalyptic reality. Christian Black is a bounty hunter charged with hunting down the infected…a "Regulator." When caught in an unsanctioned kill, Christian sets about to clear his name. A fairly deep character, whose flaws are an important backstory to his adventurous life.

Dusty's Diary: One Frustrated Man's Zombie Apocalypse Story (first in a series)

Fun and crass…be careful if you're easily offended! Has some great advice about what to pack in your post-apocalyptic bunker (don't forget the porn!). Dusty's Diary has an uncertain future…people like it, so I'll probably write more in the future. This is a short story.